Praise for Gwen Florio

"With the chops of a world-class journalist and an unsurpassed knowledge of the Rocky Mountain West, Gwen Florio weaves a compelling tapestry that combines family saga, social consciousness and human frailty, making *Disgraced* difficult to put down."

—Craig Johnson, author of the Walt Longmire Mysteries,
the basis for the hit Netflix drama *Longmire*

"Gwen Florio achieves what few others can in the field of crime fiction. She creates characters with real depth and places them in a story that is so hard-hitting and believable, it's easy to imagine it being in tomorrow's headlines."

—J.J. Hensley, Award winning author of *Resolve*
and *Measure Twice*

For Kate, the original Margaret.
And for all of the strong women
who trusted me with their stories.

DISGRACED

GWEN FLORIO

MIDNIGHT INK
WOODBURY, MINNESOTA

FIRST EDITION
First Printing, 2016

Book format by Bob Gaul
Cover design by Ellen Lawson
Cover images by iStockphoto.com/4063329/©mbogacz
　　　　　　　iStockphoto.com/783720/©Lokibaho
　　　　　　　iStockphoto.com/47661006/©ghoststone
　　　　　　　iStockphoto.com/48933926/©4x6
　　　　　　　iStockphoto.com/19841940/©4x6
Editing by Gabrielle Simons

Midnight Ink, an imprint of Llewellyn Worldwide Ltd.

Library of Congress Cataloging-in-Publication Data (Pending)
ISBN: 978-0-7387-4766-8

Midnight Ink
Llewellyn Worldwide Ltd.
2143 Wooddale Drive
Woodbury, MN 55125-2989
www.midnightinkbooks.com

Printed in the United States of America

PROLOGUE

THE AFGHANI SHEPHERD DIED beneath the hard bright light of the stars, his unexpected emergence in the black-and-white landscape of night a stroke of luck for the soldiers, if not for him.

It was finished before he could run, rifles jerked into position, *crack-crack-crack*, the impact lifting his body right out of his cheap plastic sandals and slamming it back onto the rocky earth several feet away, his unused rusting AK-47 clattering down beside him. The sheep bleated and shat and ran this way and that, in the idiotic way of sheep the world over. Two of the soldiers slung their rifles over their shoulders and re-formed the band with quiet, competent movements, the action unnecessary but somehow comforting with its echo of childhood ranch chores. They turned their attention from sheep to the shepherd's body, hefting it by wrists and ankles, what remained of his head dangling almost to the dusty ground, shreds of turban dragging behind.

"Count of three," one whispered, and the body swung once, twice, thrice, and sailed through the air, thudding beside the dead

1

American soldier. Starlight silvered the American's face. The grin slashed across his neck leaked inky blood. That same black blood covered the hands of the woman leaning over him and stained the ends of her pale hair that, torn free of its military regulation bun, dipped into the corpse's terrible wound.

A voice floated into the darkness above the woman's head. "Let's go."

The woman didn't move. The two soldiers reached down, grasped her shoulders, and raised her to her feet. "We got to get back to the base."

A third soldier kicked the dead Afghani. The body rolled to one side and fell back. The woman shook off the hands and stumbled away. The third man raised his voice so the woman could hear. "Get over it. Karma's a bitch."

Her reply a promise so soft he barely caught it.

"I'll never get over it."

ONE

THE SHOUT COULD HAVE been one of happiness, the *pop*—coming as it did amid a teary jubilation of the military homecoming ceremony in Casper, Wyoming—anything at all. A teenage daughter cracking her gum in excitement. A burst balloon among one of the dozens of celebratory bunches. A compression of bubble wrap from a torn-open welcome home gift.

Reporter Lola Wicks knew better. She shoved her five-year-old daughter, Margaret, to the hangar's concrete floor and fell atop her, reaching simultaneously for her phone to tap a quick tweet as Margaret's body shuddered beneath her. "Shot fired, Casper airport, soldiers' homecoming." The returning soldiers knew, too, scuttling toward the sound in a battle crouch, reaching for the weapons they no longer carried. Lola rolled off Margaret and shouted to the strange young woman she'd just met. "Take her. Get her out of here. Go. *Now!*"

She waited the second it took to ensure the woman indeed headed with Margaret toward the hangar's entrance, then turned and followed the sprinting soldiers in the other direction. Above them, balloon bouquets flew in brilliant starbursts toward the hangar's domed ceiling. Lola raised her phone as she ran, snapping photos of the fleeing civilians, images that in her experience would look just like every other photo of people making the split-second transition from normalcy to a flight for their lives, whether from earthquake or school shooting or suicide bombing. Arms pumped for greater speed. Faces twisted in screams. Eyes rolled wild, not yet glazed against the reality that would hit home too soon. Lola stopped to tweet a photo, then headed for the far corner of the hangar where the soldiers converged. She shouldered her way through the cluster of fatigues, thinking not for the first time that soldiers were far more polite in moving aside than elbow-throwing television cameramen, several of whom over the years had left her with bruises, one once lobbing an actual punch.

Lola reached the inner circle and wished she hadn't. She worked the phone yet again. "Soldier down. Shot appears fatal, possibly self-inflicted. #CasperShooting." She concentrated on the words, the need to inform without jumping to conclusions. The necessity of the ass-saving "appears" and "possibly." Even though there was no *appears* about it, no way for 140 characters to convey the mess that had once been the soldier's head. Soon enough, crime scene technicians would note the powder burns on what was left of the skin of his face, would verify that the gun was his own, that the bullet that had killed him had been fired from the pistol cooling in the hand already going gray; would write a lengthy report that would supply all the details that Lola and the cursing veterans around her could see with their own eyes.

Lola's phone buzzed with a text alert. She edged her way back through the circle. The text was from Jan Carpenter, her friend and colleague at the newspaper in Magpie, Montana, more than five hundred miles away. "WTF? You're supposed to be on vacation. Not your state. Not your story. Walk away. Is Margaret OK? What about my cousin?"

Shit. Lola ran through the now-deserted hangar, dodging the duffel bags and purses that people had abandoned in their haste to escape. The crowd outside surged toward her, shouting questions. She ignored them, calling for her daughter. "Margaret? Margaret?" And, oh hell, what was the name of Jan's peculiar cousin, the woman who'd hustled Margaret to safety? Something as odd as the woman herself. "Palomino? Pal? Pal Jones?"

"Hey." A voice like a hard swipe of sandpaper, unexpectedly close at hand.

Lola snatched Margaret from the woman's arms. "Oh, baby." She pressed her cheek to Margaret's, inhaling her wheaty scent.

"Boom, Mommy." Margaret patted Lola's face with soft hands.

Lola lifted her head and scrutinized her daughter. Margaret had her father's lustrous ebony hair, bound this day in braids, stick-straight in contrast to Lola's chestnut tangle. Margaret had Charlie's skin, too, albeit a lighter shade of brown, but her eyes were Lola's own, grey and skeptical, and for the moment, wide with a question. So she didn't know what had happened. Only the sound. Lola let her breath out.

"Yes," she said. "Boom. A big noise. Nothing to worry about. We should get going now. We're just in the way here." That last said with obvious reluctance, a nod to the fact that on most days, it was Lola's role to be in the hot center of whatever was happening.

Palomino Jones hitched a shoulder, noticeably bony even in her disguising fatigues, settling the strap of her Army-issue duffel more firmly upon it. "Ready when you are." She was a head and more shorter than Lola's near-six-foot lankiness, but her appearance of fragility went beyond height. Her slight body swam within her fatigues, wrists protruding twiglike from her sleeves. During her own time in Afghanistan as a foreign correspondent, Lola had worn her hair cropped close and spiky, but Pal's head was frankly shaved, the

5

pitiless June sun highlighting the pink scalp beneath the blond fuzz. Her features were all sharp points, chin like an arrowhead, nose a blade, cheekbones that threatened to slice through skin. Above them, eyes blue and cold as winter pond ice.

Lola led the way to her truck, back braced against the woman's glare. She'd agreed to meet Palomino at the airport as a favor to Jan. "You're going to be in Wyoming on your stupid vacation and I can't get time off because of it," Jan had said. "Just pick her up and drop her off at the ranch on your way to Yellowstone."

"It's not a vacation, it's a furlough. I'd rather be at work, getting paid, and you know it. Doesn't she have any friends? Neighbors?"

"There's a neighbor who's been like a surrogate dad since her parents..." Jan didn't have to finish the sentence. Lola knew about the car crash a few years earlier that had killed Jan's aunt and uncle, an occurrence so unremarkable on Wyoming's ice-sheeted winter roads as to merit little more than a brief mention in the local newspapers. "His car is unreliable. To put it mildly," Jan said.

"Casper is a hell of a detour from Yellowstone," Lola pointed out, reminding Jan of her vacation destination. But the observation only spurred Jan to the unusual tactic of personal revelation.

"She's like a sister to me, as much as she could be, given how far apart we lived. We spent most summers together. I get the feeling she had a rough time in Afghanistan. Her emails stopped months ago. You could pick her brain on the ride to the ranch, let me know how she's doing. You're the perfect person to talk to her, your having been there and all." Jan rarely missed an opportunity to jab at Lola's previous experience as a foreign correspondent in Afghanistan, usually when she thought Lola wasn't taking her job in Montana seriously enough. Lola couldn't remember a time when Jan had treated her background as an advantage.

"Come on," Jan pressed. "There's a month of free date-night babysitting in it for you."

Lola knew, and knew that Jan did, too, that finding a babysitter for Margaret was never an issue. Margaret's father, Sheriff Charlie Laurendeau, was from the Blackfeet Nation, its border just a few miles north of Magpie, with no shortage of aunties and elders willing to take Margaret on a moment's notice. But for the sake of Jan's dignity and her own, she appeared to value the offer.

"Six weeks," she said.

"Done," said Jan.

Lola reached her pickup, red as a bullfighter's cape and equally irresistible to highway patrol officers eager to fill their day's quota of tickets. At least it was easy to spot in the parking lot jammed with the more sensibly hued vehicles of families come to take their service members home. A dark, wet nose twitched at the truck's partially open window.

"We're back, Bub," Margaret called.

Lola unlocked the pickup door—no matter how long she lived in the West, she'd never abandoned her old Baltimore habit of locking vehicle and house alike—and stood aside as the border collie leaped from the driver's seat and landed on three legs at Pal's feet. A suggestion of a smile touched the woman's lips. Lola started at a recent memory. There'd been a moment, just a split second really, as the airport erupted in chaos around her. Lola had thrown herself atop Margaret, awaiting the sound of more shots. Heard none. She raised her head a couple of millimeters and took in the blur of fleeing feet. Except for the booted pair beside her. Everyone else in the hangar was in motion except Jan's cousin. Pal stood frozen, staring toward the corner where the unseen soldier lay dying, and just then, so quickly Lola still wasn't sure she'd seen it, a glorious smile lit up her thin, thin face.

TWO

THE WIND SCREAMED PAST Lola, snatching at the cellphone in her hand. She was used to wind in Montana, constant and battering, but at least there it had a visual component. Slender trees bent double, groaning beneath the onslaught. Grasses bowed and rose in sealike waves. Soaring birds veered abruptly off course. But as far as she could tell, trees didn't grow at all in this part of Wyoming. The sagebrush, low, tough and woody, appeared as impervious to the wind as the boulders and sandstone formations that littered the valley floor. The Wind River Range floated blue and spectral in the distance, reminding her of the Koh-e-Paghman mountains that so many years earlier had briefly lulled her into terming Kabul picturesque. In fact, she thought, throw in a few flat-roofed mud houses, some flocks of shaggy, fat-bottomed Arabi sheep, and bearded men in pajama-like shalwar qamiz toting AK-47s, and Wyoming would look just like Afghanistan—a fact not inclined to endear the state to her. She would not have been surprised to hear the wavering melody of a muezzin's evening call to prayer rise around her as the sun dipped below the mountains. Lola turned her back to the gusts and yelled into the phone.

"The woman is a freak, Charlie. You should see her. I can't wait to get out of here in the morning." She stood atop a rise about a hundred yards from Pal's house. It was a typical high plains ranch, a nondescript frame house with haphazard add-ons, scoured largely free of paint by the wind, smaller than any of the more essential outbuildings. Lola noted an equipment shed, a calving shelter, and sturdy corrals, all in good repair. But no sign of livestock. This time of year, cattle and sheep alike grazed high pastures miles away from ranches. But there should have been some horses in the corrals, a retired herding dog or two lazing in the shade, some barn cats slinking around. Pal must have shut down the ranch operations when her parents died, Lola thought. If Pal had been more talkative—which is to say, talkative at all—Lola would have asked her about it. As it was, Lola had fled the silent house as soon as she'd put Margaret to bed, telling Pal the cellphone reception would probably be better outdoors. Mostly, she just wanted to talk out of earshot from Pal.

But Charlie had no interest in the peculiarities of Jan's cousin. "Tell me again about the shooting," he said in what Lola thought of as his sheriff voice.

"A guy shot himself. Which you'd have seen if you'd ever check out my Twitter feed."

She should have known better. Bad enough, Charlie maintained, that he had to waste valuable time checking the social media posts of the various ne'er-do-wells who populated and repopulated his jail. The last thing he wanted to do was track his girlfriend, too. "The only people I follow are the ones I can't trust," he'd say when she pressed. "Should I put you in that category?"

Now, he ignored her and repeated his demand. "From the beginning. You got to the airport—"

"Right." She sighed. After nearly six years with Charlie, she'd learned, even if the repeat offenders had yet to figure it out, that it was quicker just to answer him. "We got to the airport right before the plane landed. There was a ceremony. A band, Welcome Home banners, yellow ribbons, the whole nine yards."

"Go on."

"The first guy off the plane, they made a gantlet for him. Everybody cheered and applauded. He must have been some big hero because the others didn't get that kind of treatment."

"That's my trained observer." Teasing her now. Charlie and Lola often compared notes about the things they noticed at different events, each agreeing that the other filled in details that one of them missed. "When I retire from sheriffing and you finally get a pink slip," Charlie often joked, "we can set ourselves up as private investigators."

It wasn't a joke anymore. Lola hadn't been pink-slipped, not exactly. But she'd been furloughed without pay for three weeks from Magpie's *Daily Express*, in a disturbing repeat of the downsizing from her job as a foreign correspondent for the Baltimore newspaper a few years earlier, an action that had led her on a roundabout route that ended up in Magpie. Where, foolishly, she'd felt safe from the unending rounds of layoffs and staff cuts that plagued larger newspapers around the country. Lola was older by nearly a decade than Jan, the paper's other full-time reporter, but Jan had seniority at the *Express*. The furlough fell on Lola, and Jan saw her long-planned trip to Wyoming to meet Pal upon her return from Afghanistan canceled. Which is how Lola had ended up stuck with Pal.

The road trip to Yellowstone had been Charlie's idea. "You and Margaret take a vacation. It'll be good for you," he said, despite knowing full well that vacation was never Lola's idea of fun. Charlie himself was busy training the new deputy that the county had, after years of pleading, finally seen fit to fund, so he couldn't come with them. But he'd upped the ante by suggesting that Lola use the time to think about his most recent offer of marriage. Matrimony, he pointed out, had worked out fine for his brother Edgar, despite Eddie's initial reluctance about the institution upon finding out about his college girlfriend's pregnancy. Now, Eddie was living in Arizona with his Navajo wife and little girl. "This is the last time," Charlie had said. "Margaret will be in first grade. She deserves married parents. If you can't commit after all this time, we need to think about a different arrangement." At which point, Lola had become even less enthusiastic about the trip.

Marriage came accompanied by the specter of a wedding, and an obligatory marshmallow dress that resided in a different universe than Lola's daily outfits of cargo pants and turtlenecks or T-shirts, depending on the season. Just thinking about a dress made her feel itchy and constricted. She'd probably have to wear makeup, too. She swiped the back of her hand across her mouth as though to wipe away nonexistent lipstick.

"I'd just met up with Jan's cousin," she told Charlie, returning to her narrative with relief. "It was pandemonium. People crying, hugging, kissing babies. Then a guy shouted something and shot himself."

"How did you know he's the one who shouted? And did you see him shoot himself?" Always the cop, Lola thought.

"Negative." Charlie already knew the answer to both questions. "But it was obvious, when I saw him, that he'd shot himself. And I asked people if he'd been the one shouting ahead of time," she said with a bit of pride. It might not have been her story, but she'd taken pains to verify the facts anyway.

"What'd they say? And what did he say?"

"Nothing that made sense. Or at least, not what people thought they heard. Nobody was really sure. He said, 'It's alive. It's alive.'"

The phone went silent as Charlie digested that piece of information. "Like in *Young Frankenstein*?" he said finally. The Mel Brooks horror movie spoof was a shared guilty pleasure.

"Except nobody laughed."

"Right."

He got around to the question Lola had hoped he wouldn't ask. "Where was Margaret during all of this?"

"Outside," Lola said.

A longer silence. "Alone?"

"With Pal."

"Lola—"

She turned into the wind and held the phone high as his voice rose, saying something else about Margaret. But not so high that she couldn't hear what he said next. "Have you thought about my question yet?"

The gusts swept past with the sound of tearing fabric. "Can't hear you, Charlie!" she shouted toward the phone. "Losing reception out here. Sorry. Talk tomorrow. Love you." Lola thumbed the phone off. She wished that in exchange for his ultimatum, she'd extracted a promise that he wouldn't bring up the topic of marriage again until she was back in Magpie. She hunched against the wind in preparation for her next obligatory call. Jan would want to know about her cousin, but Lola didn't have much to tell her. The two-hour ride from Casper to the ranch had passed in near-total silence but for Margaret's chattering, an ongoing conversation with Bub in a language that only girl and dog understood. Lola had asked Pal about the suicidal soldier, only to be silenced with a bitten-off, "Didn't know the guy."

She tried a few other questions, about Pal herself, about Jan, about suggestions on what to see in Yellowstone, eliciting only monosyllabic answers and, finally, the flat statement, "I'm tired." Pal leaned back against the headrest and closed her eyes. In the jump seats behind them, Margaret and Bub had already succumbed to sleep. But for air shrieking past the open windows, cooling only by virtue of motion, Lola drove in silence through a landscape that increased in desolation as the miles passed. Montana, with its overlay of postcard mountains and trout streams and movie-mogul ranches, was a gift to tourism marketers. Central Wyoming was the same landscape stripped to bleached skeleton, barely enough dirt clinging to hardrock to anchor sagebrush, and wholly inadequate for trees, which all but disappeared along with any hint of human habitation the farther west Lola drove from Casper. Towering rocks banded with red angled abruptly out of the ground, as though shoved by an unseen fist below. Alkali patches stretched across the flats between them, bouncing back the glare of the heat-whitened sky.

Lola wished the truck had air-conditioning. Pal had already shrugged out of her fatigue jacket, her Army-issue brown T-shirt revealing arms braided by slender ropes of muscle. Her hands were large and capable-looking. Lola guessed Pal was stronger than she appeared at first glance. Of course she was, Lola admonished herself. Carrying one of those big rifles, humping that bulky pack and body armor through the vengeful heat of an Afghan summer. Lola had hoped to compare notes with Pal, maybe get an update on how things had changed—or not—in Kabul, but their conversation had been too brief for Lola to mention her own years there.

Pal stirred and muttered in her sleep. Her hands, which had been clasped in her lap, fell apart, the tension in her body easing. One arm fell to her side. Lola glanced and gasped. She forced her gaze back to the empty road ahead. But she couldn't keep it from straying to Pal's forearm, to the four faint scars there, a row of slashes, the skin tough and whitened.

The scars were old, she reminded herself now as she punched Jan's number into her phone. No need to mention them. Jan spoke without preamble, as was her habit. "How's my cousin? Is she all right? What's the deal with the shooting?"

"You probably know more about the shooting than I do. There's got to be a story online about it somewhere," Lola told her. As to Pal—she looked toward the ranch house crouched at the bottom of the hill, edges dissolving into the gloaming. Lola was sure she'd snapped on the porch light when she'd set out up the hill, but now the house lay in darkness, nothing to suggest life within. Earlier that afternoon, they'd stopped at a town about twenty miles from the ranch so that Lola and Margaret could get dinner—Pal declined— while Pal stocked up on groceries. As far as Lola could tell from the bags Pal toted back to the truck, Pal was going to subsist on canned goods. While Lola and Margaret waited in the truck, Pal ducked into a package store and returned with a clinking bag, at which point, Lola set her internal alarm for the earliest departure possible the next morning. She and Margaret could drive back to the town and have breakfast there before heading to Yellowstone. They wouldn't even have to see Pal at all. Jan would surely call her cousin, and figure out on her own what was going on with Pal. Lola mouthed some noncommittal phrases into the phone and rang off.

She shoved the phone into her pocket and jogged back to the house. She ran her hands over the wall just inside the door, seeking the light switch. She wished she hadn't found it; that she'd simply felt her way through the darkness to the back bedroom where Margaret slept, Bub plastered to her side. Then she wouldn't have seen Pal, passed out at the kitchen table beneath the glare of the naked overhead bulb, one of the just-purchased pint bottles of bad bourbon nearly empty beside her. One arm cradled her head. The other, the one with the scars,

14

stretched across the table. Lola tiptoed close. Sometime during the late afternoon or evening, Pal had added a new scar, a slash across one of the earlier ones, turning it into an X. The line had already started to scab over, but the skin around it remained red and angry.

Guilt washed through Lola as she remembered how she'd ended her conversation with Jan. "She's not the most talkative person," Lola had told her. "But I remember those flights home from Kabul. I could barely stand up when I got home, and I was flying coach, not rattling around inside a cargo plane. She's exhausted. Aside from that, I think your cousin is just fine."

THREE

Lola's pickup crept along in a line of traffic, exhaust fouling Yellowstone's crystalline air. In Montana, she lived within an hour of Glacier National Park, and she knew the best way to negotiate its roads with the minimum amount of aggravation during tourist season. But in Yellowstone, she was the tourist, stuck on the main roads along with what appeared to be about one million other people. Behind her, Margaret slumped in her booster seat, no longer excited by herds of bison and the occasional far-away grizzly that caused the entire crawling procession of vehicles to come to an interminable stop.

Bub sprawled on the passenger seat beside Lola, every so often lifting his head and regarding her with his bifurcated gaze, one brown eye, one blue, reassuring himself that nothing had changed since the last time he'd checked. "Go to sleep, buddy," Lola told him. "You might as well sleep, too, Margaret. We're in this for the long haul." She checked her map, reminding herself that the distance to the park entrance had barely changed since the last time she'd looked. Forty-eight miles. What on earth had possessed her to make the long loop through the park at the height of tourist season? "Right," she reminded herself. "I didn't have a choice about when I got furloughed." She and Margaret only had been on the road a few days. She had another two and a half weeks to kill. Charlie and Jan and her editor, too, all had urged her to stay out of town for as long as possible.

"You won't be able to help yourself," Charlie said. "Something will happen and you'll want to cover it. They'll fire you if you do any reporting while you're on furlough."

The plan had been to spend a few days in Yellowstone and then go on to the Tetons. Lola thought they might cut the former short in favor of the latter. The Tetons, at least in the photos she'd seen, looked more like Glacier, with heavily forested mountains, their peaks foreboding with mist. Yellowstone's vast sunlit savannahs lacked the swirling sense of mystery that Glacier always evoked. Visitors complained about the latter. The park in northwestern Montana was scary, they said. All those trees pressing in close, roots grabbing at the unwary ankle, while from above skeins of black moss brushed scalp, shoulders, an unwisely exposed neck. And the fog, descending without notice, rendering a clearly marked trail tunnel-like, obscure. You never knew when a grizzly would charge out of the gloom. Or so Lola enjoyed telling the tourists.

Ahead of her, lights flashed red. Lola hit the brakes. Bub stood up. He saw the distraction before Lola did. His hackles raised, then smoothed. He lay back down with a yawn more outrage than exhaustion. "Good lord," said Lola. "It's only some stupid mulies." Back in Magpie, mule deer were nearly as common as dogs, making short work of newcomers' flowerbeds and finding clever ways to destroy the wire fences of the old-timers at constant war with them. Lola looked at the map again. Forty-six miles. She reached for the newspaper she'd picked up from a bench outside a ranger station and propped it against the steering wheel, alternately scanning its pages and the road ahead of her. A story about the soldier's suicide dominated the front page. He was, the story noted, one of a tight-knit group of companions from Thirty who'd enlisted upon graduating from high school. Lola recognized the name of the town where they'd stopped for dinner before they'd delivered Pal.

"Wait a minute," Lola said aloud. Bub opened an eye. "Tight-knit," the story said. But Pal had told her she didn't know the man. Lola had assumed he'd been from a different part of Wyoming. She cracked a rueful smile and repeated the mantra of every editor for whom she'd worked: "Assume makes an *ass* out of *u* and *me*." When would she ever learn? Apparently Pal and the suicidal soldier had gone to high school together. From what Lola had seen of Thirty, the high school couldn't have been that big. They must have known each other well in school, and even better after enlisting and serving together overseas in the same unit. Pal probably had just been trying to deflect conversation, Lola told herself. She read on. The soldier was, it turned out, the second casualty among the group from Thirty. Another had been killed in Afghanistan only a few months earlier.

"Maybe that's why he did it," someone speculated in the newspaper story. "Survivor guilt. Isn't that what it's called?"

Lola flipped through the pages to the jump, checking out other stories along the way. Wyoming, she read, was in the midst of a drought. Ranchers were already importing hay from neighboring states. Oil prices were up, good news for the folks working in the on-again, off-again boomtown of Gillette. Seemingly every town of any size in the state was making preparations for its Fourth of July rodeo, a phenomenon that caused the holiday to be known throughout the West as Cowboy Christmas for its multitude of purses. But for the names of the towns, Lola thought, she could have been reading the *Daily Express* back in Magpie, rural news the same around the region. She came to the jump of the Page One story. A companion headline caught her attention.

"Pair Charged in Bar Ruckus."

Again, standard fare, albeit with more than the usual amount of ink devoted to such a recurring story. Only the bar fights whose circumstances were so ridiculous as to make for amusing reading rated a newspaper story. Lola checked the road ahead, assuring herself of the twin streams of brake lights, and bent over the story, searching for the quirky detail that she could text to Jan. Within two paragraphs, she knew it was a different kind of story. The two pugilists were veterans, fresh off the plane from Afghanistan. They appeared to have gone straight to a local watering hole and picked a fight that ended with their victim being airlifted to an intensive care unit in Seattle with head injuries so severe as to make permanent brain damage a possibility. The perpetrators'—the *alleged* perps, Lola reminded herself—names were unfamiliar. But the name of their unit was entirely too familiar. As was their hometown: Thirty.

Lola paged back to the front and re-read the story about the soldier who'd killed himself. A half-dozen soldiers from Thirty had gone to Afghanistan. Now, two were dead and two more in jail within days, hours maybe, of arriving home. She looked at the byline on the lead story, and turned back to the one about the bar fight. They were the same—Dave Sparks.

"Congratulations, Dave Sparks," she said aloud. "You missed the forest for the trees."

Because it was clear to Lola, as obvious as the pulse that thrummed with quickened interest at her wrists and temples, that the story was bigger than the recitation of events tragic in two cases, criminal in the other. She looked to Bub. He stood at full alert, as always divining any change in mood before she felt it herself. "What do you think, buddy?" she asked him. "What the hell happened to those folks over there?"

Twinges of empathy, for the people of Thirty, and of jealousy for the stories that lay ahead for Dave Sparks, sparred within her. In a town the size of Thirty, the death of any veteran would send ripples of shock and sorrow throughout the community. In Magpie, such funerals were elaborate affairs, beyond the capacity of the small churches, filling the high school gymnasium. Afterward, people lined the streets as the hearse rolled slowly past, motorists flashing their headlights in tribute. At least those other funerals had been years apart. She'd never seen a single community hit so hard in such a short time. The fact of two dead, one of them by his own hand, and two more in trouble of their own making, would increase the effect exponentially. People questioned themselves in such circumstances. Wondered what they could have done differently. And, inevitably, some turned on one another. A thin bright line of anger nearly always underscored grief. Stories about such situations were complicated, tangled affairs, the best of them reflecting larger truths about individuals in particular and humanity in general.

Steak, Lola labeled such stories, in comparison to her usual diet of the hamburger that comprised police briefs and weather reports. One or two such stories a year was the best she ever hoped for, but those one or two sustained her through the routine of the other months. She caught herself compiling imaginary headlines, her way of focusing her thoughts. "*War's Trauma Writ Large in Small Town.* Something like that," she suggested to Bub. His head bob almost certainly had more to do with avoiding a particularly blistering gust through the window, but Lola decided to take it for assent.

The cars began to move again, crawling up a hill. Lola supposed there'd be another delay when people stopped to take in the view from the top. She banged her head against the steering wheel and groaned. Bub bestowed a quick, anxious swipe of his tongue upon her cheek. Her phone buzzed, a welcome distraction. Cell service in the park was spotty. Apparently the truck had just rolled into a hotspot.

She held the phone before her. A text—no, several texts—from Jan. "Call me." "Call me." "Call me." "Goddammit, call me."

Lola called. Jan's voice filled the cab.

Lola glanced in the rearview mirror. "Hush," she hissed. "Margaret's asleep."

Jan lowered the volume, if not the intensity.

Lola thrilled to the possibility that Jan offered. Knew better than to show it. "No way," she hissed into the eventual pause. "I am not going back there."

"You have to," Jan said. "I've been trying to call her ever since she got back. She won't answer. I even called her neighbor to make sure she was still alive."

"Why can't he look after her?"

"He's got his own issues."

Lola wondered what those were. Was he an alcoholic, as Pal apparently was, or at least was on her way to becoming? Did he, too, cut up his arm? Refuse to speak? Because, as far as Lola was concerned, that would make him the perfect person to look after Pal. Birds of a feather and all that—thoughts that Lola deemed best kept to herself. A moment later, she was glad she had.

"His grandson got killed over there. Pal emailed me something about it, back when she was still in touch. But that was months ago."

Another surge of blood warmed Lola's face. If she were writing a story—which she wasn't, not yet, anyway—the neighbor would go at the top of the list of people to interview.

"We're right in the middle of our vacation," she protested, to herself as much as to Jan.

"You? Vacation? Bored out of your skull yet? How do you like Yellowstone? Making friends with all of the tourists?"

Jan knew her too well, Lola thought. Jan pressed her case. "Look. Go back to the ranch, stick around a couple of days, make sure she's doing okay. I can head down there the minute your furlough is over."

Again, Lola delivered the expected reluctance. "What's my excuse for showing up again and imposing on her? Because I sure as hell wouldn't like it if some stranger just dropped in on me and announced she was staying awhile."

Jan threw out one implausible reason after another. Margaret was sick. Bub was sick. They wanted to see more of that part of Wyoming. Lola was out of money.

"Why don't I just tell her the truth?" Lola said. "That you're worried about her and you asked me to check back in."

"Because it'll piss her off."

As far as Lola could tell, Pal existed in a permanent state of pissed-offedness.

Jan played her trump card, letting real need leak through. "Lola, please?"

Their friendship was based on the shared belief that each was self-sufficient, able to function without the relationships that burdened other people. Lola had slipped a rung on the alpha-female ladder when she'd taken up with Charlie, farther still when Margaret had come along. On the rare occasions when she admitted it to herself, that was partly why she'd resisted Charlie's frequent and until now good-humored proposals of marriage.

"Fine," she said now. "The woman clearly has some sort of PTSD. In fact, from what I can tell, the whole unit was pretty messed up. I'll make sure she's not too out of control. And if it looks like she is, I'll call the VA. Okay?"

"Call me, too," Jan said. "In fact, call me first."

"Right."

Lola hung up. The conversation had only used up a single mile. But suddenly she was glad for the syrupy traffic flow; hoped, in fact, for a grizzly sighting or two, maybe even a pack of Yellowstone's famous—or infamous, depending on whether you were greenie or rancher—wolves. Anything to give her time to figure out two things. First, where to pitch the story already taking shape in her mind. "The *Daily Express*," she told Bub, "isn't going to go for something out of Wyoming, no matter how good it is. Which is just fine. A nice fat freelance fee will help make up for the furlough." Never mind that freelance fees hadn't been fat for a long time. She'd take a trimmed-down one. She still had connections at big newspapers and, better yet, knew reporters who had moved on from those papers to the online sites that were an increasing source of long-form journalism.

And the second issue, the same challenge she'd faced repeatedly in places ranging from Baltimore's dicier neighborhoods to countries on the other side of the globe: how, in a strange place where she knew no one, to go about reporting the story that she was sure was there.

FOUR

The smell hit Lola when they walked into the unlocked house. She sat Margaret in a kitchen chair and ordered Bub to stay with her while she made a quick search, not knowing precisely what she was looking for.

Not a body, thank heavens; it didn't have the whiff of putrefaction with which she'd become all too familiar during her time overseas. Lola held her hand over her face as she ran from room to room, flinging open doors. The house was empty, the smell receding the farther she got from the kitchen. She retraced her steps, opening windows in each room so the wind could chase away the reek she at first attributed to the empty, unwashed cans of ravioli marching down the kitchen counter, and finally to a trash can under the sink, soupy with the rotting remains of what appeared to be most of the contents of those cans. The neck of an empty liquor bottle poked up through the glop, as if seeking oxygen. Lola thought of the blast-furnace temperatures of the last few days, of the pasta and sauce breaking down with the plastic confines of the trash can, of the microbes swimming through the stinking mess, multiplying exponentially every few seconds. Even Bub, who'd crept away from Margaret's chair and across the kitchen floor to Lola, wrinkled his nose in fastidious distaste.

At least Pal had had the foresight to line the can with a trash bag. Lola gathered the crusted cans from the counter and tossed them into the bag, then knotted it and carried it out onto the porch and beyond, leaving it in the yard. She noticed a long-handled shovel by the front door, and gave a moment's thought to burying the bag. They'd left the house, what—three days earlier? Not a long time for such serious disarray. She searched for rubber kitchen gloves, thinking to scrub down the counters, but found none, determining only that canned goods appeared to be the sole form of sustenance in the house. The ravioli alone was new. The rest of the cupboards' contents, including several neatly labeled jars of home-canned jams and vegetables, were so outdated that Lola consigned them to a fresh trash bag. She turned her attention to the duffel she'd seen in the bedroom. She hadn't noticed the smell when she'd picked up Pal at the airport. But the bag had ridden in the bed of the truck. Now, in close quarters, it reeked. Lola unzipped it. "Pee yew, Mommy," Margaret protested. Lola averted her face and upended the contents into the washing machine that stood in one corner of the kitchen. It was possible, she thought, that Pal hadn't washed her fatigues at all for her last few months in Afghanistan. "Bet she was a treat to be around," she said aloud. Someone must have forced Pal to shower, to put on clean clothes for the trip home, she thought.

She located a box of laundry detergent that appeared prehistoric, its contents solidified into a sort of cement. Lola retrieved a paring knife and jabbed away at it, chipping off pieces into the washing machine. Pal didn't have anything in the way of delicates, as far as Lola could tell. Her underwear was industrial-strength cotton; her bras, yellowed sports varieties.

The screen door banged open. Lola spun around. Margaret slid from the chair and ran to her side. Bub stood his ground and barked. Lola couldn't hear Pal's words over Bub's racket, but had no problem at all making them out.

"What the fuck?"

Eyes boring straight through Lola as she said it, no concern whatsoever that a child was within earshot. Bub shut up, so that when Pal said it again, the words rang through the kitchen. "What the ever-loving fuck?"

Margaret tugged at Lola's jeans. "Quarter in the jar, Mommy." It was their rule that whenever anyone cursed—*anyone* mostly being Lola—a quarter went into a jar. Every so often, Margaret was allowed to spend the quarters on a book.

Lola picked her up. "I don't think she plays that game."

Pal stood backlit in the doorway, face in full shadow, but her fury palpable, not just in her words but her stance, leaning forward, balancing on the balls of her feet, hands clenched.

Lola threw some anger of her own right back at Pal. "Jan was worried about you. And with good reason. You've trashed this place in just a few days. It stinks in here. Don't you ever take out the garbage? Your clothes are disgusting. I'm probably going to have to wash them twice, just to get the smell out. You just cursed—twice—in front of my daughter. And speaking of my daughter, you've been drinking in here, too. That shit—sorry, Margaret—stops now. At least, not in front of my daughter. I don't know if you smoke. God knows, that's the one smell I didn't pick up on. But if you do, you're not to smoke around Margaret, either. In fact, not in the house at all. I'm going to stay here until I'm sure that you're eating decent food, wearing clean clothes, and generally taking care of yourself. And then, believe me, I will be gone as fast as I can drive that truck away from here. Are you getting all of this?"

Pal stepped into the room. The door slammed behind her. She wore a sweat-soaked tank top and abbreviated shorts and wide-soled running shoes. Lola gave herself a moment to be impressed. Pal didn't look as though she had the strength to run, especially given the ferocious hangover she had to have. The woman had grit. And some sort of discipline, which apparently fled the moment she stepped into the house and confronted the basics of nutrition and cleanliness.

"You need to leave. Right now," Pal said.

Lola's ire flared anew. "We're not going anywhere. Margaret, you take your things into the bedroom where we stayed before. Bub, go with her." As long as Margaret was safe, she reasoned, she could handle whatever Pal might throw at her—perhaps literally.

"What the—"

Lola cut her off before she could curse again. "Not in front of Margaret. I'm serious."

"What gives you the right to do this?"

"Your cousin. She's a pain in the ass—it seems to be a family trait—but she's the closest thing to a sister I've ever had. Which apparently is how she feels about you. Here's why you're going to let me stay."

Sweat ran into Pal's eyes. She swiped an arm across her forehead and shook the moisture from it, wincing.

Lola pointed to Pal's forearm. "That had to sting, right? All that salt in those cuts?"

Pal looked at her arm as though she'd never seen it before.

"Either we stay here until you're back on your feet—and that had better only take a few days—or I'm telling your cousin about those."

Pal folded her arms across her chest, too late to hide the fact that she'd added two new scars across two of the old ones, three X's now marring the skin covering her scrawny forearm.

FIVE

LOLA WOKE ALONE THE next morning. The single bed, in which Margaret and Bub had also spent the night waging an apparent contest to suffocate her, had gone roomy and cool.

Voices reached her. Margaret's declarative confidence. A low-pitched response, barely above a whisper—Pal. And, a man's. Lola hadn't heard anyone knock. She threw the covers aside and bolted for the kitchen in her nighttime attire of threadbare T-shirt and a pair of Charlie's boxers, sliding low on her hips. She hitched them up. Three heads turned. Four. Bub bounded to attention. Margaret sat in Pal's lap, comfortable in comparison to Pal, who held herself rigid as though Margaret were somehow breakable and that movement would send her shattering against the floor. The man at the table raised a hand in greeting. Before Lola had lived in Afghanistan, before she'd moved to Montana—dry places where sun and wind and dry air sucked moisture from skin, causing it to collapse upon itself in folds and crevices years before its time, Lola would have put his age at eighty. Now she knew better. Seventy, max, she figured, and likely

28

closer to sixty. There may have been a stray tooth or two somewhere in his caved-in mouth, but if so, they were in the back, where they rarely saw the light of day. His nose had been broken so many times that whatever arch it once held had disappeared within a bulbous mass. The braids that hung to each elbow were woven with grey, his skin a darker brown than Charlie's, and certainly than Margaret's. No wonder she hadn't heard a knock. Indian people were far too polite to go around banging on other people's doors. Lola watched as his eyes strayed Margaret's way, the nod of recognition as he assessed her complexion, the hair that gleamed like onyx in the early morning light.

"Delbert St. Clair," he said, when no one else spoke. So he did have a couple of teeth after all.

"This is Lola," Pal said into the silence. "Delbert's already met Margaret here." She gestured stiffly toward the child in her lap, who turned a beatific smile upon her. Pal flinched and stretched her lips in return.

Lola stepped to the table and held out her hand, barely touching her fingertips to Delbert's, shaking hands the Indian way, not the hard handclasp and firm pump she'd have used with a white person.

Delbert pursed his lips. "Huh." He clutched a paper sack in one misshapen hand. "Brought Pal here some breakfast. If I'd known she had company, I'd have made sure there was more. That girl down the convenience store gave me extra yesterday. She sees handsome and starts throwing doughnuts around like they're free."

Margaret slid from Pal's lap and scooted to Delbert's side, eyes fixed upon the sack. Lola shook her head at her daughter, whose list of approved foods was far too short, at least as far as Margaret was concerned. Diabetes was rampant among the Blackfeet, the legacy of poverty and the lack of access to the fresh fruits and vegetables, whose price soared the farther they were shipped from cities. Charlie did most of the cooking in their own household and as a result,

Margaret's diet was relentlessly healthy and Lola's had vastly improved. But Lola remained wary of the fry bread and fast foods that flashed enticements at every turn, and was determined that Margaret not succumb. On the other hand, there was nothing to eat in Pal's house but ravioli. And coffee. Lola inhaled in gratitude. Thankfully, it existed and someone had made a pot.

"That girl at the convenience store isn't a day over seventeen," Pal said. "You're dreaming, Delbert."

Lola started. She hadn't thought Pal capable of anything approaching humor.

"I'd say she's the one who's dreaming. Dreaming of what life could be like with a man who's done some living."

Lola poured herself a cup of coffee and joined the mismatched group at the table that sat in the center of the large kitchen that also functioned as living and laundry rooms. Whatever feminine touches Pal's mother might have lent to the room had vanished upon her death. A garish green easy chair sat next to a worn brown couch patched with duct tape, facing a TV table absent its television. Jan had said that Delbert had taken care of Pal during the two years after Pal's parents died, and before she and Delbert's grandson had enlisted in the military. Lola imagined Delbert and his grandson batching it with Pal during those years, eating meals of canned food in front of the television in companionable silence. The TV, she guessed, had gone to Delbert's house during Pal's deployment.

"Delbert thinks he knows a thing or two about women," Pal said now. "All evidence to the contrary."

"Evidence to the contrary, my ass. I've buried three wives. Wore 'em right out. Now I'm fighting off one who fancies herself as Number Four."

"Dolores Wadda still after you?" Pal said. "Woman needs her head examined."

Lola thought she and Margaret must look like a pair of metronomes, their heads swinging back and forth from Delbert to Pal. Margaret almost certainly didn't understand the conversation, and for that matter, neither did Lola. The body language was all wrong for the banter, Pal staring a hole in the table as she spoke, Delbert peering just as fixedly at Pal, the pain in his eyes contradicting the smile that revealed a third tooth. It was almost as though the two of them were putting on a show for Lola and Margaret.

Delbert opened the bag, retrieved a doughnut, and pressed it into Pal's hand. He wiped his fingers, powdered with sugar, against his work pants. Pal held the doughnut without tasting it. She took a sip of the coffee. Red lines threaded the whites of her eyes. One cheek was crimson and flattened, as though she'd slept all night with her face pressed against the table. The sack rustled. "Here." Delbert withdrew another doughnut and broke it into two uneven pieces and handed one to Lola and one to Margaret, who looked a question to her mother. Lola took a bite. It was stale. She considered a breakfast of ravioli, saw again the seething mass in the trash can, and forced a smile. "Go ahead. It's fine."

Pal nibbled at her own doughnut, barely breaking the surface. Sweat beaded her forehead. Sweating out the alcohol, maybe, Lola thought. The night's cool still lingered in the kitchen.

"The Fourth's coming," Delbert said. "Everybody'll be out at the cemetery."

Pal ducked her head and rubbed at the scars on her forearm. The scab broke off one of the fresh wounds. Blood threaded its way down her arm. She bent her head and licked it away.

"The cemetery?" Lola asked. The silence lasted long enough for Lola to wish she hadn't posed the obvious question.

"Delbert's grandson—" Pal began.

"Mike. Got killed over there last year."

The odds would have been against Mike, Lola thought. Proportionally, more Indians than any other ethnic group volunteered for military service, a warrior tradition dating back to the first World War, even though all the Indians living within the United States didn't get the right to vote until 1957. Send-offs and homecoming ceremonies for soldiers, Marines, and the rare sailor were common occurrences on the Blackfeet Nation. Lola covered them all for the *Daily Express*, thankful for each story that involved anyone completing a tour of duty without serious physical injury. The mental toll on those who returned—that was a matter she had yet to explore.

"Firefight?" she asked. "Or IED?" The questions were automatic, based on her own years in war zones, where the roadside bombs known in military jargon as improvised explosive devices seemed to claim as many casualties as actual battle.

"Neither," Delbert said. "They say—"

Pal's doughnut fell from her hand. A mushroom cloud of powdered sugar puffed up from the table. "Never mind about that shit they say."

Margaret opened her mouth. Lola shook her head at her. Delbert and Pal seemed to finally have strayed into the dangerous territory they'd been avoiding.

"You go on and eat all of that doughnut now," Delbert said. Concern sharpened his voice. Pal picked it up, took another squirrel-sized bite, and changed the subject. "Delbert lives down the hill," she told Lola. "On the reservation."

Lola thought of the house she'd seen just before the turnoff to the two-mile gravel road that led up and over a series of hills to Pal's place.

It was a typical Bureau of Indian Affairs shoebox, and just about as sturdy, barely a step up from a trailer, with a cone of tipi poles rising beside it. "What reservation?"

"Wind River. Arapaho and Shoshone. Historic enemies, assigned together to the same reservation. Maybe somebody thought they'd finish each other off." Pal made a coughing sound that could have been a laugh. "Delbert here's Shoshone. There's about three times as many Arapaho as Shoshone."

"But we're tougher."

Lola looked again at Delbert's nose, the cauliflower ears. She was willing to bet he'd gotten the best of his opponents.

"Ladies'll be making the flowers," he offered.

Once again, Lola was forced to ask.

"What flowers?"

"For the graves. They decorate them fresh for the holiday. Might be Mike won't get any flowers, though."

Lola feigned interest in her doughnut, trying to disguise how badly she wanted to hear more about Mike.

"Enough about the cemetery!" Pal banged her hand onto the table, smashing her own unfortunate doughnut. Bub, alert to the burst of food scent, shot to Pal's chair. Pal swept the doughnut's remnants to the floor, where Bub hoovered them up. Breakfast was clearly over. Delbert pushed back from the table and headed for the door. One of his legs worked better than the other.

Lola hurried after him. "Nice to meet you, Mr.—" She needed to fix his name in her brain.

"St. Clair. Delbert St. Clair."

She held out her hand to him again. Delbert's fingers shook in hers. His eyes were moist.

"Make sure she eats," he said. "She tells me she's fixing herself dinner every night. But there's barely anything to her."

Lola thought of the empty ravioli tins and the full trash can, as though Pal had dumped the cans' contents after a single taste. "Yes," she said. "She's fixing dinner." He hadn't asked whether Pal actually ate it.

"You take care," he told her.

But he looked toward Pal as spoke.

SIX

THE TRIP FROM THE ranch to town took half an hour. Lola gasped anew whenever the pickup crested another rise and the horizon leapt away, mile after treeless mile in every direction. The landscape's unwelcome resemblance to that of Afghanistan struck her again. She reminded herself of the differences: the luxury of a smooth paved road, a truck that she could drive without hiring a man to do it for her, and the absence of anyone intent upon killing her. Still, the old tendrils of unease, her constant companion during her years overseas, curled insistently around her spine.

The outskirts of Thirty arose, sudden hard angles amid the rolling hills and wind-rounded rocks. Lola left her memories behind and pointed the truck toward the offices of the *Last Word*, Thirty's weekly newspaper. She intended to find out everything she could about the soldiers who went to Afghanistan, starting with the first body blow that had come in the form of Mike St. Clair's death. She'd gone to the newspaper's website on her phone the previous night, looking in vain for an online archive, but beyond posting a sampling of stories from each week's edition, the *Last Word* had yet to go fully digital. She drove around the block, seeking a parking place in the shade, and retraced her route on foot with Margaret to the newspaper office, forcing herself not to look back at Bub, whose drooping ears and tucked-in tail telegraphed a full sulk. A woman behind the front desk removed a cherry popsicle from her mouth at the sight of Lola and Margaret. Her face glistened.

"Sorry about the heat. Air conditioner's broke. Been broke for two weeks now. Every day, the publisher passes out popsicles to help us keep cool. He musta got a crate of 'em the last time the store had a sale. Cheap S.O.B." Her lips were stained red. A scarlet droplet ran down the popsicle stick, skittered across her thumb and wrapped itself in a line around her wrist. Lola explained their mission.

"You wait here. I'll see about those back copies. You want a popsicle?"

"No, thank you," said Lola, over Margaret's hopeful intake of breath. While they waited, Lola read a plaque summarizing the *Last Word's* brief history. She'd already surmised that newspapering and the town were inextricably linked, given that, back in the long-gone days of hot type, the notation "—30—" signaled to pressmen that they'd reached a story's end. The plaque confirmed her guess. A newspaperman had founded the town after the Conestoga wagon that had hauled his printing press across a thousand miles of prairie irreparably foundered on the banks of the nearby Popo Agie River. The receptionist returned, sans popsicle, and held open a door for Lola and Margaret. "You can come back now. Honey, I think I can find a toy or two for you to play with while your mommy does her work."

"She's fine," Lola said. Margaret had spent much of her young life in the *Daily Express* office, learning early how to entertain herself, drawing flaking pictures on pieces of printer paper with red grease pencils and old bottles of Wite-Out that nobody had gotten around to throwing away. Lola handed Margaret a pen and looked around. The people in the room spoke into phones tucked between ear and shoulder, or tapped at their computers. Lola filched a couple of pieces of paper from a printer tray and gave them to Margaret, then she approached the daunting stacks of what looked to be decades' worth of newspapers.

"Looking for anything in particular?"

Lola took a single glance at the guy who'd posed the question and knew him for a reporter. Shave a little past due, shirt a little too wrinkled, demeanor a little too pleasant. The old competitiveness flared, the resistance to telling another reporter what she was working on. But she wasn't actually doing a story. Technically, she was still on vacation. Even though she'd felt far more relaxed than at any point on her so-called vacation the minute she'd stepped into the *Last Word* and inhaled the comforting scents of dust and ink and the never fully eradicated smoke of now-forbidden cigarettes; more at home in a newsroom than she was anywhere else. "Just checking out something for a friend," she said. "We're here on vacation. "

"You've got a funny idea of vacation."

About Jan's age, she figured, getting his start at a small newspaper, where he'd spend as little time as possible before jumping to the first big daily that would take him. If the bigs were even hiring anymore. Which, in Lola's recent experience, they weren't. He came out from behind his computer terminal and sauntered toward her, lanky and loose-limbed. Lola took in the cargo shorts made of some sort of indestructible material, the wiry calves knotted with muscle, the Vibram-soled sandals that would have eaten up a good part of his weekly salary, and revised her opinion. The Wind River area was home to an internationally renowned outdoors school, priced accordingly, that attracted people from all over the country who wanted to acquire the skills necessary to kayak off the Australian coast, climb mountains in Patagonia, backpack in the Yukon. Some of those folks came, completed the programs, and left again, but others stayed in the area, working jobs that kept them afloat during the week, heading into the Winds—as locals called the Wind River Range—on weekends and vacations for more of the sorts of near-death experiences in which the school specialized. At least, that's how Lola viewed their activities. The *Last Word's* reporter, she decided, was most likely a trustafarian, slumming in Wyoming with the safety net of mommy and daddy's money. Such good bone structure and straight teeth went beyond vitamins and orthodontia, bespeaking generations of good breeding. The confident slouch she attributed to prep school and a history of success with women.

"Dave Sparks." His thin lips quirked in a smile. He held out his hand.

She took it, feeling the roughness in his fingertips, and slid her gaze along his arms. From a distance, Dave Sparks looked like a scarecrow, but up close his biceps challenged the seams of his shirt. Rock climber, then. She imagined him spread-eagled halfway up a cliff, that expansive wingspan to his advantage.

"Lola Wicks." She let go of his hand and held her hair away from her neck. The newsroom was, if anything, even warmer than the lobby. "Don't you rate a popsicle?"

"I don't eat sugar." He flashed his perfect teeth.

Of course you don't, she thought. She pointed to the yellowing newspapers crammed into the slotted shelves. "Is there a system here?"

"If you can call it that. You looking for any particular time frame? That's the easiest way."

Again, she went with vague. Soldiers served one-year stints in Afghanistan and Iraq. Lola had called Jan to try and pinpoint the date of Mike St. Clair's death, without success. "Last spring," Jan had said.

"That's more or less the last time I heard from Pal. She told me a friend of hers had gotten killed, and that was it. Why do you want to know?"

"Just curious," Lola had said. Which was true enough. "I'll start with March," she told Dave Sparks now.

He led her to the correct shelves. She looked at the stacks of newspapers. She'd come to take for granted the search-term-and-click efficiency of Google. It had been years since she'd resorted to microfiche, let alone paged through actual hard copies. Hanging around a newsroom, especially the one offering the sort of scenery that Dave Sparks offered, was momentarily pleasant, but putting a lot of work into only the vaguest notion of a story was another matter. Thirty was small, but Lola had already noted a coffee shop, a bookstore and, most important, a compact but newish supermarket that undoubtedly would offer more than canned ravioli. She had better things to do with her time than dirtying up her hands with newspaper ink. She decided to forego pride in favor of speeding up the process.

"How long have you worked here?" she asked Dave.

"Couple of years."

She blinked. Most trustafarians, no matter how they rhapsodized about the great wide open, soon fled back to the delights of a city, unleashing their love of wilderness in two-week vacations.

"Does the name Mike St. Clair ring a bell? Got killed over in Afghanistan a few months back?"

"Remember him? It was a big story here. Local boy and friends enlist together, serve together. Every last one of them grew up here. They'd all known one another since grade school. Losing one of them hit all the families hard. And now—" He started to say something else, then stopped.

"What?" said Lola. She reminded herself that, as far as he knew, she remained unaware of the suicide.

He shook his head. "I've got a story to finish. You read all the coverage, then maybe we can grab coffee. You'll probably have some questions." He started toward his desk, then turned back. "Mike died in April. But you'll want to go back before that. There was a story when they all enlisted, right after graduation last year. Start there."

Lola moved along the shelves until she'd located the previous June. She heaved an armload of papers onto the table and set herself to the task at hand. She'd have questions, Dave had said. So she'd be looking as much for what wasn't in the stories as what was. She muttered under her breath as she turned page after page. "What the hell could that possibly be?"

SEVEN

An hour later, Lola had learned that Palomino Jones once had a mane of blond hair that did justice to her name. It swung nearly to her waist in the photo of her with the group who'd enlisted in the Army the day after graduation. They stood, arms around one another's waists, laughing into the camera, the picture of youthful health and optimism and absolute ignorance of the world in which they were about to be immersed.

Lola pulled out the reporter's notebook she always carried with her, even on vacation, and wrote down their names. The third name stopped her. Cody Dillon, the soldier who'd killed himself at the airport. Lola repeated Pal's words aloud. "'Didn't know the guy.' What a bunch of bullshit." Lola glanced Margaret's way to be sure she hadn't heard. She was running low on quarters. The next two names rang a bell. She unzipped her bookbag and pawed through its detritus, seeking the newspaper she'd picked up in Yellowstone. Sure enough, the names of the recently jailed soldiers were in the caption below the photo. She copied them into her pad, doodling stars next to all three names. Such a small group. Such big trouble. Such a good story. "*No*," she said aloud. She didn't have to write it. Could stay another day or two with Pal, just as Jan had asked, and then resume her vacation.

"Mommy?" Margaret looked confused. She wasn't doing anything wrong.

"You're fine," Lola reassured her. "Mommy's just talking to herself. Here." She fished through the bookbag again until she found a previously overlooked sandwich bag of whole-wheat crackers for Margaret that she'd packed before leaving home. She turned her attention back to the papers, taking care with pages already going brittle. A brief story ran a few weeks after the one about the enlistment, just a notice that the whole group had successfully completed basic training and had been assigned to the same unit, headed for Afghanistan. She replaced the June papers and wrestled an armful from the following spring onto the table. April yielded the terse notice that a local soldier, Mike St. Clair, died there.

So far, so standard, Lola thought. She checked on Margaret. The crackers were gone, the baggie dutifully deposited in a trash can. Margaret lay on the floor, covering pieces of paper with scribbles, murmuring the story that went with the pictures. Good. The paper wrinkled beneath Margaret's sweat-dampened arm. Lola tore a blank page from her notebook and accordioned it into a tiny fan. She handed it to Margaret and made another for herself. It didn't help. Lola wiped her ink-smeared fingers on her pants and paged through the next few days' newspapers until she came to a longer story about Mike's death, this one accompanied by a photo. Delbert's own face had been so rearranged over the years that it was impossible to discern familial resemblance in his grandson. Lola thought that if it had once existed, Delbert must have been a striking man in his youth. Mike had wide eyes under bushy brows, a straight nose, a long jaw, and a serious expression behind which an incipient smile lurked. She knew she should just ask Delbert about his grandson. But the depth of sorrow in his eyes when he'd spoken of Mike, and the knowledge that to question him would increase that sorrow, had stopped her. It would amount to causing pain to an elder, as unthinkable as it was unforgiveable.

She turned her attention to the story that, as had the others, carried Dave's byline. It started with the standard recitation of Mike's achievements—good enough student, better athlete, eager to follow the family tradition of military service that had seen his grandfather serve in Vietnam and his father one of the cruelly few casualties of the first Gulf War. Then it got around to Mike's own death.

"Mommy?"

Lola knew she must have gasped aloud. "Nothing," she said. "A tickle in my throat." She coughed a couple of times and for good measure put her hand to her neck, covering the same place where Mike St. Clair had suffered the gruesome wound that killed him.

———

"Was that the issue? That his—" Lola looked toward Margaret, who was busy dissecting her sandwich and rearranging it in a way that better suited her. Still, Lola was unable to bring herself to say the words aloud. She drew her finger across her throat.

She and Margaret and Dave Sparks sat at a table in, of all things, an organic foods café that existed to serve the outdoors school's participants. At least, that's what Lola thought when she first saw it. She scanned the room and thought again. The people at the mismatched kitchen tables and whimsically painted wooden chairs would have looked at home in Nell's Café back in Magpie, ranchers who'd traded in their wintertime coveralls for lightweight canvas summer pants and long-sleeved work shirts that provided protection not only against the sun but dust, itchy chaff, and bedeviling insects. A few, like Lola, wore running-style shoes, but most wisely stuck with work boots, opting for safety over comfort.

Dave noticed her look. "Good food is good food," he said. "A lot of the people who come here pull the sprouts from the sandwiches"—as Margaret herself was doing, piling up a miniature green mountain range along one side of her plate—"but they seem to like the rest just fine."

Lola thought the rest was more than fine. The ham in her ham and cheese between generous slices of what tasted like homemade bread was thick and moist, nothing like the floppy processed slices at Nell's, and the cheese had a fine sharp bite. Usually she saved part of her sandwich for Bub, but he was going to go without his customary treat today. She thought of the canned ravioli back at the house and took a bigger mouthful. "Mike," she mumbled around it, bringing Dave back to the topic at hand.

"What a tragedy. You must know how important military service is to the tribes." He looked at Margaret. There was no mistaking her for a white child.

Lola nodded and chewed.

"When somebody gets killed after falling asleep on watch, that's hardly a hero's death."

Lola forgot about manners. "What are you talking about?" she said past a fresh mouthful of sandwich.

Dave reached for Margaret's sprouts and stuffed them into his own sandwich. He'd gone for hummus, Lola noted. No sugar, and probably a vegetarian, too. Lola wondered if he drank coffee. She didn't trust reporters who foreswore caffeine. Just as the thought occurred to her,

Dave signaled a waitress and asked for a cup of coffee. She decided to forgive him for calling it java. "Two," he said. "Black? Iced?"

"Yes," said Lola, "and no." The café's air-conditioning was in fine working order, a welcome respite from the newsroom. But no matter how high the mercury climbed, Lola considered iced coffee only slight less of an abomination than coffee ruined by cream and sugar.

Dave waited until the mugs sat steaming before them. "There's talk around town about Mike," he said. "People say Mike was on watch while the rest of them slept, but that he fell asleep, too, and the guy crept up on him and cut his throat. Could have killed everybody else. Just luck that he didn't."

Lola lifted her mug and blew wavelets across the coffee's surface. "That's impossible. Those bases have got perimeters that Superman couldn't bust through. It must have been an inside job. One of those American-trained Afghani soldiers who turned out to be a Talib."

Dave ran the heel of his hand over close-cropped hair. "Nope. They were on their way back from a village, just a small group of them. As I understand it, their vehicle broke down and they were waiting for a replacement. They were close, only about a mile away. But this guy came across them and took advantage of the situation, I guess."

Lola turned her attention to the fries, sweet potato, and obviously homemade, as was the tangy ketchup that accompanied them. "What was he doing out of the vehicle? That's not exactly standard procedure."

"I wouldn't know what standard procedure is," Dave parried.

You could ask, Lola thought. It's what reporters do. She reminded herself that it would hardly serve her purposes to insult him. Then came close, anyway. "None of this was in the paper. So it's just gossip, then."

"Gossip, maybe." He dunked a fry into the pleated paper container of ketchup. "Maybe more. It'll never be in the paper because the editor didn't think it needed to be. The idea was that Mike's grandfather had suffered enough, losing him. Why make his shame public?"

"But what if that's not how it happened?"

Dave's shoulder lifted. "We'll never know, will we? Besides, what if it's something even worse? This seemed the best thing for all concerned." He changed the subject. "You're going to want to try the dessert."

Margaret's face lit up. Lola's darkened. "We don't do dessert."

"You might change your mind. Look here." He turned the menu toward her, pointing out the no-sugar, vegan-crust benefits of the pie. "It's good. Really," he said, an assurance accompanied by a look so simultaneously earnest and droll that Lola succumbed, admitting aloud after the first bite that he might just have been right. Dave touched his tongue to his upper lip to remove a crumb. Lola crossed her legs. She'd been away from Charlie—what, less than a week?—and here she was, going all swoony for a good-looking, barely-more-than-teenage guy in shorts. Dave wore a bracelet on his left wrist, a complicated affair of woven leather thongs and an occasional silver bead, the kind of thing no man wore unless a woman bought it for him. Lola pointed her fork at it. "Doesn't that snag on things when you're climbing?"

"How'd you know I climb?"

Lola sat her fork down and took his hand and turned it palm-up. *Shame, shame, shame,* her internal voice scolded. She ignored it. It had been a long time since she'd flirted with anyone. There was no harm in enjoying the feeling, she told herself, as long as flirtation was as far as it went. She traced his calluses with her thumb. "You didn't get these pushing a pen across a notebook or banging away on a keyboard."

He folded his hand around hers. "Why's a reporter from Montana working on a story in Wyoming?"

"How'd you know—?" Lola stopped, nodding acknowledgment. He'd gone back to his desk and Googled her name the minute she'd introduced herself, exactly as she would have done if the roles had been reversed. "You got me," she said. "But I'm not working on a story."

"Then why?"

"Just curious," she said. "I was at the airport when that guy killed himself in front of everyone. It got to me and I didn't even know him. It has to affect the community. You must be working on something about that."

Dave withdrew his hand. "No. Nothing more than what I've already written."

Margaret fidgeted in her chair, her own sliver of pie, shaved from Lola's piece, long gone. Her accusing look at Dave mirrored her mother's, albeit for different reasons. Margaret just wanted to get out of the restaurant. But Lola had one more question.

"Why not? It's such an obvious story." So much for flirtation, she thought. Nothing killed an urge like the implication of incompetence or, at best, indifference. To his credit, Dave Sparks met her gaze directly. His eyes were clear and hazel and extravagantly lashed, a softness at odds with the rest of his lean, spare body. "I live here," he said. "But I'm not from here. Just like you're not from that town in Montana. You know the drill."

Lola did indeed. Poking a stick into war wounds would stir up resentment. Locals would blame the paper in general and Dave in particular for airing whatever dirty laundry he might uncover. Advertisers might decide to spend their money elsewhere. All the old reasons. "If you're going to stay in this business"—she spoke aloud despite herself—"you've got to grow a way thicker skin."

"So noted." He might not have been in the business long, but he'd already developed a practiced, professional smile, nothing like the endearingly crooked grin he'd turned upon her earlier. Just as well, thought Lola as she said goodbye. The last thing she needed was a distraction like Dave. Still, he'd been distracting enough that she'd finished her grocery shopping and was on her way back to the ranch, Margaret asleep in her booster seat, before her mind returned to the ominous phrase he'd shoehorned into their conversation about the rumors surrounding Mike's death.

"What if it's something even worse?"

EIGHT

LOLA ARRANGED THE GROCERIES on the kitchen counter with a sense of dread. She'd grabbed some of the items Charlie routinely brought home without giving much thought to the fact that she had only the vaguest notion how to prepare them.

They sat there—the mushrooms, the carrots, the lettuce, the tomatoes, the ground beef (extra lean, something Charlie always emphasized), the brown rice (again, Charlie's insistence), the bananas and the cereal and the soy milk for Margaret, whose Indian heritage rendered regular cow's milk intolerable. Bub plastered himself to her leg, alert to the fact that the appearance of food meant that some might find its way to the floor.

Margaret played in the cool shade of the porch, investing pieces of kindling filched from the box near the woodstove with names and personalities. Pal was MIA, as were the running shoes she usually kicked off just inside the front door. Lola turned her attention back to the food. It was late afternoon. Soon Margaret would be hungry again. Despite the café's substantial sandwich, Lola already was. What in heaven's name was she supposed to do with the things in front of her? She studied them awhile. Hamburgers, she decided. Despite the fact that she'd forgotten buns, or even bread. Rice. And a salad, even though she hadn't bought any dressing. She mentally compiled a new shopping list. She tore the plastic wrap from the hamburger, washed her hands, and began shaping the meat into lumpy patties, recoiling from its clammy chill, relieved when Margaret's summons interrupted her.

"Mommy, come see."

She rinsed watery hamburger blood from her hands and stepped out onto the porch. Margaret was in the yard, crouched before a tall clump of sagebrush. Bub stood between her and the bushes, nose extended, tail stiff, body quivering. Lola shielded her eyes against the sun. She caught a blur of bright-colored movement along the road. Pal jogged toward them, nearing the end of one of those inexplicable runs.

"What is it?" Lola joined Margaret, the heat slamming her as soon as she left the porch, the same blast-furnace intensity that had marked summers in Kabul, once again resurrecting warring emotions of nostalgia and fear. She'd worked hard to put her years in Kabul behind her. But in this landscape that so resembled that of Afghanistan, the memories had begun to reassert themselves, pricking at her like a too-stiff tag on a new shirt.

"Listen." Margaret stamped her foot.

Lola heard a dry rattle. She peered beneath the sagebrush. Saw fat coils, a raised, spadelike head. She snatched up Margaret and leapt back screaming in a single motion. Bub barked and bounded about. Pal charged up in a flurry of pounding footsteps and swirling dust.

"What's going on?"

"Snake," Lola gasped. Margaret squirmed in her grasp.

"Snake!" Margaret said in an entirely different tone.

"Snake." The look Pal shot Lola's way was pure disgust. "Another snake, I should have said." She marched off toward the porch, dust clumping on the sweat running down her arms and legs. She returned with a shovel. "Stand back."

Lola stepped away. Pal swung. It was Margaret's turn to scream. "You killed it!"

Pal nudged the head, the fanged mouth slowly opening and closing, farther beneath the bush, then slid the shovel under the snake's body and flung it away. A circling raven landed nearby. Bub shot past it and nosed about the still-writhing coils. The raven croaked at Bub and flapped its wings.

"Of course I killed it," Pal said. "Just like I killed the last one, and just like I'm going to kill the next one. Otherwise, when we walk outside, they'll be sinking their fangs in our ankles. What do you think about that?"

Margaret allowed as to how she didn't think much of that at all.

"Besides," said Pal, "there's a present in it for you." She walked over to the snake's body, dragging the shovel behind her. She nudged Bub aside, and stood over the squirming remains. The shovel rose and fell again. She returned and held out her closed hands. "Pick."

Margaret's gaze moved from Pal's hands to her face and back again. Lola sighed. Margaret was like her father in that regard, considering all the options, taking forever to make a choice. Which, Lola had to admit, was usually correct.

"That one." Margaret pointed with certainty to Pal's left hand. Pal uncurled her fingers. The snake's rattles lay across her palm. Margaret lifted them with thumb and forefinger, held them beside her ear, and shook them. "Put me down."

"Please," Lola reminded her.

"Uh-huh," said Margaret. "Put me down."

Margaret called to Bub and they scampered away with her new toy. The porch door banged shut behind Pal. Lola took a long look around to make sure no more snakes lurked, then followed Pal into the house to once again confront the issue of dinner.

———————

A half-hour later, three people sat at the table in silence, moving food around on their plates, Pal's usual modus operandi when it came to meals. This evening, it was Lola's and Margaret's as well. The burgers lay charred and black on their plates, the cut pieces oozing red. Bare lettuce leaves found their way to the edge of the thick crockery plates and floated off onto the table, where hands nudged them beneath the plates' edges. As though she wouldn't find them there later, Lola thought. Even she had to admit the meal was damn near inedible. She'd also forgotten to buy the ketchup and mustard that might have made the burgers palatable. The rice would have been a welcome addition, but the burgers were already sizzling in the pan by the time Lola realized the rice needed nearly an hour's preparation.

"Not a cook," Pal said. It wasn't a question.

"No."

"She looks healthy enough." Pal nodded toward Margaret.

"Her father cooks."

"I miss Daddy." Margaret sounded more angry than sorrowful.

"Me, too." Lola heard the echoing emotion in her own voice. Why had Charlie been so insistent that they go on this vacation that was turning out to be anything but? At least back in Magpie, they could have eaten in the café. Slept in their own beds at night. Walked outside without fear of being set upon by poisonous reptiles. Maybe she could have persuaded her editor to a wink-and-nod arrangement to work on a couple of long-term projects while she was off—knowing, even as the thought occurred to her, that was why Charlie had wanted her out of town. She collected their plates, scooping up the stray leaves of lettuce, and scraping the contents onto a single plate, which she set on the floor for Bub. He took a single sniff and turned an incredulous gaze upon her before setting dutifully upon it, probably afraid if he turned down an offering of leftovers, there might never be another.

"Tomorrow night will be better," she promised. Even though she wasn't sure how. "What would you like to eat?" Maybe if she started planning now.

"Ravioli is fine with me," Pal said.

"No," Lola and Margaret chorused.

"Whatever, then."

Margaret spoke into the silence. "Chicken."

Chicken, thought Lola. They ate a lot of it at home. How hard could it be?

"I'll call Delbert, ask him to pick some up," Pal offered. "He usually goes to the convenience store before he comes up here for breakfast. Maybe he'll bring us some more doughnuts, too." She looked at Margaret as she said it. If the woman had anything regarding a soft spot, Lola thought, it was for Margaret, as improbable as that might seem. Lola wondered if she could somehow use that to get more information out of Pal. Her stomach growled. Food was the more immediate issue. But having Delbert stop at the convenience store was no solution. If it were anything like other reservation stores she'd been in, the only available chicken would be fried, with the added insult of being wildly over-priced.

"Never mind about calling Delbert," she said. "I've got to go into town again tomorrow. I'll pick up the chicken myself. Along with everything else I forgot today."

Pal made a show of yawning and stretching. In a few minutes, she would retreat to the bedroom, passing unobtrusively by the cupboards, making a quick grab for the bottle she'd shield with her body as she left the room. Lola knew Jan would expect her to discourage Pal from drinking. A worthy goal. But not on this night. The last thing Lola needed from Pal was any uncomfortable questions as to why she'd head back into town herself rather than have Delbert pick up the groceries for her. While the *Last Word*'s archives had been of limited help, the daily paper had informed her that two men who'd been arrested in the bar fight had bonded out of jail. Lola had every intention of tracking them down the next day and talking to them about whatever the hell had happened to their unit in Afghanistan.

NINE

TYSON GRAFF MUST HAVE moved the instant the photographer snapped the photo that accompanied the enlistment story, his head a blur atop an angular frame. So his face was new to Lola, a freckled square beneath gingery curls already challenging the remnants of his military buzz cut. But the rangy body had filled out since that post-graduation portrait; muscle, mostly, but the beginnings of a gut, too.

Lola shook a doughy hand, reminding herself that the average MRE contained 1,250 calories, and that it wasn't unheard of for soldiers to consume more than one per sitting. More to the point, the food at the bases was just as heavy on starches and fried crap as anything offered on the reservations. Tyson had been easy to find. He worked in Thirty's hardware store, a fact divulged in the story about his release. The store's owner had stood up in court and offered to hire him on the spot. "We all know what these boys have been through over there," he said. "Well, we don't. But that's the point, isn't it? They've got some big adjustments to make, being back home. We're all here to help them out. There won't be any more problems." No such offer, Lola noted, had been made to Tommy McSpadden, the soldier who'd joined Tyson in the bar fight.

Lola stood with Tyson in the hardware store's cool dimness, in an aisle lined with bins of nails and screws, their metallic, oily scent mingling with that of the varnish on the wooden floorboards and the sweet saltiness emanating from a popcorn machine by the front door. "Is there anywhere private we can talk?" she said. "If you're not busy, that is."

That last, a formality. She and Tyson were alone in the store but for the owner, who cast dark looks their way from his position by the front door. Margaret turned a winsome smile upon the man and his expression softened. Lola hadn't been wild about dragging Margaret back to town with her, but the notion of leaving her at the ranch with Pal was unthinkable. She hadn't considered that Margaret's presence might lessen people's resistance to a stranger asking questions. Tyson raised his voice. "Okay if I take a smoke break?"

The owner nodded, once, the warning in his eyes clear. Tyson was not to say anything untoward to this strange woman from out of town. And Lola was not to stir up any trouble. Tyson led her to a back door that opened into an earlier era. Many of Thirty's storefronts sported updated facades, and wrought-iron lampposts with hanging flower baskets lined the sidewalks, evidence of the coal and oil money that had washed westward from the mines and oil fields on Wyoming's eastern border. But progress had yet to wrap itself around the buildings' backsides, all rough bricks adorned by ghostly painted signs from a bygone era, advertising saddleries, dry goods, farm implements. Lola retreated, wedging herself into the few inches of shade afforded by the store's back wall. It wasn't much of an improvement. The bricks radiated heat. Dust hung like a veil. Lola licked lips gone dry and cracked. She loved the crisp, dry air of the

West, but Wyoming took desiccation to a new level, extracting moisture with ruthless efficiency. Tyson stood in the full sun, not even breaking a sweat, grinning at her discomfiture. Lola remembered how long it had taken her to acclimate to Afghanistan's savage heat, and how quickly she'd lost that resistance upon returning stateside. Give Tyson a month and he'd lose that cocky smile.

"What's this about?" he said.

Nothing shut people down faster, especially people who'd recently tangled with the law, than knowing they were talking with a reporter. Lola would have been required to let him know as much, if she'd actually been working on a story, but on this day she could tell herself in all honesty that she wasn't. Yet.

"I'm just down here on vacation. A friend of mine back in Montana has a cousin, Palomino Jones, who served over there with you. Her cousin is worried about her. She wanted me to check around with her friends, make sure everything's fine." Again, it was almost true. Jan hadn't said anything about talking with Pal's friends. But it was a logical move, Lola reassured herself.

Tyson dropped the cigarette into the dust of the alley and turned his heel atop it.

"Pal Jones, huh? Know her?"

"Met her. Briefly." Again, true. Every encounter with Pal was brief. "Interesting woman," Lola hedged.

Tyson moved farther into the alley, forcing Lola to follow him into the sun. Margaret stayed in the shade. Lola thought of Bub in the truck. She'd rolled down the windows as far as she'd dared and parked it beneath one of the spindly oaks lining Main Street. The trees were another effort at civic improvement, one that had yet to realize its potential. She felt sorry for the dog, panting in the front seat. Moisture trickled from her hairline down the back of her neck, dampening her shirt. Tyson grinned again.

"Hot enough for you?"

"It's nothing compared to Paktika." She named the province on the Afghanistan-Pakistan border where Mike had lost his life.

That was the end of the grin. "What do you know about that?"

"That Mohammed Gul is one rude sonofabitch." Gul was one of the region's minor warlords. The day Lola had interviewed him, Gul had motioned to a servant, who brought the inevitable cups of tea. But instead of serving her one, Gul drank from one cup, then the next, tossing the dregs of each into the dust at her feet, an insult so stunning that even his battle-hardened men had exchanged fearful glances.

"You're not military." Tyson stated the obvious.

"Hardly."

"Then what?"

Lola ignored the question. "Sounds like you all have had a tough time. First Mike getting killed, then Cody Dillon shooting himself in front of all those people. And now your own ... issues."

Tyson's nostrils flared. His freckles ran together across the bridge of his nose, a brown blotch suggesting a mask across his face. "Fucker asked for it."

Lola thought of the account she'd read, and imagined the victim in his hospital bed in Seattle, tubes snaking from every orifice, the machine beeping slowly beside him, the relatives sitting braced against the possibility of any change in that ominous rhythm. "I didn't come here to talk about that," she said. Even though she hoped to get around to it later. "Pal's cousin thinks—"

"I heard you the first time," he said. "Here's what you can tell her cousin."

Lola leaned in, close enough to see the coppery stubble forcing its way through the skin of his chin and jaw. He'd have a five o'clock shadow by two in the afternoon. "What should I tell her?"

"That any problems Palomino Jones has are very much of her own making. Karma's a bitch. Know what I mean?"

Lola moved out of the alley's incandescence into the steadier, ovenlike heat of the shade. "No," she said. "I have absolutely no idea what you mean. Maybe you can tell me."

She spoke to a closed door. The interview—even if it wasn't one, not really—was clearly over.

———————

Lola crossed Tyson Graff's name off her list. Next up, Tommy McSpadden. She was grateful for his unusual last name. There'd been no reference in the newspaper to a hardware store job, or any sort of job or other connections, about McSpadden. She'd meant to ask Tyson how to find him, but he'd ended their conversation before she got the chance. Lola clicked through sites on her phone, finding references to only a single McSpadden family in Thirty. The address, she saw with relief, was in town. She didn't even want to think how much time she could have wasted negotiating one after another of the gravel roads that ran like strands of a comb-over across the bald hills surrounding the town.

The house stood a few blocks off the main street, across from an elementary school. The playground's monkey bars and metal swing-sets sat in full sunlight. Lola thought it could have used a sign warning parents that their children risked third-degree burns if they used the equipment. Not that any of Thirty's young mothers were foolish enough to bring their children to the playground during the day's baking heat. The McSpaddens' house stood in cool contrast, its square of grass well-watered and green, shielded by cottonwoods whose girth and deeply ridged bark indicated stately old age. Cheerful geraniums planted in coffee cans marched up the front steps. Lola parked in the pool of shade beneath one of the trees and rolled down the windows, fighting an urge to simply stay in the truck and enjoy the brief respite from the heat. In just the short ride from the hardware store to the house, Margaret had fallen asleep, her lips puckered around a chubby thumb, wisps of hair stuck to her high damp forehead. Her features were a streamlined version of Charlie's blunt visage, the nose tamed to mere assertiveness, chin like a small smooth stone. She'd be a string bean like Lola, her visits to the pediatrician since birth showing her at the top of the growth charts for height and near the bottom for weight. Lola's heart lurched as she gazed upon her sleeping child. Until she'd had Margaret, she'd never understood the stories about mothers who rushed headlong into flames, dove into churning seas despite their inability to swim, offered themselves to would-be killers, all in the name of saving their children. Comprehension came the moment the nurse had placed newborn Margaret in her arms. "Stay with her," Lola told Bub now. As though he'd do anything else. He curled beside Margaret's booster seat, well aware of his job.

A slight woman answered the front door, wiping her hands on a dishtowel, squaring her shoulders with a visible effort. Exhaustion scribbled the delicate skin beneath her eyes and around the corners of her mouth. She wore a starched pink camp shirt and pink-and-white flowered shorts. Toenails a shade deeper than her shirt winked from her sandals. Lola made a mental note of the effort it cost the woman to maintain the appearance that Everything Was Fine. She wondered what wasn't.

The woman held the door wide, wordlessly inviting Lola in before even ascertaining her name. Lola glanced over her shoulder at the truck, assuring herself she'd have a clear view from the doorway, and stepped inside. The assumption of goodwill that seemed to be first nature in the West, as opposed to the deep suspicion of East Coast residents, still surprised her. "I could have been an ax murderer," she always wanted to say to all the people who, like Tommy McSpadden's mother, ushered her into their homes without an apparent second thought. "A thief. A scam artist."

She might as well have said it, because Mrs. McSpadden found her voice as soon as Lola asked to see her son. "He's asleep," she said, backing deeper into a living room that owed its refreshing cool to closed windows and heavy, drawn drapes rather than air conditioning. The towel slipped from her hands and lay ignored on the floor. Her face flushed red. "Are you from the VA?" She folded her arms, and took a few steps sideways, blocking a hallway that Lola guessed led to the bedrooms, exactly the sort of protective maternal instinct that had tugged at Lola moments earlier. Lola guessed that if a stranger had knocked at her own door, asking about Margaret, she'd have done the same thing.

"No." Lola hovered—reassuringly, she hoped—by the door. "I'm, well, I guess I'm a friend of a friend."

Mrs. McSpadden wasn't buying it, not yet. Her round, wire-framed glasses caught a shaft of sunlight sneaking between the drapes and shot it back at Lola. "What friend?"

Something moved in the hallway. Lola tried to look out of the corner of her eyes, not wanting to draw Mrs. McSpadden's attention to the young man who'd emerged from a bedroom in nothing but his briefs. He was short, like his mother, ribs showing prominent beneath slumped shoulders.

"The friend?" The mother again.

"Palomino Jones. She goes by Pal. I guess they've known each other since school—" She got no further. Mrs. McSpadden moved fast to Lola's side, grasped her elbow, steered her onto the stoop and gave her a shove. Lola caught her balance just before she fell. A shout followed her. Tommy, not his mother.

"That little slut," he yelled. "She's just lucky she didn't get us all killed."

"Tommy, get back to bed." His mother's voice was full of concern. It changed when she spoke to Lola, her words like a slap. "Whoever you are, wherever you came from, you go right on back there. Leave my son alone."

The door closed. A lock clicked. Lola wondered when it last had been locked. She turned to the truck, only to be confronted with two sets of wide-awake eyes. Margaret bounced in her booster seat and pronounced judgment as Lola climbed back into the truck.

"Scary lady."

Lola started the truck and looked back at the house. The drapes twitched. She pictured mother and son peering through the opening, watching to make sure she left. "Not scary," she said. "Scared. People who get mad and yell are usually scared of something."

She steered the truck around a corner, imagining the relief in her wake as she disappeared from Mrs. McSpadden's sight. She wondered what in the world about the very mention of Pal's name could have triggered such a reaction. One thing for sure, she wasn't going to bring up Pal with whomever she interviewed next.

TEN

Lola's Wyoming map had been unfolded and refolded incorrectly so often that it had begun to separate along the seams. She located the pieces that comprised central Wyoming and held them together, seeking anything that resembled a tourist attraction. It had been a morning of rejection, and more awaited in the form of Pal's inevitable surliness when she returned to the ranch. Margaret had been patient with her for most of the day. They were both ready for some time off.

The map was unwieldy, but she preferred it to the phone app that seemed unable to encompass the region's immensity and emptiness in any way that made sense, urging routes through high country that lay beneath snow until well into summer, or suggesting shortcuts over gravel roads so rough as to make the paved route, although fifty miles longer, the faster option.

Lola brought a square of map close to her face and peered at the tiny print within the shaded area that marked the Wind River Reservation. A familiar name caught her eye. Sacajawea Cemetery. "It has to be the same one," she said to Margaret. "The woman who led Lewis and Clark." Margaret turned a blank look upon her. She didn't know about Meriwether Lewis and William Clark yet, but she would the minute she started school. Montana was lousy with Lewis and Clark this and Lewis and Clark that, the famous—infamous, if you were tribal—explorers who'd led the way to white development. Or, again depending upon your point of view, to the destruction of the West.

"We're going to a cemetery," she said. Margaret knew about cemeteries, already having visited the Blackfeet burial ground several times in her young life to pay homage to various elders. Lola had objected at first, falling back on her own memories of chilly Catholic ceremonies populated by stone-faced adults in black standing among regimented rows of granite. But she'd quickly learned that Indian cemeteries were far more intimate places, graves as likely to be defined by wooden markers as imposing stones, and decorated with personal mementoes. Lola's heart broke at the sight of toys on children's graves, and warmed again at the realization of the comfort it must have given those bereaved parents to know their children were surrounded by familiar, well-loved things.

She told Margaret a simplified version of the story of Sacajawea on the way to the cemetery, pointing out that Delbert, the man who visited Pal every day, was Shoshone, just like Sacajawea. "The same way you're Blackfeet," she said.

"Pikanii," Margaret reminded her, using the tribe's own name for itself.

"Right." Lola experienced the familiar sensation of being on the other side of a door, looking into a room that Margaret and Charlie shared, but unable to enter. A sign caught her attention. "Here we are," she said, a bit too brightly. With her first glance, she forgot about her status as a perennial outsider.

Scarlet paper flowers carpeted the hillside, making shushing noises as the wind moved across them. Lola eyeballed Bub so severely that he abandoned his raised-leg stance beside the cemetery gate and instead did his business by the truck. "You stay here," she told him. She didn't mind him burning off energy in the deserted parking lot, but it seemed disrespectful to allow him to cavort among the graves.

Lola led Margaret through the gate and stooped to examine the first site. It was, like the others, covered in flowers made of red tissue paper with green wire stems. The flowers were going pink beneath the punishing sun, their petals tattered by the wind's daily assault. Lola and Margaret wandered among the graves that but for their crimson blankets, were much like those of the Blackfeet, simple wooden crosses or low, narrow stone markers adorned with carved feathers or horses. A single granite monument loomed above the others, announcing Someone of Significance. Lola wondered if white people had been responsible for Sacajewea's marker, and whether she lay unquiet beneath it, oppressed by its weight, longing for the airiness and simplicity of her tribespeople's resting places.

Tobacco, a gift denoting respect, speckled the ground beneath the headstone, along with coins and a few notes on pieces of scrap paper. Lola resisted the temptation to read them. Her phone buzzed. Lola checked on Margaret, who wandered among the rows, stopping to examine the offerings at various graves, and answered it. "Jan?"

"You texted me."

"Right." Lola had tried to call Jan after leaving Tommy McSpadden's house, but Jan hadn't answered. So Lola simply texted 9-1-1, their signal for important calls.

"What's so urgent?"

"Your cousin—"

"Oh, God. What's wrong? Do I need to come down there?"

"Whoa, whoa." Lola held up her hand, a calming gesture that Jan couldn't see. "Take it easy. First of all, you can't leave until I get back. You'll get fired. And anyway, nothing's wrong. I just had a few questions for you."

Jan's sigh was audible. "You're sure nothing's wrong?"

Lola was not sure; in fact, was certain something was very wrong. But she didn't want to alarm Jan until she knew what it was.

"She's fine. Just a little closed off. I thought if I could get a better sense of who she is, it'd help me talk to her."

"Shoot." Jan's voice was thick. Lola could picture her talking past the end of the long braid that she usually wore, chewing on it when she was upset or merely thinking hard.

"Well—" Lola wondered how many innocuous questions she'd have to ask before she could get around to the ones for which she really wanted answers. "Was she a good student? Into sports?"

"Yes to both. She pulled down A's without breaking a sweat. And if by sports you mean rodeo, we all did that growing up."

"Why'd she go into the military instead of college?"

Jan's voice regained the sure footing of superiority. "You've been in this part of the world long enough now to know the answer to that one. No way that two-bit ranch ever brought in enough money for her parents to be able to afford a college fund. The military was a great way to make some money fast and still give her the option of college later. Half the kids graduating from any of these schools enlist. Afghanistan and Iraq are the best things to happen for them. Otherwise, they'd be juggling three shit jobs, trying to stay afloat."

Lola bit back her knee-jerk response. Jan was right, she knew. But she couldn't help but think of the kids who came back in boxes. The wars hadn't been good for them at all. "What about her personal life? Did she have a boyfriend?"

"No. Why?"

Lola had veered more quickly toward the key question than she'd planned. From the sudden caution in Jan's voice, she knew Jan had realized it.

"Just wondering." Tommy McSpadden's voice echoed in her head. *That little slut.*

"I'll bet you were. Why were you wondering?"

Lola sidestepped. "It seems like the whole bunch of them who went over there from Thirty were under some kind of strain. One guy, the friend you told me about, got killed there. Another killed himself at the airport—well. You know about that, too. And two more got arrested a day or two after coming home for beating the ever-loving shit out of somebody in a bar. That's a lot of trauma for just a few people."

"Yeah." Jan's voice rang clear. She'd spat out the braid, maybe was on her feet, pacing back and forth across the newsroom, voice rising as she spoke. "You know what it sounds like to me?"

Lola waited.

"Sounds like somebody sees a story for herself."

Lola tried to summon up some righteous indignation. "That's ridiculous. You said it yourself. It's not my state. Not my story. Besides, I'm on vacation."

"Bullshit."

Lola glanced again toward Margaret, as though Jan's voice could have ridden the wind toward the far end of the cemetery. Margaret assessed quarters from whomever she could. Jan spoke even louder. "You've said it yourself, more than once: A reporter is never on vacation."

Jan's end of the call went to garble. Lola heard the squawk of a police scanner in the background, followed by their editor's raised voice. Jan returned to the phone. "I gotta go. You're off the hook. For now. But fair warning, Wicks. This conversation will be continued."

Lola blew out a breath and called to Margaret. The wind carried her own words back to her. She leaned into it, narrowing her eyes against the swirling dust it raised, and trekked to the cemetery's far corner.

"What are you doing all the way back here?"

The face Margaret lifted to her was somber. "This one's lonely, Mommy."

Compared to the floral extravagance atop the other graves, the site seemed forlorn, its plain white marker free of mementoes or other adornment. Lola bent to read the name. Knew before she even saw it.

"Michael St. Clair."

ELEVEN

PAL JABBED AT A hamburger with her fork. It scooted across her plate, coming to a halt against a mound of rice. This time, Lola had flattened the burgers and fried them to a crisp, rendering their interiors a uniform gray, even though their exteriors posed a danger to Margaret's young teeth.

"Guess you decided against chicken," said Pal.

"At least the burgers are cooked through," Lola retorted.

"Unlike the rice," Pal pointed out.

The rice was a bit crunchy, Lola had to admit. Unlike the previous night, she'd started it in plenty of time, but hadn't paid attention to the final direction to let it sit and steam after she turned off the heat.

"I'm sorry about the chicken," she said. "I forgot about stopping by the store when I was in town." She'd been so rattled by her encounters with Tommy McSpadden and Tyson Graff that she hadn't given the groceries a second thought until she'd had to confront dinner again.

Pal tapped her knife experimentally against the burger's crust, whacking it a little harder each time, waiting to see when it would break through. "Didn't you go to town just to get groceries?" *Tap, tap.* "You were gone a long time. If you didn't buy food, what'd you do instead?" *Tap.*

It was the first time Pal had shown the slightest bit of interest in her. Lola wished she hadn't.

"We went to the library," she said. Pal didn't need to know it was the newspaper's library, and that they'd actually gone the day before.

Margaret turned to her. "*Mommy*—" Lola had long given her to understand that lying ranked right up there with cursing and junk food.

Pal's expression, usually so flat, came alive. Her blue eyes went to slits. Lola wondered if that's what she'd looked like as a soldier, rifle raised to her shoulder, sighting her target. "Where are your books?"

"We're not going to be in Wyoming long to make it worthwhile to get a library card and check out books. But it was nice there, in the air conditioning." Thirty had to have a library. And every library she'd ever been in—with the exception of the one at Kabul's university—was air-conditioned.

"Where's your phone?"

"What?" Was Pal going to check out her story? Maybe call the library, see if an out-of-town white woman and her Indian child had been there that day? "Why do you want it?"

"You'll see." Pal held out her hand. Her new scars were healing. She saw Lola looking. "Your phone."

Lola gave it over. "Don't you have your own? What about a land line?"

Pal punched some numbers. "Who was I going to call in Afghanistan? As to the land line, I canceled that when I went overseas. Hey, Delbert."

Lola heard Delbert's voice, his confusion clear, on the other end. Pal cut him off.

"This is Lola's phone. Listen, we've got ourselves a problem." Lola braced herself. She couldn't think of a single good explanation of why she'd been in town, not one that wouldn't tip off Pal, anyway. Pal would probably ask them to leave. This time, they'd have to comply. Lola felt a tug of regret for the story she'd never be able to write. At least she hadn't tried to sell it to anyone yet.

"Yeah, Delbert. I'm fine with ravioli, but we've got a couple of picky eaters up here with us. Lola was going to get some chicken in town today, but she forgot. She forgot a few other things, too. What things? Normal things. Bread, stuff like that. From the supermarket down in town, not the rez store." She paused. Delbert's voice remained unintelligible to Lola's ears. Pal nodded. "Could you? That would be great. Maybe some ice cream for Margaret, too." She ignored Lola's vigorous head shake. "Be sure and keep the receipt so she can pay you back. Oh, and Delbert? If it were me, I'd tack on some kind of surcharge, for gas or delivery or whatever. Thanks."

Lola forced her mouth closed. It was the longest speech she'd ever heard from Pal. The woman looked at Lola with something like triumph in her eyes. Lola nodded acknowledgment. Anything was better, she told herself, than that dead gaze. Besides, the exchange with Delbert had distracted Pal from any further quizzing on the reasons for Lola's trip to town.

———

Lola had learned to listen for the rattle and wheeze of Delbert's fossil of a car, which labored so slowly up the hill to Pal's house that she had time to throw on a T-shirt and jeans and be in the kitchen with Margaret and Pal by the time he arrived for breakfast each morning. But on this day, she somehow slept through its arrival, padding

71

barefoot and late into the kitchen, only to be greeted by a counter crowded with grocery sacks, along with three pairs of eyes suspiciously full of mischief as they regarded her from their places at the table. Even Bub seemed friskier than usual, dashing from Lola to Margaret and back again, tail a blur.

Lola avoided the groceries and poured herself a cup of coffee.

"Delbert got eggs," Pal offered.

Lola gulped coffee. Pal sounded less surly than usual. Whatever these three were up to, she wanted none of it.

"You could cook them," Pal added.

As though you'd eat any, Lola thought.

"Eggs, Mommy. Eggs, eggs," Margaret chanted.

"And bread, too," Delbert chimed in. "For toast."

Lola drained her coffee cup, silently apologized to her scalded throat, and poured another. They'd trapped her. She didn't trust Pal to make breakfast—the woman would probably poison them—and of course Margaret was too little. As for Delbert, custom demanded both that she cook for an elder and serve him first.

"Fine," she said. She tried to remember if she'd ever cooked an egg. When she'd lived alone, if she'd eaten breakfast at all, she'd simply poured herself a bowl of cereal, which she consumed standing at the kitchen counter. But Charlie cooked eggs all the time. She was pretty sure she'd watched him at least once or twice.

"Frying pan?" she said.

Pal pointed to a low cupboard. Lola retrieved a cast-iron pan, set it upon the stove, and twisted the knob until the gas caught. She went through the bags and found the eggs and the bread, along with a wealth of vegetables and condiments and even more soy milk for Margaret. She calculated—no use wasting more than a single egg on Pal, who probably wouldn't eat it anyway—and broke a half-dozen eggs into the pan, recoiling as the white dripped from her fingers.

"Maybe you want a spatula," Pal observed. "There's one in the drawer."

Maybe you want to come over here and cook these damn eggs yourself, Lola thought. She found the spatula and prodded the eggs. The yolks broke and immediately adhered to the bottom of the pan in an immovable mass.

"There's butter in one of them bags," Delbert offered, a little late. That would have kept the eggs from sticking, Lola realized. At least she could butter the toast. She found the bread and popped a couple of pieces in the toaster. By the time she turned back to the eggs, they'd begun to burn about the edges.

"Something stinks, Mommy."

"I'm well aware of that." Lola scraped the mess of eggs onto four plates, tiny amounts for Margaret and Pal, somewhat larger ones for Delbert and herself. A good portion of the eggs remained stuck to the bottom of the pan. The smell of burning bread warred with the eggs' sulfurous reek. Lola whacked the toaster and two carbonized pieces of bread popped up. She ran a knife across the surface, scattering black crumbs into the sink. "I'll take these pieces, if you don't mind, Delbert," she said. She strove to keep her voice even. She wanted to scream. She managed a tight smile. "Let's see if I can do better with the next batch."

"There's some Tabasco and ketchup in those bags," Delbert said. "Might help with the eggs."

It did. By the time Lola was done doctoring her own eggs into edibility, they were more sauce than egg. She gnawed at her pieces of toast, which had lost all resemblance to bread, tasting instead like wooden shingles. Not that she'd ever tasted shingles. The room had gone ominously silent. Even Bub sat frozen in some sort of expectation. Lola tried

73

to come up with an adequate apology, one that would mask her own resentment at being forced into a role for which she was so obviously unsuited. She raised her eyes and opened her mouth to begin.

No one was looking at her. Instead, Margaret, Delbert and Pal all exchanged glances, obviously in some sort of cahoots. Margaret and Delbert shook with silent laughter, and even Pal's typically frosty mien had thawed a degree or two. Lola wondered what else they had planned.

"Jesus H. Christ on a crutch," Lola said. "Whatever the hell you three are up to, out with it." How much worse could this morning get?

"Quarter, Mommy," Margaret said. "Two quarters." She burst into giggles.

"Just for the record, I don't think hell is a particularly bad word."

"Three quarters now, Mommy." Lola told herself that Margaret's superior counting skills indicated her daughter was a math genius, and not just a mercenary little soul.

Pal put a single bite of eggs into her mouth and choked them down, making sure Delbert saw her. The minute he looked away, she put her plate on the floor. Bub heaved a martyred sigh and trudged to do his duty. "You might want to put the chicken away," Pal said. "It could go bad fast in this heat."

"Right." Lola was grateful for any excuse to leave that dreadful table. She searched the bags on the counter. "I don't see any chicken. Did I miss it?"

Margaret had the whooping belly laugh of an adult, so forceful she slid from her chair and rolled onto the floor.

"Delbert," Pal said, raising her voice above Margaret's laughter, "did you forget the chicken?"

"It's not in them sacks?" All three of his teeth showed.

Lola went through the groceries again. "I don't see it," she said. Just as well, she thought. One less thing for her to ruin.

Delbert slapped his leg. "Must be in that bag out on the porch." He left the room. Margaret climbed to her feet and jumped up and down. "He's going to get the chicken, Mommy."

Damn the whole lot of you, Lola thought. This time, she vowed, she'd go to her phone for recipes for chicken. She'd follow directions. She'd make an edible, nay, a delicious dinner, and shut them all the hell up. For just a moment, she thought of Charlie's ultimatum, and of the fact that, if she didn't accept his proposal, she'd be forced to learn to cook. A point in the "yes" column, for sure. The door opened and all thoughts of Charlie and his offer of marriage vanished.

Swinging upside-down from Delbert's hand, its legs bound with twine and its baleful yellow eyes fixed firmly upon her, was a very large, very angry, and very live chicken.

TWELVE

LOLA'S REACTION TO THE chicken assured Margaret of a lavish book fund for months to come. Whenever Lola stopped for air, the chicken squawked, inspiring her to new levels of creativity.

Margaret finally intervened, taking the chicken from Delbert and cradling it in her arms. Once right-side up, it quieted, closing its eyes in bliss as Margaret stroked the top of its head. Its feathers, save for a glossy black band around its neck and chest, were a burnished gold and extended even over its feet, creating an illusion of fluffy boots. "Is it a boy chicken or a girl chicken?"

"This here's a hen," Delbert said. "That's a girl," he added. Just in case.

"Then her name is Jemalina," Margaret pronounced. "Untie her." She cast a glance toward her mother. "Please."

Delbert fiddled with the twine binding the chicken's feet. Margaret put Jemalina down. The chicken fixed eyes like agates upon Lola. It bobbed its head twice, then dashed to her and jabbed its beak into her bare feet, first one, then the other. Once again, the air around Lola purpled as she danced away from Jemalina's unerring aim. Bub dashed to Lola's defense, only to receive a sharp peck on the snoot. He yelped and tumbled backward. Margaret laughed so hard she ended up on the floor again. She held out her arms to the chicken, who scooted back to stand beside her protector. It did not, Lola noted as she rubbed her own reddened toes, seem to have anything against Margaret's feet.

"What am I supposed to do with that thing?" Lola asked. Bub pasted himself against her legs and flashed his incisors at Jemalina. She fluffed her feathers and turned her back on him.

"You said you wanted chicken," Pal reminded her.

"And this here is a chicken," Delbert said.

"No way am I going to cook that."

"You think all meat comes shrink-wrapped on Styrofoam trays?" Pal, always ready with a challenge.

Help came from an unexpected quarter. "We can't eat Jemalina!" Margaret was on her feet, Jemalina back in her arms.

"You might change your mind after a couple of days," Delbert said.

"I won't. Where did she come from?"

"I ran into Dolores Wadda down at the store. When I told her I was after chicken, she said she had some for me."

"Chicken," Pal murmured. "Is that what they're calling it these days?"

"Mind your manners," Delbert said. "Dolores said this one is a good layer, but she's always pecking at people. Dolores was about ready to put her in the soup pot herself. Oh, I almost forgot. I left something else out on the porch, too." He left and came back with a package of supermarket chicken. It went into the refrigerator.

"Jemalina! You're saved," Margaret cooed. Jemalina made a chortling noise and nestled deeper into her arms.

Lola looked at Bub. "Looks like you and I are outnumbered. Here's the deal," she told Margaret. "The chicken is your responsibility. She lives outside. You feed her, you collect her eggs. And you keep her away from people's feet. Sorry, Bub."

The dog slunk to the far side of the kitchen, casting occasional looks of betrayal over his shoulder. The wattage of Margaret's smile could have powered entire cities. "We'll bring her back to Montana with us. Right, Mommy?"

Lola tried to imagine the look on Charlie's face if they showed up with a chicken. If she rejected Charlie's proposal, she'd be stuck with the thing. "I am not," she muttered to herself, as she turned her attention to putting away the rest of the groceries, "basing my decision to get married on a damn chicken."

The good thing about Jemalina was that she occupied Margaret for the rest of the morning, leaving Lola free to tap out elaborate emails on her phone. Charlie had forbidden her to bring her laptop on the trip—"You'll just end up working," he'd said—but now she wished she'd sneaked it into the truck after all. She'd brought a flash drive, but it was little use without a computer. She wrote out a query letter longhand and two-thumbed it into her phone, emailing it to various news outlets.

Then she looked up chicken recipes, clicking through them until she found one that looked both easy and required only the ingredients from Delbert's sacks of groceries. She did a quick tour of the house. No Pal. Nor did she see Pal's running shoes parked in their usual spot beside the front door. Good. She stepped out onto the porch—and hopped back inside, slamming the door behind her, when Jemalina made a beeline for her feet. Lola opened the door a crack. Her daughter stood beside the blasted bird, stroking its head as it turned a look of beady-eyed avian devotion upon her.

"Say goodbye to Jemalina for a little while," Lola said. *For forever*, she wished she could say. "Today, we really are going to the library."

Thirty's library indeed was air-conditioned, and clearly had undergone an upgrade, an interior version of the prettifying throughout the town. The library's improvements were practical as well as attractive. Rows of computers filled one side of the room, books the other. At one end of the stacks, a nook with a sofa and wingback chairs invited a pleasurable few hours of reading. At the other, an oversized stuffed bear and low tables strewn with brightly colored books lured children. Back in Magpie, Lola had often given thanks that the oil boom and its accompanying social and environmental devastation hadn't reached their part of Montana—yet—but now she took a moment to appreciate the benefits of the tax monies it reaped. She stood just inside the front door, pores contracting in the chill, as Margaret ran past her to the children's section. Lola resisted the temptation to follow her, to grab a novel from a shelf, to sink into one of the inviting armchairs and while away the day in cool delicious escapism.

A woman behind a desk raised her head and looked a question her way. Lola reminded herself that she was here to work. "Do you have high school yearbooks?"

"For every town in the county. They're in alphabetical order by town. Over there." She pointed.

Lola found Thirty and pulled the previous four years' books. Early in her career, she'd discovered the font of information that lay between yearbook covers. Activities, athletics, best friends—all helped flesh out portraits of the people she'd written about, whether hero cop or serial killer. A single scowl in a smiling group photo, a star athlete who was also a member of the chess club, an excess of extracurricular activities or an utter lack of participation in same, all of it the rich fodder of telling detail that lifted a story above the mundane.

She pulled out her notebook and her phone, the latter to reproduce photos. An hour later, she had several pages of notes and a dozen photos. Pal barrel-racing, long ponytail flying behind her. Tyson Graff and Tommy McSpadden, bulky in football shoulder pads—no surprise there, Lola thought. Only a few photos of Cody Dillon, the suicide, a youth with a tendency to look away from the camera in all of his photos. In contrast, Skiff Loughry was all over the yearbooks. Student Council. Boys' State. Honor Society. Football, of course. Prom King, with Pal as one of the court princesses. Lola's grimace at the discovery mirrored Pal's expression in the photograph. Lola wasn't the only one who didn't see herself as the poofy-dress type. On the other hand, Pal was clearly no outcast. Lola wondered when the antipathy toward her had begun. In school? Basic training? Or had something happened in Afghanistan? She'd already decided that her next interview would be with Thirty's high school principal. But she'd learned her lesson. She'd leave it up to him to mention Pal. She started to close the final yearbook. Then checked her list. Someone was missing. She leafed through all the books again, knowing even as she looked that the name wasn't there.

"Excuse me." She stood before the librarian's desk, assuming as she spoke that the librarian was, along with everyone else in town, familiar with the story of the six childhood friends who'd gone into the military together. "I'm looking for information on someone who went to school here. He and his friends all went to Afghanistan last year. But he doesn't seem to be in any of the yearbooks."

Lola waited for the stiffened shoulders, the crimped chin, the outward signs of resistance that preceded a refusal to divulge information. Her years working in Baltimore had taught her to expect it at every turn, even when she sought documents available by law to the public. The tendency wasn't nearly as pronounced in small towns, but Lola expected it anyway, so it always came as a pleasant surprise when someone delivered.

"You're talking about Mike St. Clair. Such a shame. But you're right, there's nothing about him in the Thirty yearbooks. That's because he went to the Indian school. We don't have their yearbooks. You'll have to go to the rez for that."

Lola returned her smile and called to Margaret. She braced herself against the blast of heat beyond the library's door. But she was thinking so hard it barely bothered her. If Mike St. Clair had gone to the rez school, how had he ended up being such good friends with the group of kids from Thirty?

THIRTEEN

"It's because of Miss Jones."

Arlie Colton, Thirty High School's principal, delivered the answer to Lola's question about Mike St. Clair with visible distaste, immediately laying waste to her plan not to bring up Pal's name. "She went to school with the others," he said. He ticked them off on his fingers "Mr. Loughry, Mr. Dillon, Mr. McSpadden, Mr. Graff. But she grew up with Mike and so she always dragged him into our activities." No corresponding *mister* for Mike, Lola noticed.

"I don't understand," said Lola.

"Miss Jones' family—I suppose her parents' grandparents, or however many generations back it happened—bought up fee lands."

The light clicked on for Lola. A few years ago, the word would have meant nothing to her. But living with Charlie, and in such proximity to the Blackfeet Nation, she'd learned that reservations were hardly all-Indian bastions. During the starvation years after the reservations were formed, and with help from a federal abomination known as the Dawes Act that further wrested land from tribes by force of law rather than war, white people snapped up prime reservation land—fee lands—sold for a pittance by desperate tribes. A century later, many tribes were trying to buy that land back, parcel by newly high-priced parcel. Lola remembered Pal telling her that Delbert lived on the reservation. Funny, Lola thought, that Pal neglected to mention that her land, too, was on the rez.

Arlie Colton was still talking. "Their parents were neighbors. Such parents as Mike had. His grandfather, mostly. His father, you know, was killed in the Gulf War. And his mother—" He tipped his hand in front of his mouth, indicating drink. "He lost her, too. Miss Jones went to the schools in town, and Mike to the Indian school. That way, he got to play for the Chiefs."

"The Chiefs?"

"You're not from Wyoming, are you? Everybody in the state knows about the Chiefs, and the Lady Chiefs, too. They make it to the basketball finals just about every year, and to the championship a fair amount of time, too. Pity that's as far as most of them go."

Lola had heard the queasy-making soliloquy about Indian athletes—great in high school, but a tendency to fall apart in colleges far from their families—too many times in Montana to want to hear the Wyoming version. She tried to steer Arlie Colton back on track. "But he attended a lot of your school's activities?"

"Miss Jones included him whenever she could at events in our school. Though why he wanted to come was beyond me. It can't have been comfortable for him. But she insisted. They were friends. Closer than most." The curl of his lip and flare of nostril indicated disapproval. "There was talk."

"What sort of talk?" Lola asked. As if she couldn't guess. A white girl, an Indian boy. Lola had grown up on Maryland's Eastern Shore, hearing the same sort of talk about white girls who had the temerity to say more than two words to black classmates. But she had to change the subject. She was not going to let another interview go astray on the subject of Pal. "Actually, I'm here to talk about the other students who went to Afghanistan." She consulted her notes as if trying to remember, even though she'd memorized their names. A little feigned stupidity never hurt. "Let's see. Here's one." She thought she'd ease into things before bringing up Cody Dillon's suicide, or Tommy McSpadden's and Tyson Graff's near-deadly hijinks. "You mentioned him just a few minutes ago. Skiff Loughry."

Arlie's round face brightened. She'd found the principal at the school after walking into the unlocked and nearly deserted building in the middle of a summer day and following the smell of floorwax. A janitor, buffing a basketball court into renewed glassiness after a year of hard use, had directed her to Arlie's office at the end of a darkened hallway. The principal hadn't seemed surprised to see her. Lola wondered if Dave Sparks had paid a similar visit. If he had, she'd missed the story he'd written. More likely, she thought, once again *he'd* missed the story.

"Mr. Loughry. We're planning some sort of celebration for him once school starts. We thought it would be more respectful to wait a few weeks after Mr. Dillon's funeral and the other, ah, troubles."

"Why a celebration?" Lola, turning to check on Margaret, whom she'd parked with a coloring book in the outer office, asked the question over her shoulder.

Arlie's eyebrows, so pale they barely showed, disappeared into the mass of wrinkles on his forehead. He was short and egg-shaped, wearing a long-sleeved white button-down shirt and khaki pants even in the heat and informality of summertime Wyoming. He had a nervous, fussy aspect, more like that of an insurance man, Lola thought, than the weary authoritarianism of a longtime school administrator.

"Because of what he did, of course," he said. "I thought you knew. Isn't that what your story is about?"

Lola had gotten the email she'd hoped for the previous night, the go-ahead for the story from InDepth.org, one of the sparkly new online journalism sites creating a buzz in an otherwise-moribund business. "Send photos, too," the editor had urged. "Some video would be nice. We'll get the graphics guys"—Lola noted the plural with an envious sigh—"started on the maps. If your own photos don't cut it, we'll send a shooter out, but give it a try."

"My story," she told Arlie carefully, "is about all aspects of the situation."

Arlie blinked rapidly. He caught his lower lip between his teeth and sucked it in, clearly envisioning the myriad ways a story might somehow make him look bad.

"Certainly," she hastened to cut off any brewing objections, "Skiff's role is a major part of it. Why don't you tell me about it?"

Arlie released his lip, sat back in his chair, and puffed up a bit inside the starched shirt. "He saved them all, of course. He's our hero. If it wasn't for Mr. Loughry, every last one of those kids would be dead."

————

Something had awakened Skiff Loughry that night. Maybe Mike St. Clair had scuffled with the Afghani—just for a second, not even long enough to cry out—before the knife nearly parted his head from his neck.

Or maybe Skiff just had a sixth sense, Arlie said. Whatever, he awoke. Saw what was going on. Shot the Afghani before the rest could rouse themselves. "They were saved before they even knew what had happened. It was too late for Mike, of course. But one could argue he got what was coming to him. Falling asleep on watch like that. They used to shoot soldiers for as much."

Lola suppressed an urge to prick the principal with the point of her pen, to see if she could deflate some of that self-importance. "Having your throat cut—that's a pretty rough way to go," she ventured.

Arlie sniffed. "Anyone going to that godforsaken place should have expected as much. How does the Kipling poem go?"

Lola hadn't figured Arlie for a former English teacher. Math, she would have said. Or shop. She hated that poem. "I know it," she said, hoping to forestall him. It didn't work. A smile hovered around his lips as he chanted:

When you're wounded and left on Afghanistan's plains,
And the women come out to cut up what remains
Jest roll to your rifle and blow out your brains
An' go to your Gawd like a soldier.

"Well, he didn't go like a soldier, did he?" Arlie said. "Asleep like that. Besides, he only got what his people had been doing to each other for years. He's lucky to have kept his hair."

Lola was on her feet, notebook in one hand, the other balled into a fist. Arlie Colton scooted back in his chair. She hadn't, she thought with some satisfaction, had to jab him with her pen after all. He'd deflated all by himself. She took a breath and reminded herself that no matter how much she wanted to slap him into the next county, or at least go upside his head with a few choice phrases, it wouldn't help to antagonize anyone just as she was starting to work on the story. If Thirty was anything like Magpie—like any small town—people would hear fast that they shouldn't talk to the out-of-town reporter.

"Sorry," she heard a calm voice say. "I didn't mean to startle you. I just remembered another appointment. I should have watched the time more carefully. You've been most helpful. And you're right. The story about Skiff's heroism deserves to be told."

She turned away. His voice called her back.

"I know what you're thinking."

"What's that?" Her fury flared new and undisguised. She didn't dare turn to face him.

"You people from away. You've got this whole noble savage idea of the Indians. But you don't live here, surrounded by them."

Given that the reservation comprised small parts of only two of Wyoming's twenty-three counties—Lola had looked it up—Thirty was hardly surrounded. But Lola kept the thought to herself.

"The crime level on the rez is through the roof. There's drinking, drugging, gangs. Your Mike St. Clair is lucky he ended up in the Army instead of prison."

Lola touched a hand to her face to reassure herself that the flush of anger was fading, and turned back to Arlie. "He ended up dead at the age of what—eighteen? Nineteen?"

"Which could have happened just as easily if he'd stayed here."

True enough, Lola thought. Just as there was a grain of truth in what Arlie had said about the reservation. The issues facing the West's reservations—remote, inadequately policed, targeted by out-side gangs—were daunting. But Lola picked up her newspaper every day and saw stories about white people arrested for those same problems, yet nobody seemed to fault them as a race.

"He and Miss Jones, they were no angels. Not everybody's a martyr."

"Mommy?"

Margaret stood in the doorway, having sat in on enough of her mother's interviews to know when one was over. Lola watched Arlie's gaze take in Margaret's braids, her coppery skin. "Oh," he said.

Lola picked up her daughter and quick-stepped through the endless dark hallway as though the very air about them were contaminated with the poison of prejudice. But even as she fled the thing her daughter would have to encounter far too often in her life, she reminded herself that just because Arlie was a bigot didn't mean he was wrong about Pal and Mike. She'd learned from hard experience that it was foolish to ignore information just because she didn't like the source. Which meant that, as much as she wanted to stay away from the subject of Pal, she was going to have to probe deeper.

FOURTEEN

LOLA HAD TO GIVE Pal credit. No matter how much she'd drunk the night before—and the routine deposit of empties in the kitchen trash can bore mute witness to exactly how much—she arose every morning in time to be at the table, nursing a cup of coffee, when Delbert arrived and Lola emerged from her own room. Lola attributed it to Pal's military training. But the morning after Lola's interview with Arlie Colton, that training deserted Pal.

Lola was already at the stove, flipping pancakes when Delbert arrived, grateful that among his earlier purchases had been a mix that required the addition of nothing but water. Delbert stood in the doorway, seemingly paralyzed by Pal's absence. His glance darted around the kitchen. "Come on in," Lola said. "We won't bite. Although, Margaret might if she doesn't get her pancakes." Lola thought that in the healthy-eating department, the pancakes probably were only marginally better than doughnuts, but they saved her from wrestling more eggs into submission. Delbert, whose default gait was a shuffle, crossed to the table in two steps. "Where's Pal?"

Lola wielded the spatula. A pancake fell back mid-flip, folding over on itself. Lola prodded it. "Still sleeping, I guess."

"You guess? You didn't check?"

"I know she likes her privacy—" Lola began. Delbert headed down the hall. Lola turned off the flame under the griddle and followed. "Margaret, you stay there," she called, even as Margaret slid from her chair. They burst into the room, four of them, Delbert and Lola, Margaret and Bub. Pal lay motionless on the bed, clad in a tank top and shorts, arms flung above her head.

"Oh, Christ, she's on her back. She could have choked." Delbert put his ear to Pal's lips and his hand to the chest that showed ribby through the flimsy fabric. "She's breathing. Thank the good Lord. Help me turn her."

Lola moved to the other side of the bed. She took one of Pal's arms and pulled as Delbert pushed at her shoulder. Pal flopped boneless onto her side. Lola dropped Pal's arm. Even in the dim light, the scars showed pale, the newer ones healing fast. Lola ran her finger over them. "What are these?"

Delbert pulled a blanket over Pal. "Her business is what those are."

Message received, Lola thought. "Fair enough," she said. A small hand slipped into hers.

"Mommy, is she sick?"

Delbert answered. "She's going through a very hard time. It's our job to help her. Make sure she eats, keep her in clean clothes. We got to do something else for her," he said.

"What's that?" Pal barely made a bump beneath the covers. Lola put her fingers to Pal's neck, seeking the reassurance of a pulse. It fluttered beneath her fingers, life trapped within a body that appeared to be doing its best to snuff it out.

"We got to get her out of this house," Delbert said. "She's turning it into a grave of her own making. She needs to be amongst people again."

Lola led the way back to the kitchen. "How do you propose doing that? Tie her up and kidnap her?"

"Fourth of July parade is tomorrow. Hard to say no to a parade. I say we make an expedition. All four of us. It'll be good for this one, too." He put his hand on Margaret's head.

The word "parade" grabbed Margaret's attention. "Candy!" Until they'd been presented with Delbert's doughnuts, Halloween candy and the treats tossed at parades had been the only sweets allowed Margaret.

"Be good for you, too," Delbert said to Lola. "You need a day off."

Meaning, Lola supposed, everybody needed a day off from her cooking. Which, despite her credible attempt at barbecued chicken the previous night (chicken pieces doused with bottled barbecue sauce, an hour at 350 degrees, turned halfway through) was just fine with her. They could eat at the café in town after the festivities. "A parade sounds like fun," she said. "What time does it start?"

————

Thirty's Fourth of July parade began late in the afternoon. "That way, people who come in from out of town for the parade don't have so long to wait for the fireworks," Delbert said. "That's the reason they give, anyhow. Me, I think it's so you don't have folks drinking all day long and starting fights by noon."

Despite the holiday, the event was better known as the Aunt Millie parade, he explained as they sat at the curb, waiting for it to start. Pal had agreed to the outing only if Delbert brought her home immediately after the parade, so Lola and Margaret had followed them into town in Lola's truck. Lola told Delbert they wanted to watch the fireworks. She didn't tell him she thought the parade would make for a perfect place for her to interview people about the veterans. She hadn't anticipated how large that crowd would be.

It seemed as though all of Thirty's residents, plus everyone from the surrounding ranches, had packed themselves into its three-block business district. Lola's time in Afghanistan had left her panicky in crowds. Women reporters learned within days of arrival in the country that the men thronging the streets took the opportunity to grab their breasts or their rear ends, to slide their hands between their legs, before melting unseen into the masses. Whenever Lola covered anti-Western demonstrations, she found herself among a line of women journalists sliding along a street, their backs plastered to the buildings, fending off at least one angle of attack. The photographers had it worse. They had to wade into the fray, subjecting themselves to the worst sorts of manhandling, or risk verbal abuse from editors safe in their offices in their home countries, wondering why they hadn't captured the same arresting images as their male colleagues. Now, as people brushed past Lola on Thirty's main street, her buttocks clenched and her elbows went up. She raised a shaking hand to her face and rubbed sweat from her temple and tried to concentrate on the fact that the day was supposed to be fun.

Margaret pestered Delbert about the parade's name. "Who's Aunt Millie?"

"Well, now. Millie's one of them Kendricks," he said, as though that explained everything.

"The Kendricks have been in Thirty forever. There are about a million of them," Pal said. Her raspy voice, when she was talking about something other than herself, rose and fell like a normal person's. "They started the town, and the newspaper, too. You know, the *Last Word*. Remind me to pick up a copy today."

Lola already had that particular task on her list. She couldn't wait to see the paper, to see if Dave Sparks had written anything more about the veterans. But she didn't want to seem too eager. She pressed Pal for more details on the parade.

"Millie Kendrick was born on the Fourth of July." As Pal told it, when Millie was still a teenager, she took to wrapping herself in a green sheet, holding up a green-painted flashlight, and marching in the parade as Lady Liberty. It didn't take too many years for the rest of the Kendricks to get into the act, following behind Millie with kazoos, playing all the patriotic songs they could think of. Now that Millie was getting on in years, she rode in a convertible from the local car dealership.

"She's upped her game in the costume department, too," Pal said. Some years back, Millie had ordered herself a new get-up from a store in Denver, with a realistic looking crown and torch, and a gown that draped flatteringly around her expanding form, and about half the town marched behind her now. People still played kazoos, but the high school band came along, too, and there was always a float or two, and the whole bunch of them ended up at the park, where Benjy's Banjos, the band that played at the Stockman on Friday and Saturday nights, set up a makeshift stage and people had themselves a time.

It was, Lola thought, the longest speech she'd ever heard Pal make. Delbert's eyes met Lola's. He gave the slightest of nods, an acknowledgment that the outing was already accomplishing its purpose. A bass drum boomed. Margaret jumped up. Lola leaned forward and took firm hold of Bub's collar. He wasn't used to parades. The last thing she needed was for him to run beneath a passing fire truck.

Baton twirlers led the way. Of course, thought Lola. She looked again. These were no teenage girls. Two women stepped high in white tasseled boots, shiny short skirts, and skimpy tops that revealed too much of their leathery bosoms. Their sprayed-stiff spit curls were more white than blond. Creases spiderwebbed their faces. They pirouetted, bent, passed the batons through arthritic knees spread wide, shook skinny bums at the crowd, all to dutiful applause. Delbert put his fingers in his mouth and whistled.

Lola turned to Pal. "What the hell?"

"The Becker Babes."

"Are they like the Kendricks?"

A high school marching band appeared, kids in red T-shirts and khaki shorts and sneakers. They raised their instruments to their lips and burst into the "Stars and Stripes Forever." Trombone slides dented the air. Margaret clapped her hands over her ears.

"Those two are all that's left of the Beckers," Pal said. "But what they lack in number, they make up for in—let's call it personality."

"What's their deal?"

"Twins. They won some sort of twirling championship in high school, so they got to lead the parade that year. Once they got that spot, they never gave it up. Never married. Twirling is their life. You've got to give them credit. The Becker Babes are about as strange as they come, but those girls figured out early who they were and never strayed from it. I think those costumes are the same ones they wore in high school."

"Looks like they've updated their routines," Lola said as the sisters circled the band, shimmying, running their tongues around scarlet lips, touching fingertips to hips and jerking their hands away as though burnt. A baton landed at Margaret's feet.

"Don't touch that!" Lola said.

Margaret picked up the baton and handed it to a Becker babe. "Thank you, little girl," the twirler croaked.

"Look there!" Delbert hollered.

A fire truck followed the marching band. Its siren whooped. Candy showered around them. Margaret scrambled. Bub lunged against Lola's grip. People rose and began to applaud. Quite a frenzy for candy, Lola thought. Then she saw the cause. A contingent of veterans followed the fire truck, the World War II vets on folding chairs in the back of a flatbed truck, the Vietnam graybeards marching behind them, and finally—the obvious cause of the crowd's adulation—veterans from Iraq and Afghanistan, led by Skiff Loughry.

"Skiff! Skiff!" People shouted, clapped, stamped their feet. Lola would have recognized him anyway, from the same square face and prominent ears she'd seen in the newspaper and yearbook photos. He marched eyes front, flushed face the only acknowledgement of the cheers. But when the veterans passed the spot where Lola and the others sat, Skiff broke ranks and veered to the curb, his shadow splashing across them.

"Pal? Private First Class Palomino Jones? Is that you?"

Lola and Delbert rose. Pal remained seated at the curb, her body twisted into itself like a question mark.

"Hey, Delbert. How you holding up? Tough deal about Mike." Skiff grabbed Delbert's hand, knuckles whitening as he squeezed. Delbert let his hand fall away. He seemed somehow diminished in Skiff's presence, shoulders rounded, head angled downward. Lola wondered if that was simply because Skiff was so big, not just tall but with the blocky shoulders and taut physique of someone who'd retained his Army workouts along with the haircut. He had a snub nose and a wide generous mouth that suggested a smile even amid the military solemnity.

"Aw, Delbert. You got to pay no mind to what people say. None a them know what it was like over there. Right, Pal?"

Pal said nothing at all.

Skiff looked to Lola, awaiting an introduction. When none came, he stuck out his hand. "Skiff Loughry."

"Lola Wicks." She put her hand in his and braced herself. He stopped just short of cracking bone. Skiff reached for Margaret. She dodged behind Lola's knees.

"Shy, huh? She'll need to outgrow that. Lola, how do you know these fine people?"

"Old family friends. Just passing through. Stopped for a visit." Lola thought she was going to have to develop a standard story for her association with Pal.

"You come on by the barbecue after the parade. It's in the park. You'd like it. All of you. Delbert, it's been too long. And Pal, I haven't seen you since we got back. Time you quit being a stranger."

Lola expected Delbert to leap at the invitation, given his concern for getting Pal out and among people. But he wagged his head, regret creasing his features. "Much appreciated, Skiff. But Margaret here, she runs down pretty quick. Afternoon is naptime." Lola shot him a look. Delbert knew good and well Lola wasn't bringing Margaret back to the ranch for any afternoon nap. "You give my regards to your folks."

"Sure thing." Skiff stepped past Lola and stood over Pal. "Invitation's open. Anytime. We can get reacquainted. Put all that shit past us. Karma's a bitch, huh?"

Pal jerked as though he'd slapped her. Skiff whacked Delbert between the shoulder blades, a guy's equivalent of a hug.

"You take care, Delbert. Lola, nice to have met you. And you, too, little girl."

Lola looked down at Margaret just in time to catch her sticking out her tongue. She never took kindly to being reminded that she was little. Skiff, already walking away, seemed not to have noticed. Lola sank back down on the sidewalk, mulling over Pal's silent reception of Skiff, as well as Delbert's own reticence. Aunt Millie cruised past, weighing down the back of the convertible, torch held high, loose flesh flapping from her upper arm. Margaret strained in Lola's grasp. Another fire truck approached. Firefighters balanced on its steps, hanging on one-handed, their other hands filled with candy. Margaret escaped Lola's arms. "Go!" said Lola, admitting defeat.

Click.

Lola turned and saw Dave Sparks, his scarecrow frame jack-knifed into a crouch. He lowered a Leica. Not from the *Last Word's* equipment closet, Lola was willing to bet. Dave examined the camera's screen. "Nice mother-daughter image. Might even make it into the paper. Want me to text you a copy?" The smile that accompanied the offer was almost innocent.

Not a bad way to ask for her phone number, Lola thought even as she gave it to him. A baton bounced at his feet. The sisters were working their way back along the parade route, maximizing their annual moment in the public eye. Dave picked up the baton and tossed it to one of the sisters. She blew him a kiss from withered lips. "Aw, hell," he said. "I'll be in a world of hurt if we don't run a picture of the Weird Sisters." He ran down the street after them, his long stride eating up the distance. Lola wondered if he'd said things like "world of hurt" before he landed in Wyoming.

"It's time to go." Delbert stood behind Lola. She clambered to her feet. People drifted away from the parade, probably heading to the barbecue at the park. She wanted to interview them before the combined effects of heat and beer took their toll. Margaret, fists full of brightly wrapped pieces of candy, planted her feet in a stance Lola knew all too well.

"No. More."

"No more," Lola echoed. She knew better than to expect a smile from Margaret. She didn't get one. "You've had enough candy for one day. For the whole week—the month in fact."

"Look here." Delbert pulled his hand from his pocket. He'd collected his own hoard of candy. "Might be that I could be persuaded to share this. But only if we leave. Pal needs to go home."

Pal still sat at the curb, bent double, arms wrapped around her head.

"Is she sick again?" Margaret asked.

"Something like that. Let's help her to the truck. Miss Margaret, if you put that candy of yours in your pockets, maybe you can hold mine for me." Margaret was delighted to help.

"Need a hand?" Skiff Loughry was back from wherever he'd been. "She okay?"

"Too much sun, maybe," Lola offered when no one else spoke.

"Doubt it," Skiff said. "We patrolled in Afghanistan when it topped a hundred in the shade, and in full packs and body armor. This girl kept right up. Sun doesn't bother her. Nor nighttime cold. Right, Pal?"

A long shudder ran along Pal's bent back.

"We got this," Delbert said. "Thanks."

Skiff stood a few moments more as Delbert took one elbow and Lola the other, not moving away until they'd started half-walking, half-carrying her toward Delbert's truck. It was like carrying a bird, Lola thought, nothing but feathers and hollow bones, her spirit weighing heavier than all of her body parts combined.

When Lola looked back, Skiff was gone.

FIFTEEN

Margaret pulled at Lola's hand, trying to turn them back toward the truck. "Go with them, Mommy," she said.

"No," said Lola. "Pal doesn't need a lot of people hanging around her."

Margaret squared her shoulders. She dug her feet into the dusty soil of Thirty's block-square city park. On the far side of the park, under the shade of some cottonwoods, dozens of people gathered around smoking barbecues. Lola couldn't see the band, but she heard the plinking of banjos. Skiff Loughry was over there somewhere and Lola aimed to find him. She tried to pick Margaret up, marveling at how a forty-pound child could turn herself into dead weight. The girl sagged in her arms, body yearning back toward the ground. Lola released her into a heap. Bub curled an upper lip, not brave enough for outright defiance, but registering clear disapproval nonetheless. "She's sick, Mommy. She's bad sick." A tear leaked from Margaret's eye.

Guilt dealt Lola a swift kick. She'd been careful, too careful, to shield Margaret to the extent possible from the realities of sickness and fear in her young life, and now—when she finally encountered them—Lola's response was to ignore her understandable reaction. She knelt in the dirt beside her daughter and rubbed her thumb beneath each of Margaret's eyes. A burst of laughter sounded from the partiers across the way. Lola took Margaret's hand. Her interviews were going to have to wait.

"You're right," she told Margaret, over ice cream cones in a shop air-conditioned to the point of discomfort. "She is sick. But not the kind of sick like when you get a cough or a cold."

The cone twirled in Margaret's hand, its stacked scoops of vanilla and chocolate dwindling with each turn. Ice cream was a rare and wonderful treat for Margaret and she was making the most of it before her mother changed her mind. At their feet, Bub polished a plastic dish with equal concentration. Lola had paid for one for him, too. Guilt was costly, she thought. She wondered how to explain PTSD to a five-year-old. "Her heart is sick," she offered.

"Like Auntie Earline's?" Fresh tears welled in Margaret's eyes. "Is she going to die?" One of Margaret's babysitters had suffered a heart attack a few months earlier.

"That was different. Let me see if I can put it another way—not so much her heart, but her soul."

Margaret's hands sketched an outline around her head and torso, and crossed over her chest. "Soul?"

"Yes," said Lola, "the thing that makes her who she is."

The ice cream was gone. Margaret's teeth crunched on cone. "Why is her soul sick?"

Where was Charlie when she needed him, Lola wondered. If she turned down Charlie's proposal, she'd face a lifetime of answering Margaret's tough questions on her own. She wondered if that realization was why he'd sent her off with Margaret. "Pal was a soldier," she began. Margaret nodded. Soldiers were always coming and going on the reservation, and every tribal ceremony featured a contingent of veterans. "She had to go to war."

"That's when people fight," Margaret said through a final mouthful of cone. "With guns."

"No talking and chewing at the same time," Lola reminded her. "But yes, war is when people fight, with guns and all sorts of other things. Sometimes people die. Soldiers see that. It can hurt their hearts. Their souls." A memory arose. She pushed it away. Others flooded its place.

Sometimes the dead weren't even the worst of it, Lola thought. The war in Afghanistan wasn't noted for big body counts. But other things were just as insidious. The constant twanging threat that each new footstep could be the one that tripped a mine, that each madly beeping Toyota pickup could be the one that bore a bomb, that each new face could be that of a potential friend—or killer. And the faces themselves, gaunt with hunger and desperation and resentment. Children so relentlessly deprived of childhood that they'd turned feral, swarming around Lola and other journalists in pint-sized mobs, faces oozing with sores, fingers worming into pockets and emerging with precious photo cards, passports, rolls of rubber-banded cash, making it nearly impossible to work. One particular memory nudged hard. She shoved it away, but still more arose, a trickle turning too fast into a flood.

Lola thought of a day she'd visited a hospital, of the scrawny cats drifting like shadows past the puddles of stinking indefinable liquids on the hallway floors, of the babies who lay gray and motionless three to a crib. A doctor lifted a little girl's gown to reveal ribs that threatened to slice through her papery skin. "Starvation," he said. "She'll be dead by morning." Lola stumbled retching from the building. That night her colleagues, singly and in pairs, tapped at the door of her darkened hotel room, where she lay curled in her sleeping bag atop the narrow pallet. "Are you all right?" they called through the flimsy plywood panel. "Can we get you anything?" Refusing her the dignity of pretending nothing had happened. At least, by the time the worst thing occurred, they'd learned to let her be.

"Really," she assured Margaret now, "she'll want to be left alone. And when we see her tomorrow morning, we're to act like we always do."

Margaret's smile was sly. "You mean hungry?"

Lola laughed at the way her daughter's humor so reliably vanquished the ghosts. "I love you, baby girl," she said. Bub, reassured by the change in atmosphere, lifted his head from the ice cream bowl and wagged his tail in approval.

————

By the time they made their way back to the park, darkness softened the day's hard edges. The crowd had multiplied. The mingled scents of smoke and beer and charred meat hung in the air. A man in a sauce-spattered apron pressed what appeared to be a quart-sized plastic cup into her hand and directed her to a line in front of a keg of beer. "Lemonade for the little ones is over there." He jerked his head toward a picnic table beside a small play area. Children and dogs swarmed around it, not a parent in sight. Margaret looked a question at Lola. She surveyed the crowd, located Skiff within the playground's sight lines, and nodded permission to Margaret, who ran without a backward glance, Bub at her heels. Lola directed a foaming stream of beer into her cup. A woman with a brew was a lot less off-putting than a reporter with a notebook. Some of the people she approached even offered to hold her beer when it came time for the notebook to emerge. They said all the predictable things. Cody

Dillon's suicide—such a shock. His poor father. And then, those boys getting in trouble barely two steps off the plane. You just knew it had something to do with the terrible things they'd seen.

In any other place, Lola thought, this would be the part where people questioned the wisdom of a far-away war that took their healthy children and returned them broken in body and spirit. But this was the rural West, with its staunch and unquestioning patriotism. She mm-hmmed and took notes and thanked people for sharing their thoughts and for holding her beer. "Where can I read this story of yours?" an elderly man asked.

"Online," Lola said. "A website called InDepth.org. People all over the country can read it. All over the world."

"Maybe they can read it all over the world, but I can't read it in Thirty. I don't have a computer."

"Give me your address and I'll print it out and send it to you," Lola said. She probably would never see this man again in her life. Then again, she might. At which time, the small courtesy of having sent him the story would pay big dividends. "I don't know when it's coming out," she said, as he wrapped an arthritic hand around her pen and printed his name and address in crooked block letters in her notebook.

"Aren't you the busy one?" Skiff materialized beside her. "I heard a reporter was working the crowd. Didn't know it was Delbert and Pal's 'old friend.'" He rolled his eyes at the phrase. So much for thinking he'd bought her explanation. "You must be hungry." He handed her a paper plate with a hamburger fat with fixings and led her to a picnic table. Lola took a bite and tried not to think of her own disastrous attempts at this most simple fare. Skiff sat across from her.

"How do you really know Pal?"

Lola shrugged and chewed.

"How well do you know her?"

Lola put her burger down. She retrieved her beer and took a sip.

A grin split his square face, letting her know he was on to her, and that he didn't mind. "Fair enough," he said. "But I take it you don't know her well. Because if you did, you wouldn't be hanging around with her."

Bingo. Lola swallowed. "And why is that?"

A shriek came from the play area. Lola ascertained it was one of happiness—Bub expertly herded a group of kids, Margaret among them, circling them in ever-tightening arcs, forcing them into a bunch—and turned back to Skiff.

"She's trouble," he said. "She was trouble in school, and she was trouble in Afghanistan."

"I heard what happened to Mike," Lola said. "But what about Pal?"

It was hard to see his expression in the fading light. "Mike," he said. "Now that's a tragedy."

Tragedy. It was the same word that Dave Sparks had used. "How so?"

"You must have heard how he died. Even if you're not from here, you only have to spend about two minutes in town. People are still talking about it."

Lola feigned ignorance and thus was treated to a second recitation of the story Dave had told—a patrol out too late, the broken-down vehicle, Mike standing sentry as they napped while awaiting a replacement, the shepherd happening upon the group, taking full advantage. "Well," said Skiff. "Not full. If he had, we'd all be dead. Instead we got lucky."

Lola noticed that he left out his own part in it, the part the principal had told her, how Skiff himself had killed the shepherd, saving his companions. She prodded him. "Lucky how?"

"We shot him," he said. "It had to be done."

We. Sharing the credit. The more Skiff talked, the more Lola liked him. "How come there wasn't anything in the paper?" she asked before remembering, too late, that the only way she could have known what was in the paper was by searching it out. Nothing flickered in Skiff's earnest gaze, no spark of realization, no jerk of suspicion.

He gestured toward the people a few yards away. "Everybody already knows about it."

It could have been a gathering in Magpie, Lola thought, the old folks at the picnic tables, the younger guys at the keg, toting beer back to their wives and girlfriends, the moms in a cluster, knocking back more beer than they should, so grateful were they for a respite from one-on-one child-rearing. Not a brown face in the crowd, Lola noted. That, too, was like Magpie. The Indians would be observing the day on the reservation, holding their own ceremony at the cemetery, leaving oranges at the graves, making sure the departed had good things to eat in the spirit world. There was no one for Skiff to point to when he evoked Delbert, again echoing Dave Sparks's words.

"Can you imagine how it would affect Delbert, the whole tribe, to have that out there in print? Best just to let it lie."

Lola's beer tasted flat. "But everyone knows, anyway. Isn't the truth always better? It's messy, but so is war. I don't know that there's even that much shame to it. An Afghan summer, all that gear. All of you must have been exhausted. It could have been any one of you. Me, I think it humanizes the situation, lets people know what things are really like over there. Gives them something to think about next time they go to vote." Lola wished she'd held back those last words. She hurried on. "Especially given what happened to that other soldier. The one who killed himself. That has to have hit people hard, too."

Skiff's expression darkened, more in sorrow than in anger, Lola decided, no heat coming off him. "All the more reason," he said, "to just let it go. People have been through enough. Want another beer?"

Lola shook her head. He wasn't going to say anymore about the suicide. Maybe he could shed light on something else that bothered her. "Why'd you let Mike out of the vehicle? You all couldn't have stayed awake until the replacement got to you? Everybody knows Afghanistan at night makes Afghanistan by day look like a picnic."

His voice was soft as the fading light around them. "What do you know about that?"

Answering a question with a question. Lola lost patience. "It's time for us to go," she said. "Margaret's got to be exhausted. She'll probably sleep all the way back to the ranch, and then I won't be able to get her to bed." Let him find out on his own that she'd done time in Afghanistan, too.

"You can't go," he said. "Look around."

People were packing up leftover food into their coolers, dousing the coals in the barbecue grills, and moving to the center of the park, spreading blankets on the ground. "The fireworks are about to start. Come on. You can sit with me." He led them through a patchwork quilt of overlapping blankets crowded with generations of families, from oldsters nodding off in lawn chairs to babies likewise asleep—at least for the moment—in bouncy seats. Lola didn't see an obvious space, but people made one when they saw Skiff. A man leaned forward to pat him on the shoulder as they settled onto an itchy green Army blanket of a vintage probably dating to Skiff's grandfather. "Helluva job over there, son," the man said. "Thanks for bringing them back." The man's grin faded as he remembered the obvious. Not everyone had made it back. And among those who had, one never made it home.

"Thanks, sir," Skiff said, giving cover to the man's embarrassment. "That's real nice of you. But I was just doing my job. You're going to like these fireworks," he said to Lola, as a way to end his conversation with the well-wisher. Bub flopped down with a theatrically superior yawn.

Most dogs hated fireworks, ranking them right up there with thunderstorms. Lola had friends who fed their dogs Valium on the Fourth. But Bub was impervious. The first time Lola had taken him to Magpie's July Fourth celebration, he'd fallen asleep. She said as much to Skiff.

"These are different. Not your usual run-of-the-mill small-town stuff. Guy who does them is some kind of expert. He lives here, but goes all over the country doing fireworks displays. He's even been to China to study fireworks. Brace yourself. Miss Margaret, don't you be scared. They're really loud, but they're like nothing you've ever seen."

And they were. The fireworks lit up the sky with a mighty blast, daylight above, all black dark and shaking earth below. The crowd's cheers drowned Lola's scream. She bit her lip, but her fear leaked free in a long moan, much like the sound she'd made that day in Kabul when she'd been standing in the security line outside a government office, lingering to chat with another reporter one minute, and found herself flat on the ground the next, knocked senseless by the same sort of explosions surrounding her now. Or, at least they felt the same. Lola caught a glimpse of Margaret's rapt expression before she closed her eyes. The memory she'd resisted all day, one that had taken her years to suppress, hit her full force—the way the world had gone silent after the blast, the way her feet and legs moved like deadweights as she staggered toward the building where her fixer had gone on ahead of her. The way she'd shoved past the guards so preoccupied with holding back screaming family members that they'd ignored her. And, finally, the unforgettable thing, the bloodied bits of clothing and flesh, the round object a few feet farther, the thing that could have been a broken melon, a squashed soccer ball, but for the fact that it bore recognizable remains of a face. Which signaled the second unforgettable thing. One of the bits of trivia floating around in Lola's head, information useless in the real world but crucial in war zones, was the fact that a suicide attack often decapitated the bomber as the blast detonated upward. The realization that had sent Lola to her knees in the scarlet-spattered dust informed her that one of the few people she'd considered a true friend in Kabul had actually been her enemy. The ground shook again. "Christ!" Lola shouted into the din. "Make it stop."

"Hey. Hey." Skiff's arm was around her, his face close. "What's up?"

"I was there," she blurted. "Kabul. I was there." It was all she could manage.

His eye went knowing. "Got it," he said. "We're outta here. Hey, Margaret. We're going to make some room for other people. How 'bout you let me carry you? That'll make it quicker. Lola, where's your outfit parked?" Once again, the crowd parted at the sight of Skiff. He wrapped his free hand around Lola's wrist and guided her with a firm, reassuring touch, not releasing her until they stood beside the pickup. Wonderment still rained from the sky, but this far away, Lola could no longer feel the blasts rising up through the ground. She drew a quavering breath. "Thank you," she said.

"When?" he asked. They were on common ground now, speaking in a sort of code, the surface shorthand that disguised the roiling emotions below. The subtext: *I know.*

"Six years ago," she said. "I've been back a lot longer than you, and this shit still gets to me." She tried to smile. His look told her she didn't need to.

"You weren't in the military."

"Journalist."

"Embedded?"

"No."

His eyebrows went up. "Tough on a woman."

"Sometimes." All the time, she thought.

"You okay to drive?"

"Sure." She forced herself to meet his gaze, to hold it. Steadied her voice. "Really. Thank you. For everything."

He helped hoist Margaret into her booster seat, leaving it to Lola to fasten the belt tight. "If you ever want to talk sometime—"

"No!" she said. "That's the last thing I want to do."

He laughed in acknowledgment of the constant admonishments, from the VA on his part, human resources departments on hers, that counseling was in order for anyone returning from a war zone. "Hell, no!" he threw back at her. "Excuse the language, but fuck that woo-woo shit."

"Damn straight," she said. She'd spent years not talking about it. She wasn't about to start. She climbed into the truck and rolled down the window. The memory slithered back to the dark crevice within her heart where it usually slumbered undisturbed. A fresh burst of fireworks lit up the sky, the kind that showered soft twinkling white lights that dissolved over the heads of the crowd. "They really are pretty," she said.

He slapped the side of the truck and stepped back. She gave it some gas. It wasn't until they were headed home she realized that, even though she'd let him get away with deflecting every single important question she'd asked him about Cody Dillon and Mike St. Clair, she'd neglected to press him on the most intriguing thing. Everyone to whom she'd mentioned Pal's name had reacted with revulsion. Skiff, on the other hand, had seemed happy to see Pal, even inviting her to the barbecue where no doubt they'd run into some of those others who so despised her. But then he'd warned her that Pal was trouble.

There would be, she vowed, more conversations with Skiff Loughry.

109

SIXTEEN

MARGARET IN FACT DID not sleep all the way back to the ranch. Lola wondered if maybe she'd sneaked some Coke or 7-Up, or possibly shared a cupcake, something sugary that on top of the candy and ice cream left Margaret wide-eyed and alert despite an afternoon romping with kids and dogs in the merciless heat. She tried a few discreet questions, only to have Margaret respond by getting directly to the point. "Mommy. You know I don't eat bad food unless you let me."

"Right." It was hardly a direct denial. Lola thought of all the times Margaret had hovered at the edges of her interviews, and wondered what sort of evasive skills she might have acquired. She trained her eyes on the long, empty road ahead. Low light still outlined the peaks to the west, and rendered eerie the rocky upthrusts from the valley floor. The day's heat fled before the darkness. The wind sliding past the open window took on an edge. Lola raised the window and tightened her hands on the wheel, glancing right and left. It was the hour when deer and pronghorns became suicidal, sauntering down to the roadside, seeking the day's warmth leaking from the blacktop. Lola suspected that somewhere in the dim recesses of their walnut-size brains, they took mute enjoyment in the startled faces within the vehicles that swerved hard when they caught sight of the deer, tires occasionally hooking the soft shoulder, cars flipping and bouncing away through the sagebrush. Intentional or not, it was a dangerous business. Lola occasionally occupied the empty miles by counting the corpses of deer. She couldn't recall seeing a flattened pronghorn. The antelope were usually too agile to lose the game, vanishing with a last-minute pirouette and a mocking flash of white rump.

"Mommy."

Lola scanned the roadside again. "Potty time?"

"No. *Mommy.*"

Bub yawned and stretched and stood up on the seat beside Lola. He turned toward Margaret, then hopped into the jump seat beside her. His tail stretched back past Lola, stiff, quivering. Something had caught his attention. "Mommy. *Look.*"

Again, Lola looked left, right. She didn't see any deer. "What, honey? Nothing's out there."

"Behind us." Margaret's voice caught. Bub growled.

Lola glanced in the rearview mirror and slammed her foot against the accelerator. Margaret cried out. Bub listed to one side, toenails scrabbling for purchase.

The truck came up fast behind them, traveling with only its running lights, inches from the pickup's rear bumper. Lola goosed the pickup. The speedometer crept past ninety. "Some idiot on a cellphone probably. Bet he doesn't even see me." She tapped the horn, trying to get the attention of the driver behind her. "Hey, idiot. Hang up and pay attention. And turn on your lights."

The truck fell back just short of contact. Lola sighed and let her foot drift upward. "That was scary. Thanks, Margaret."

The truck behind them—something silvery, it was getting too dark for Lola to make out the exact color or model—pulled into the passing lane. "Better yet," she said. "It's going to go around us. Then we won't have to worry about it anymore." She wished she'd left the fireworks sooner. In Magpie, she'd learned to leave such events early, wary of back roads full of folks who'd spent the evening partying in town. Drunk drivers claimed an unconscionable number of lives. Charlie pulled them over when he could, but the savvier ones knew to refuse the Breathalyzer and hired the lawyers who got the charges dropped, then continued their boozy ways, gaming the system time after time until the night their luck—or, more likely, the luck of the unfortunates they hit head-on—ran out and they finally ended up behind bars on a vehicular homicide charge. For a little while, at least. Judges were only slowly coming around to the concept that a person was just as dead after getting hit by a drunk as if he'd been shot.

"Mommy!" Margaret shrieked. Bub flung himself across her in a crescendo of barking. The truck was beside them and then it was in their lane. Lola stomped the brake, and braced herself against the jolt when the truck's rear bumper clipped the front of her pickup as it slipped past. She caught a glimpse of a man with a ball cap angled low over his eyes, a license plate with Wyoming's bucking bronco, Steamboat.

"Goddammit!" she yelled, as though anything could be heard through closed windows, the roar of challenged engines, and Bub's racket. "I've got a child in here." Bub increased the volume, something she wouldn't have thought possible. "And a dog, too." She let the pickup coast to a crawl. The farther ahead of them the truck got, the better. "Everybody okay?"

Bub regained balance on his three legs. Margaret met her mother's gaze in the mirror and nodded, eyes stark and staring. The truck was nothing but taillights in the distance, too far away for Lola to catch the license number. She reached for her cell phone anyway, thinking to call 9-1-1. She could at least describe it—a little—and let dispatchers know when it happened. Even before she saw the phone's "no service" message, she knew it was an exercise in futility. Lacking a license number, it was hopeless. Charlie always fumed about such emergency calls, especially if they came from locals, who—as opposed to the tourists—knew full well Charlie was likely to be at the far end of the county, as much as fifty miles away from whatever mishap someone was trying to report. The ugly downside of law enforcement in the remote reaches of the West was that people were mostly on their own.

"Suppose," Charlie said to Lola one night, "Old Man Baggs starts beating on his wife. Again." Lola's mouth twisted downward. The Baggses' domestic issues were an open secret. She'd heard there was a pool among the regulars at Nell's Café as to when Lorene Baggs would finally turn up dead by her husband's hand. "Only this time," Charlie continued, "he takes it up a notch, gets his gun out, waves it around, holds it to her head, that sort of thing."

"Hasn't he already done that?"

Charlie thought a moment. "You're right. I'm getting the Baggses mixed up with the Howards. But, anyway, suppose whatever Old Man Baggs does this time, Lorene's lucky enough to sneak away, maybe says she's got to pee, calls me on her cell from the bathroom, saying this time looks like he's gonna make good on all those threats to kill her. But maybe they live out by Annie's Tit, and it's just rained and their road has gone to gumbo, so even after I've driven a half-hour at a hundred miles per, then I've got to hike in the last mile. I told Mrs. Baggs to get her own damn gun and learn how to use it. Which, if she ever does, there's still somebody dead, and it'll be the wrong damn person on trial." By the time he was done talking, his face was gray. He'd only been sheriff for a few years, but he'd already dealt with too many actual cases like the hypothetical one he'd just outlined. City amenities such as counselors and support groups and shelters for the likes of Lorene Baggs and Jeannie Howard were unknown in their part of the world.

Lola's pickup topped a rise. Ahead of them, the taillights that had glowed so far away moments earlier were close. Too close, almost as though the truck had been waiting for them. Lola felt a sudden affinity for Lorene Baggs; wished, in fact, she had a gun at hand, that she'd learned how to use it, even if the wrong person, that being her, would end up in jail. If it was a choice between her and someone who might hurt Margaret, then it was the easiest choice she'd ever make. She scanned the road beyond the waiting truck, and did a quick check behind them, too. No other cars, and she hadn't seen a house in miles. To the west, a pinprick of light shone within the purpling dark. Maybe a porch light. But, just as likely a security light over someone's supply of ammonium nitrate, used as fertilizer but also in homemade bombs and thus occasionally stolen from remote fields by wannabe terrorists intent on wreaking their own Oklahoma City-style havoc. Lola and Margaret and Bub were on their own with the truck that had slowed to a crawl ahead of them. Lola touched the brakes. Margaret began to sob. A chill moved through Lola, not of fear, but fury. She'd spent five years protecting her child from the dangers of sugar, had assiduously rubbed her brown skin with sunscreen the moment the temperature rose above seventy, had assured her that ghosts and goblins were fake and that even the Blackfeet's Under Water people were nothing to fear, and now this creep in the truck in front of her had scared her child half to death. Lola wanted to get out of the pickup, march over to the truck so brazenly awaiting their next move, yank open its door, seize the driver by the scruff of the neck and throw him onto the hardpan, administering a few swift kicks before turning Bub loose on him. She'd seen Bub take on a coyote, larger and possessed of its species' legendary hatred for dogs. Things had gone badly for the coyote.

Lola's fingers twitched on the door handle. To leave the pickup would be to leave Margaret alone. Her daughter was already terrified. She flashed her lights at the truck, serving notice. She narrowed her eyes and reached a hand back to Margaret, grasping her ankle, giving it a reassuring squeeze. "Hold on, you two," she said. "This guy doesn't know who he's dealing with."

"Who, Mommy?" Margaret's voice was barely audible.

Lola turned and looked her full in the face, flashing a wide smile that in no way reflected the twin surges of anger and panic within her.

"Margaret Wicks's mommy, that's who. You know how mad I got that time you jumped into the creek with your last set of clean clothes? Or when Bub stole that roast off the counter?" The pickup moved more slowly still. Lola released Margaret's ankle and tugged at the belt holding her booster seat in place. Margaret's sobs diminished to hiccups as she remembered. "You were really mad, Mommy."

"Well, that wasn't even close to how mad I am now." The truck in front of them swung broadside across the road. Lola threw the pickup into four-wheel drive and faked a confidence that she in no way felt. "All those carnival rides I wouldn't let you go on? We're about to make up for that. Come on now. Everybody holler."

She threw her head back and shouted her terror and rage as she steered off the road and carved a path across the prairie, the pickup nearly taking flight in its escape from whoever was trying to hurt them.

SEVENTEEN

Rocks rushed toward her so fast that Lola could barely steer among them. She didn't even try to miss the low ones, and prayed she'd see the bigger ones in time to swerve. The light ahead of them grew incrementally larger even as the truck roared closer. Its driver switched on the lights. The glare of high beams bouncing off her rearview mirror nearly blinded Lola.

She forgot to yell, forgot to feign any semblance of fun, forgot everything other than the need to keep the pickup upright and ahead of the truck gaining inexorably upon them. The pickup jolted down into a gully, pitching Lola forward so abruptly she clipped her chin on the steering wheel. She horsed the pickup up the other side, scanning the horizon for the light. She didn't see it. "Oh, Jesus, Jesus, please," she begged, forgetting she was a nonbeliever. A jagged rock loomed. She jerked at the wheel. And just like that, there was the light, farther to the left than she'd remembered, larger, too, the unmistakable outline of a building beside it, some sort of shed, probably, but maybe, just maybe, a house. Lola wrangled the pickup in its direction, giving thanks to Jesus and some other deities, too. Maybe they were going to make it.

The pickup shook with the force of the blow to its rear. This time, nobody screamed. Even Bub was silent, three legs planted solidly on the passenger seat, staring fixedly ahead. Lola braced herself for the truck's next strike. It came from the left, the truck's nose scraping along the pickup's side, both vehicles slewing sideways, their headlights highlighting the house looming before them. Lola leaned on the horn. The truck pulled even with them. The door to the house opened, a rectangle of yellow light silhouetting the person standing within, holding what even Lola, eyes awash in tears, could see was a long gun. He raised it.

"Head down, Margaret!" Lola yelled. She wrenched the wheel, throwing the pickup into an intentional skid. Lola ducked as it spun, expecting it to hit the truck. Or the house. Or to rotate smack into a bullet.

But the pickup slowed unimpeded to a stop and Lola, when she finally unclenched her hands from the wheel, decided she was unhurt. A ragged gasp from the backseat reassured her that Margaret was at least alive. Margaret lifted her head and provided more reassurance still.

"Holy shit, Mommy."

————

By the time the man from the house reached the pickup, Lola was alternately laughing and sobbing with relief, holding Margaret so tightly the child protested she could barely breathe. Bub's growl gave her notice. The pickup door flew open and Lola and Margaret blinked in the overhead light that revealed a wisp of a man and his very substantial rifle.

"You'd best come out of there now." His voice was reedy and halting. The rifle shook in his hand. She took him for elderly.

Lola considered the possibility that they might not be out of danger. She had scrambled into the back seat with Margaret as soon as the pickup stopped. Now she unlatched the belt that, just as advertised, had held Margaret solid in the booster seat. She extricated first herself and then Margaret from the truck, thinking as she did that the man seemed so fragile that whatever threat he posed might be easily neutralized. At least, if she could get that gun away from him. But she had a more immediate concern.

"Where's the other truck?"

"Went tear-assing on by. Probably in the next county by now. You mind telling me what sort of foolishness you people are up to? This here is private property, not somebody's goddamn playground."

Bub's hackles rose apace with the man's voice. His presence made Lola feel better about her odds. "Foolishness, my ass. Some crazy man tried to run me off the road, rear-ended my truck, sideswiped it, scared the hell out of my little girl."

A different note crept into the man's voice. "Says you."

"That's right. Says me. Look, could we please use your phone to call 9-1-1?" It would do, she knew, little good. But she wanted to get Margaret indoors where she could get a better look at her, make sure she was truly okay, and truth be told, to close a door behind her, shutting out the blackness where she feared the truck still lurked.

The man lowered the gun and led the way to the house. The kitchen light jumped as the door slammed behind them, throwing startling shadows around the same sort of kitchen-dining room-living room space as Pal's. All resemblance ended there, though. The counters and tabletop gleamed bare. Light bounced off a floor buffed as shiny and antiseptic as an operating theater. The man replaced the gun in a rack beside the front door and Lola got her first surprise. She'd imagined the white equivalent of Delbert, all caved-in cheeks and stove-up body, but the man was young, maybe only ten years older than she was, the sorrow in his eyes so deep and commanding that it jerked her attention away from the stubble on his cheeks, the only thing about him or his home that appeared untended.

Those eyes. Her gaze came back to them after wandering the room and fastening on the feature that explained them, the sort of wondrous coincidence that would never fly in fiction but that, Lola had learned over years, occurred more often in real life than would have seemed possible. The clippings were magneted with military precision to the refrigerator door, each and every one of them about Cody Dillon, the soldier who'd shot himself at the Casper airport.

———————

Shirl Dillon told her about his son over coffee as they waited for the sheriff's deputy the dispatcher had sounded reluctant to send.

"Cody was crazy to sign up. I told him so. But he had to go along with the crowd. If somebody he looked up to said, 'Jump,' it wasn't just, 'How high?' but 'Over what cliff?' Always looking for a way to impress people. Those so-called friends of his signed up and he couldn't wait to be next. 'You think gettin' yourself killed will do the trick? Think they'll be some kind of true friends now?' I asked him. Some friends. Not none of them's come around. Well. One has. Not come around, but at least he's talked to me about it. The rest, you'd never imagine they'd known Cody since he was in short pants."

At some point, thought Lola, she was going to have to tell Shirl Dillon she was working on a story. Her chat with Skiff earlier in the day didn't count as a formal interview. She'd get another crack, a lengthier one, at Skiff. But she sensed that this moment would be her only time with Shirl. She glanced again around the room and shivered at its order, so purposeful as to make her suspect Shirl was preparing to follow his son into the hereafter. "There's something you should know," she began. "Maybe you want some more coffee first."

She waited until he'd poured himself some, and then she told him who she was and how she'd wanted to write the story ever since Cody had shot himself at the airport while she was standing right there, and especially since she'd read the story about his two compatriots who'd gotten in trouble so soon after their homecoming.

He held up his hand. "Wait a minute. What was a reporter from Montana doing at the airport in Casper? You writing a story down here? Or you have family on that plane?"

Damn, thought Lola. He hadn't been so sunk in sorrow, nor so angry at the unwelcome arrival of two battling trucks just outside his front door, that he'd failed to notice the Montana license plates on her truck. "Something like that," she said. "I was in the area and a friend of mine asked me to pick up her cousin and give her a ride home." She was careful to leave Pal's name out of the equation, and was glad when he didn't ask for more information. "These people, your son and his friends, they've all been through so much. Losing Mike St. Clair over there. That must have been a terrible thing."

"Mike St. Clair!" Shirl set his coffee cup down so hard the liquid sloshed over the rim. "He was half the problem."

Lola rose before he could, tearing a paper towel from a roll above the sink and mopping the table clean. She didn't want him distracted. She tossed the paper towel into a trash can beneath the sink and tore off another one and wiped his mug free of any drops, and added a fresh splash. Margaret fidgeted in her chair. Lola cut her eyes at her and shook her head. Margaret employed her lower lip to maximum pouting effect, but she stayed put.

"Why was Mike a problem?"

"Carrying on with that woman. The two of them rubbing everybody's noses in it, in front of all those other boys, no chance for them to get women of their own, not in a small unit like theirs. Don't get me wrong. I got nothing against girls in the military. But that sort of thing messes up discipline, ruins morale."

It also was, Lola knew, a blatant violation of regulations—and probably the regulation most blatantly violated. Still, other than the principal's dirty-minded presumptions, this was the first she'd heard for sure that Pal and Mike were more than friends.

"How'd you know they were a couple?" Jan had said her cousin didn't have a boyfriend. Pal and Mike must have hooked up overseas, friendship at long last turning into something else. Cody probably emailed his father, she thought, grousing about everything from the food to the injustice of a flaunted affair. The answer surprised her.

"Skiff—one of the other boys who went over—he told me at the funeral," Shirl said.

Lola offered a silent apology to the deceased Cody. He'd had enough smarts, and loyalty, too, not to blab in an almost certainly monitored email about his companions' breach of regulations. Still. "Why would Skiff bring up something like that at the funeral?"

"There was talk, you know. That Cody wasn't tough enough. Falling apart the way he did, killing himself in front of all those people. Skiff wanted me to know what Cody had been dealing with over there. He pulled me aside after and told me."

Skiff couldn't have been happy that Pal and Mike were so obviously involved, Lola thought. Which made it more inexplicable still that he'd seemed so glad to see Pal earlier that day. On the other hand, she thought, he seemed determined to shield the families from any more pain than the unendurable blow they'd already suffered, wanting to keep the news about Mike falling asleep out of the paper, trying to reassure Cody's dad that the pressure on his son in fact had been too much to bear. The thought rose that she would structure her story around Skiff, the group leader struggling to hold his friends together against increasing odds, losing first Mike and then Cody, but still fighting for them, even back on home ground.

"Did Cody ever write to you about what it was like over there? What'd he say?" Hoping for real-time tidbits, something to give a reader a sense of what the soldiers from Wyoming saw every day in Afghanistan, what they ate, how they amused themselves during the down times (although now she knew how Mike and Pal had done so) and, most important, what it was like to be on patrol where death lurked behind every rock, every mud hut, every herd of sheep.

Shirl shook his head. "Not a word beyond, 'We're all fine.' Made a joke of it. 'Not dead yet,' stuff like that. I think he didn't want me to worry. We lost his mom a few years back. Cancer. I probably hung on to him too tight after that. Might be what drove him to enlist." The grooves around his mouth deepened. The coffee cup jittered anew in his hands.

Lola resisted an impulse to cover one of them in her own. Such moments made her doubt her choice of career, the way it demanded that people rip the scabs off unhealed wounds and displayed the raw, bleeding depths of their souls to her. Their sadness straitjacketed her, leaving her struggling against its bonds hours, even days, sometimes months later. Margaret looked toward the door. Bub rose from the floor. Lola heard it, too, the rumble of an approaching vehicle.

"Mr. Dillon. Shirl," she said urgently, "your son shouted something before he … in the airport. 'It's alive.' What did he mean?"

Shirl's head jerked. "I didn't hear it. I was late getting there. Truck blew a tire on the way in. Maybe if I'd gotten there sooner—"

Lola sucked in her breath, imagining herself in the same sort of position with Margaret, the nightmare scenarios that present themselves to any parent. Lagging to retrieve some forgotten item as Margaret skipped toward a creek running high with snowmelt; turning her back to tend to some inane task as Margaret, sometimes still unsteady on her feet, poked a marshmallow into a blazing campfire. She talked past her own hovering fears and Shirl's realized one, thinking back to that day in the airport, the incoherent shout, so like all the others around her as people recognized their relatives. "I heard him say something, but I couldn't make it out. I asked somebody and that's what she said."

A car door slammed outside.

"'It's alive. It's alive.' What did he mean?"

Shirl shook his head in emphatic denial. "I do not have a single goddamn clue."

———

The deputy had been around awhile, long enough to acquire the air of detached courtesy that covered the fact that he knew the long drive out to Shirl's place was a colossal waste of his time.

All Lola could tell him about the truck was that it was light-colored and large, far bigger than the compact Toyota pickup she'd inherited after her friend Mary Alice's death. "American-made," she told the deputy uselessly. Most pickups in that part of the world were. "Wyoming plates. Just the driver, nobody else. Big guy. Ball cap."

The deputy pressed his lips together, containing his exasperation. Lola had described every other vehicle—and its driver—on Wyoming's roads. "And you say this truck actually struck yours?"

"He rammed us from behind. Clipped the front bumper. Side-swiped us, too."

The deputy removed a flashlight the size of a small table leg from his duty belt. "Let's take a look."

The flashlight threw a beam like midday sunshine, highlighting the scrapes on the front and rear bumpers, the long gouge down the driver's side of the pickup. Lola permitted herself a twinge of satisfaction. The deputy's skepticism had been clear. "Huh. Hold this for me." He handed her the flashlight and she pointed it as directed as he snapped photographs of the damage and then scraped bits of silver paint that glittered against her own truck's red into an evidence bag. He retrieved the flashlight just as Lola's arm was beginning to sag from its weight. "You know this is a long shot. But we'll do everything we can. I don't suppose you saw anyone else on the road while this was going on."

Lola acknowledged the impossibility of his task with a rueful smile. "Not a soul. Wish we had." Her smile vanished in the memory of those moments of terror, the sense that she was alone with someone bent on hurting her and her child, with no one around to help them.

"Anybody around here pissed off at you?"

Lola thought of Tommy McSpadden's mother, slamming the door on her; of the principal, angry at the way she'd taken offense at his racism. But neither seemed the type to play bumper cars with half-ton trucks. "I hardly even know anyone around here."

"Could be it was just somebody out for a thrill. Happens every so often. Guy comes across a woman driving alone after dark and senses opportunity."

"I wasn't alone," Lola pointed out. "And it wasn't quite dark yet."

He considered that, his eyes straying to Margaret and Bub. "Could be it was a worse kind of guy. You maybe dodged a bullet. Or worse."

Lola didn't even have to reach for Margaret. Girl and dog pressed against her legs, gone goosebumpy beneath her jeans. He was right, she knew. She'd done enough stories about just such wrong place-wrong time-very wrong guy situations to know that the deputy's speculation was well within the realm of possibility.

"Where were you headed?"

"A friend's house. We're staying with her. Palomino Jones."

The deputy pursed his lips at the mention of Pal's name, but said only, "On the rez. Long way yet."

"Yes." Maybe, out there somewhere, the guy in the truck patiently awaited his chance.

The deputy's sigh was audible. "I'll follow you on back. No sense taking chances. I'll have to turn back at the rez line, but you'll only have a couple miles left by then."

Lola wanted to throw her arms around him, hug him tight, kiss him full on his fleshy lips. She restrained herself to "thank you," hustling Margaret and Bub into the pickup before he changed his mind. She turned to Shirl and took both his hands in her own, feeling his grief flow into her and shoehorn its way into a too-crowded corner of her heart.

"Thank you for everything, Mr. Dillon. You take good care of yourself." She knew better than to offer false promises that his pain would ease in the foreseeable future. She trained her eyes upon the taillights of the deputy's truck, forcing herself not to look back and see Shirl once again outlined in his doorway, waiting for the one person who would never return.

EIGHTEEN

THE NEXT DAY FOUND Lola back at the park in Thirty, empty this
time but for a few crumpled napkins and the occasional stray plastic
beer cup, the detritus of the previous day's party that had escaped an
unusually efficient cleanup crew.

Lola positioned Margaret at the picnic table and retrieved an array
of distractions from her backpack. Books. Snacks. Drawing paper and
crayons. A few toys. Lola was about to get on the phone with the Department of Defense and knew from hard experience that the process
was likely to be interminable. But she wanted to arm herself against
the likelihood that Skiff would refuse to talk on the record about his
role in saving the others after Mike's death. Best to have the official
account of the incident. Despite the military's propensity to gunk up
its reports with convoluted phrasing, such narratives—once translated into words used by normal humans—often contained unexpected drama and pathos. She'd ask Pal, too. She wanted to have all
the facts at hand first, though. Lola's hand strayed to one of Margaret's
toys, a plastic rooster that despite his gender Margaret had renamed

Jemalina in honor of the hen that continued to bully Lola whenever she ventured outside Pal's house. On this morning, Jemalina had spoiled Lola's plan to slip quietly away while Pal slept off her most recent hangover, chasing Lola all the way to the truck with Bub in voluble pursuit. Lola didn't dare risk Pal overhearing her phone calls. Hence, another trek to Thirty, on a day so blindingly bright as to render almost unreal the previous night's shadowy attack. Lola encountered various vehicles along the way, their drivers all staying decorously on their own side of the road, each raising a couple of fingers from the wheel in the time-honored greeting of rural motorists.

"Mommy." Margaret removed the toy from Lola's hand and said in her most accusatory tone, "You're supposed to be working." The sooner Lola finished her phone calls, the sooner they could do something fun. At least, that's what Lola had promised. Even though she had no idea of what comprised fun in Thirty. She'd assured Margaret there would no repeat trip to the ice cream shop, and they'd already seen what appeared to be the region's lone historic attraction, the cemetery. Lola reached for a toy horse, a wooden pinto with a flowing yarn tail, and galloped him across the table. As far as she knew, the horse didn't have a name.

"*Mommy*." Margaret rescued the horse, too, and shoved Lola's phone toward her mother. "You work."

The DOD number was on speed dial. It was, Lola reflected as it rang, likely to be the only speedy thing about the process.

———

An hour's work netted nine transfers—four of them to wrong numbers—along with two hang-ups, three endless sessions on hold and five full pages of doodles in her notebook. At long last, Lola was instructed to send an email with her questions. "When will someone get back to me?" she asked. Just for the hell of it. She crossed her eyes at Margaret, who made her toys laugh in response. The answer was so mechanical Lola nearly forgot she was talking to a real person. "Your question will be answered in the order it was received."

"In which," she said.

"Pardon?"

"The order in which it was received." Stupid. The last thing she wanted to do was piss off the DOD, ensuring her request would be removed daily to the bottom of the list. Fortunately, her grammatical gibe seemed to have gone over her tormenter's head. Lola hung up and made a note to herself to send a Freedom of Information request for the same information. The feds at least were required to respond to such requests within twenty days. Although, by then she would be long gone from Thirty. It was possible she'd end up writing the story after her return to Magpie, which made it even more imperative that she do as much on-the-ground reporting in Wyoming as possible. She turned to the *Last Word* and the story that had caught her eye, a brief notice that Tyson Graff's and Tommy McSpadden's beating victim had been released from the Seattle hospital and was expected to recover. It was possible, according to the story by Dave Sparks, that the attempted murder charges against Tyson and Tommy would be downgraded to assault, still a felony but one with considerable sentencing latitude. Lola tapped her pen against her teeth. Tyson and Tommy might be more willing to talk now—at least, if she could get past Tommy's mother. It would help to return with someone local. Someone like Dave. She even managed to persuade herself that if another reporter had written the story, she'd be calling that reporter instead, trying unsuccessfully to suppress the smile that curved her lips as she punched the number for the *Last Word* into her phone.

The smile faded when the *Last Word*'s receptionist informed her that Dave had the day off. It returned when the woman added, "Is it important? I can give you his cell number." Lola allowed as to how it was very important. She shook her head as she jotted down the number, still amazed at the readiness with which people divulged such information. Dave picked up on the first ring. Margaret raised her head, alert to the change in her mother's usual brusque tone. Lola shot her a sidelong glance, cleared her throat and lowered her voice as she explained her mission. Dave offered a plan. Margaret put down her toys and watched her mother's end of the conversation.

"Sure," Lola said.

And, "That's a nice idea. But Margaret and the dog are with me."

And, "It's no trouble? Really? Can we bring anything?"

Margaret frowned. Lola grinned into the phone. Margaret's frown deepened.

"What did I tell you?" Lola said after she'd rung off. "I promised you something fun. We're going on a picnic." She turned her head so that her daughter wouldn't see the combination of excitement and guilt flaming her cheeks.

———

"Say the name again," Lola ordered Dave.

He shifted a rolled-up blanket beneath his arm and pointed to the water boiling grey and furious around jagged rocks far below. "Po-*po*-jah," he said.

"Spell it."

"P-o-p-o A-g-i-e."

Lola had seen the words on signs beside the stretch of river that slid tamed and picturesque past the outskirts of Thirty. She'd never have connected the two bodies of water, let alone those words and Dave's pronunciation.

"Po*po*jah, Po*po*jah," Margaret repeated, making a song of it, dancing to the words.

"Stay away from the edge," Lola said. Bub had already positioned himself between Margaret and the bluff above the disappearing river. The water plunged through a canyon, over rocks slick and covered with moss, and then dove into a cave. "It's called the Sinks," Dave said. "For the way the river just sinks into the earth."

Lola looked around for a flat place for them to picnic. Despite the drama below, the overlook offered nothing but dun earth, gray rocks, and dusty, silvery-green sagebrush. Dave gestured toward a dirt trail that led away from the parking area. "We've got a little ways to go."

Lola started back to the truck.

"Where are you going?"

"To get the picnic things."

"We aren't picnicking here. I just thought you should see this. Come on."

They picked their way along the path, Lola leading, not trusting Dave to be as wary of rattlesnakes as she. Bub stalked beside her, picking up on her unease, ears pricked forward. The trail began a descent, then took a sharp jog into a different world. Lola stopped so abruptly that Dave bumped into her, lingering a moment before stepping away, the warmth of his body a distraction from the oasis before her. They were at an overlook. Below, a glassy pool reflected the towering clouds, their inverse image leading Lola's eye down, down through the water's green depths, serene and untroubled in contrast to the muscular river they'd just left. Trout, the biggest Lola had ever seen, lolled near its surface, so confident that she knew their protected status even before she saw the "no fishing" sign. "What is this place?"

Dave's lips quirked. Lola looked away. "The Popo Agie," he said. "This is what it looks like on the other side. It's called the Rise."

Lola thought of the churning cataract not a half-mile behind them. "It seems impossible that it's the same river. It's not even a river here. It's a pond."

Dave pointed to the far end of the pool, where a tendril of water wandered away through a tangle of scrubby willows. "There's your river. Such as it is, at this point. You know how quickly we walked from the Sinks to the Rise?"

"Uh-huh." Even slowed down by Margaret, it had been a short walk.

"Given how fast that water dumps into the Sinks, you'd think dye would shoot right through to the Rise, wouldn't you?"

Lola nodded. She seemed to have lost her voice. Dave stood so close that she could feel the heat from his body. She edged a half-step away.

"But when they dumped dye in, it took more than two hours for it to show up in the Rise."

Lola offered a croak that she hoped indicated interest. In the river. Margaret came to her rescue. "Where are we going to have our picnic?"

———————

As far as Margaret was concerned, the picnic spot was even better than the mystery of the Sinks and the Rise. Easy for her to say, Lola pointed out. Margaret hadn't toted picnic gear during the mile-and-a-half hike in. Lola dropped the rolled-up blanket she'd carried. Even Dave looked relieved to dispense with the cooler. "Worth it, though, huh?" His gesture took in the river tumbling over the smooth rocks that surrounded a natural swimming hole.

Margaret brushed past her, stopping just long enough to tear off her shoes and socks, leaving a trail of pudgy footprints to the water's edge. Lola started after her. "Careful," she called. "It looks deep."

"It's okay." Dave trotted beside her. "It is deep, but not for a long ways out. If she stays near the edge, she'll be fine."

Margaret was already in up to her calves. Bub paddled back and forth a few yards ahead of her. "No deeper than your knees," Lola warned.

Dave unrolled the blanket, spread it on the sand, and opened the cooler to reveal sandwiches from the hippie café where they'd eaten a few days earlier. "I brought this, too," he said, emerging with a six-pack of good microbrew, not the watery stuff that had been in the kegs at the Fourth of July celebration. "This, too," he said. A lidded paper cup—recyclable, of course—from the café contained orange juice for Margaret. "Fresh-squeezed," he said. "Not that store-bought junk."

Margaret splashed reluctantly ashore when Lola summoned her. "Can I take mine down to the water?"

"As long as you don't take it *in* the water," Lola said. Bub hesitated. His job was to stay with Margaret. But there was more food on the picnic blanket. Lola shook her head at him. "You know the drill. Do your job, and there's a little something in it for you." She tore off a corner of her sandwich and set it aside. Bub's ribs bellowed in a sigh. He followed Margaret back to the shoreline. Lola wondered when Margaret would grasp the concept of delayed gratification as well as Bub had learned it. The hiss of an opening beer interrupted her thoughts.

"Here." Dave handed her a bottle, then held up his own. She clinked hers against it.

"What should we toast?" His eyes met hers, his intent clear, the question rhetorical.

At some point, Lola thought, she was going to have to tell him about Charlie. Although, Margaret's presence surely implied someone in her life. She raised her bottle.

"To good stories," she said, and drank deep, trying not to choke on the laughter that arose at the look on his face.

———

She waited until they were halfway through their pieces of pie before bringing up her story, telling him what she'd learned about Pal and Mike's relationship. "So many people I talked to dislike her. This could explain why."

Dave handed her another beer. "It also could explain why he was so tired he fell asleep on watch." He laughed. Lola didn't.

"I can't imagine anybody wanting to have sex in a place like that. Back on base, sure, but not on patrol." Maybe soldiers were different, she thought. She'd had her own fair share of fun during weeks of relative inactivity in Kabul, but the field was different. She loved her forays out of the city—the best stories were out there—but they were fraught with danger in a way that, at least for her, precluded any thoughts of sex. Not to mention the heat, the dirt, and the lack of plumbing.

"Spoken by one who knows," Dave prompted. But Lola rarely talked of her time there. Charlie had learned better than to probe too deeply, and Dave was about to learn the same lesson.

"I want to talk to Tommy McSpadden and Tyson Graff again," she said. It was, after all, the real reason that she was meeting with Dave. The only reason, she reminded herself.

"You mean T-Squared?" he said. "That pair is trouble. They almost killed that guy."

She pointed her beer bottle at him. "Apparently not, at least according to your story."

"Yeah, but that was just dumb luck. The guy could just as easily have died. Really, you want to stay away from them."

Lola snorted at the idea that despite their bar dustup, a couple of yahoos like Tommy and Tyson could present a serious threat, especially in the middle of the day and the middle of town. Going unarmed into a hostile warlord's territory with only a driver and a fixer who'd become the closest thing she had to a friend in Afghanistan, drinking endless cups of tea surrounded by men crouched beside grenade launchers—*then* she'd worried about getting hurt. And she'd worry the next time she drove back to the ranch in darkness, she thought. She pushed the notion away. She'd already considered that Tommy or Tyson might have been the truck's driver but, even though she'd barely seen the driver, he'd seemed bigger than either of them.

Dave tried another tack. "You're really going to pursue this?"

"I have to. I got the go-ahead to do a story. It's important. The same sort of ripple effects in Thirty are playing out in towns all over the country as soldiers come back."

He tilted his head back for another swig of beer. His Adam's apple bobbed. A tuft of pale hair curled from the top of his T-shirt. Lola swallowed hard. "I thought you said Tommy and Tyson wouldn't talk to you," he said.

"Tyson did, a little. Tommy's mother wouldn't let me get near him. I thought if I went back with someone local—" She let it hang there, not directly offering him a piece of the story, waiting for him to ask. Any reporter would, especially the hungry ones at the beginning of their careers. It's how she'd forged her friendship with Jan, although with Jan, she'd offered. But she'd been new to the West then, less sure-footed. Besides, she got the feeling Dave had skated through life on things being offered to him. She wanted to know that the guy could break a sweat, at least on someplace other than a rock face.

"Let me think about it."

Lola finished her beer and replaced the empty in the cooler. "Don't take too long, okay? I'm only here for another week. Maybe I can call you tomorrow?"

Dave reached for the cooler. Another bottle cap hissed free. "Hell," he said. "You can call me anytime."

A pair of damp and sandy arms wrapped her from behind. Lola turned to Margaret in guilty relief. "Sleepy, Mommy." Margaret sagged against Lola and closed her eyes. Bub flung himself down on the blanket, off the clock for the moment, and claimed the bit of sandwich she'd saved for him.

"This never happens," Lola mouthed to Dave. The prospect of the hike back to Dave's car, so short on the way in, seemed infinitely less desirable with the burden of a sleeping child. She said as much to Dave.

"Not an issue," he said. He pointed to a tall sagebrush casting a fat shadow. "Why not let her nap in the shade? She'll wake up full of energy." He stood and shifted things off the blanket, and tugged it beneath the bush. Lola followed, looking hard once again for snakes. She didn't see any. She prodded the base of the bush with her foot, wishing she'd opted for boots over the thin-walled running shoes in which she had never once run. Nothing rattled.

"All right, I guess." She laid Margaret in the shade and looked around for Bub. He rose, shook sand from his silky fur, and positioned himself beside the sleeping child.

"Sweet," said Dave. He kicked off his sandals and shucked out of his shorts.

"What the hell are you doing?" Lola hissed.

He pulled his shirt over his head. "Going for a swim," he said. He stepped out of his underwear as he walked away. Clothed, he looked skeletal. Bared, his long body revealed itself as lean muscle, deep tan lines bisecting his upper arms and thighs. "You coming?"

Muscle, thought Lola, and one very sweet ass.

"Hell, yes," she whispered, as she peeled off her own clothes and jogged behind him toward the water.

NINETEEN

DAVE WAS RIGHT ABOUT the long expanse of shallows. Lola floundered toward him, desperate for deep water to cover her small, high breasts and the profusion of curls between her legs. Although she refused to wax, she understood that women just a few years younger considered it an integral part of grooming. For all their male contemporaries knew, adult women remained as bald down there as the little girls with whom the boys once had played doctor.

She wondered if Dave would find that a turn-off, then told herself it didn't matter, because nothing was going to happen between them. The skinny-dipping was just a lighthearted romp, something she could have done as easily with her friend Jan. *Bullshit*, a voice said within. The water lapped at her thighs. She dove into it, closing her eyes against it, letting it flow into her ears, blocking out the inconvenient voice. When she came up, crouching so that only her head and shoulders were above the water, Dave was beside her.

"Let's go out to the middle." He put both hands on her shoulders and slid them down her arms, fingertips brushing her breasts along the way. He locked his hands around her wrists and towed her into deeper water, seemingly unconcerned that standing to do so momentarily exposed him. Lola glanced away, although not before noticing that he was proportionate to those long arms and legs. The footing fell away beneath them and Dave dropped her hands. Lola paddled backward to a safe distance and let her feet sink beneath her, treading water.

"What do you think?" Droplets of water sparkled on Dave's lashes.

Think of what, Lola wondered? His naked self? His naked self and hers, together?

"Pretty amazing, isn't it?"

Unless Dave's ego exceeded even that of any healthy young male of the species, he was talking about the lake in which they hung suspended.

His arms skated across the top of the water, bringing him closer. Lola forced herself not to move away. She didn't have anything to worry about, she told herself in the silent reminder quickly becoming a mantra, because Nothing Was Going To Happen.

His foot encountered hers again. He slipped it up her calf.

They sank below the surface, his hands running over her body, her pulling him close, sinking down, down into the darkness before she kicked free and shot for the surface and air and sanity.

"Charlie," she gasped into the sunshine.

"Say what?" Dave surfaced behind her, wrapping her in his arms, hands to her breasts, moving himself between her legs. They sank again, Dave pulling her down against himself. Lola's breath escaped in a moan, and then she needed air, blessed indispensable oxygen, its necessity saving her from herself. She twisted free and clawed toward the light, gasping as she broke the surface, spinning to face Dave before he could latch onto her again.

"Charlie," she said. She sucked in more air.

"Who's Charlie?"

"Margaret's." Gasp. "Father." Lola took a deeper breath still as his feet found hers again. Her body yearned toward him in eager betrayal, her legs twining with his. He stroked the water with one arm—they'd stay above the surface this time, no last-second salvation—and let the other slide between her breasts and down her belly until the heel of his hand was pressed against her. He held it there, leaving it up to her to move against him. Which Lola felt herself do.

"Charlie," she whispered.

"Charlie's not here."

"But. *Oh.*"

His hand moved, its motion timed to hers. "He'll never know," he said, his breath warm in her ear. "I've got a girlfriend back in Massachusetts. She'll never know, either. Nobody gets hurt. Everything's good. It *is* good, isn't it?"

His tongue slid into her mouth and his hand moved to her breast and she wrapped her arms around him to keep from sinking, and her legs, too, and he was between them again and she knew in a second he'd be inside her, and God, she wanted him there, she was hot in a way she'd forgotten during the years of once-in-awhile, almost-married, hurry-up-the-kid's-asleep sex she had with Charlie. She closed her eyes and saw Charlie's face, broad and brown, his slow smile dissolving the harshness of its planes—"No!"

She shoved at Dave's shoulders, disentangled her legs, and swam toward shore in a thrashing backstroke. The smooth rocks beneath her feet were the foundation she needed, each step on solid ground one more away from wavering madness, the water and all its seductive power sluicing from her body. She stumbled toward her clothes, yanking hard to pull them on over her dripping flesh, and fell onto the blanket beside Margaret. Only then did she turn and look toward Dave, following her out of the water, striding easy through the shallows, still hard, letting her see what she'd missed.

She turned away again and shook Margaret more roughly than necessary. "Wake up, honey. It's time to go."

Dave dropped them off at the supermarket parking lot where she'd left her truck. He'd chatted casually on the way back to town, letting her know everything was fine. Which was how guys like Dave operated, Lola supposed. He didn't have the creepy vibe she associated with predators. He merely saw opportunity and gave it a shot, and moved on cheerfully if he got turned down. It had, in fact, been her own modus operandi in the years before she'd met Charlie. What bothered her was that Dave had sensed something receptive in her, and what bothered her even more was that she couldn't deny it had been there.

TWENTY

THAT EVENING, LOLA TURNED off the ringer on her phone so she'd be able to tell Charlie, truthfully, that she hadn't heard it when he'd called.

Which of course didn't stop her from seeing the calls stacking up in the "incoming" box, along with the texts and finally an email. "Check in. I'm worried about you." The phone sat on the windowsill above the sink, blinking guilt at her as she washed the dinner dishes. Lola was worried about herself, too. Was her near-miss an impulse toward a last fling, one final romp before settling down? Or was it a sign that a fatal flaw lurked within her relationship with Charlie? More than anything, she resented the fact that his proposal brought such questions to the forefront of her consciousness. She'd have preferred things to remain exactly as they were, ignoring the need—if such a need existed—to probe deeper. "Cleopatra, Queen of Denial," Charlie had called her more than once.

"Denial is a fine coping mechanism," she'd retorted. "How do you think I got through all those years in Afghanistan without denying the reality that I could end up dead at any moment?" Which once again brought up the uncomfortable fact that, beyond such flippant remarks, she'd refused deeper discussions of Afghanistan, deflecting Charlie's questions with, "There's no way to understand unless you were there."

"I'm here," he'd said.

They'd been on the reservation at the time, on their way home from visiting some of the aunties, the pickup rolling past settlements of flimsily built bungalows that, for lack of any alternative, housed far too many people; past the jobless young men smoking on the street corners; past the older ones who'd given up looking for work and turned to drink, the same way people in Afghanistan got hooked on the heroin that was for all practical purposes the only viable part of the country's economy. Lola had, in fact, often spoken of her desire to write a series called "America's Afghanistan," a way to funnel her outrage over the way the government found it acceptable to let the reservations languish. "Five billion a month over the wars in Iraq and Afghanistan!" she'd sputter. "Put a single month's spending into the reservations. That would fully fund the Indian Health Service, build enough houses for all the people on them, do real job training—"

Charlie's indulgent smile, full of patience for the newly informed, stopped her. "I know, I know," she'd smiled back. "Here comes another white person, charging in with all the answers." But at least, she thought privately, her rant ended his questions about her own experience in Afghanistan.

A sharp pain in her ankle interrupted her reverie. "Ow!"

Jemalina shot squawking across the kitchen, Bub in respectful pursuit, close behind but not close enough to risk another peck on the nose. "Who let that goddamn—that flippin'—chicken in the house?" Lola scooped up a handful of soapy water and flung it Jemalina's way, succeeding only in creating a slick spot on the floor. Bub hit it full tilt and slid into Jemalina. Feathers and fur flew. Margaret waded in, fearless, emerging with Jemalina in her arms. Bub retreated to a corner, licking new wounds, his blue eye, full of indictment, turned upon Lola.

Pal wandered out of the bedroom, eyes heavy with sleep or booze. Lola no longer cared which. At the moment, she was disenchanted with just about everyone she'd encountered that day—Dave and his damnable charm, Bub and his accusing stare, the fuzzy-footed chicken and her razor-sharp beak, and even Margaret for rescuing the creature from what might well have been certain death from Bub and resulting sweet relief for Lola.

Pal rubbed the stubble on her head and fell into one of the kitchen chairs. "What's going on?"

"Somehow the chicken got in the house."

Margaret scurried for the door, which Lola was pretty sure had not swung ajar by accident. "Good night, Jemalina," Margaret sang out theatrically and made sure Lola could hear the door click closed.

"Couldn't sleep?" Lola dried the dishes and put them away with rather more noise than necessary, emphasizing the fact that one of the adults in the house was doing all of the work.

"Too much racket," said Pal. "Don't sleep much, anyway." Her eyes were red.

Could've fooled me, Lola thought. Pal retreated to the bedroom immediately after dinner each night, not emerging until Delbert's arrival each morning. Lola, a longtime insomniac herself, often listened for the telltale rhythm of pacing footsteps, of the gurgling that would indicate a glass of water filled in the kitchen, or the flush of a toilet, but had yet to hear anything. She'd just assumed Pal drank herself into a nightly stupor. Well, she was sick of speculating about Pal. Time for some direct questions. Or at least, less indirect.

"Gotta be tough, losing a boyfriend. No wonder you can't sleep." Even to herself, Lola couldn't pretend her voice held the least bit of sympathy, her words sounding exactly like the accusation they were.

Pal's hands fell to the table. Her head snapped upward.

"Boyfriend? What boyfriend?"

"Oh, please." Lola ran a towel around a final pot. She'd done a credible job with spaghetti, funneling her confusion over the afternoon with Dave into meatballs that to her surprise had turned out exactly the way the online recipe had promised. Both Pal and Margaret had had seconds, much to Bub's dismay. Lola turned to face Pal, bracing her back against the kitchen counter. "Mike. Mike St. Clair."

Pal passed a hand across her eyes. "Mike wasn't my boyfriend. Where'd you get that crazy idea?"

So this was how it was going to be, Lola thought. First, Pal said she didn't know poor suicidal Cody Dillon. Now she denied the man with whom she'd been in love. Or at least in lust. Given that she apparently was dealing with a pathological liar, Lola thought it best not to divulge where she'd learned what everybody in town already knew.

"I guess I just assumed," she said. Hoping Pal didn't know enough about reporters to realize that "assume" was a word that eclipsed the worst of curses.

Pal didn't know. She stood up. "You assumed wrong," she said. She strode from the table down the hall toward the bedroom, slamming the door so hard that Lola felt the reverberation in the kitchen.

"Three," Lola said.

"Three what, Mommy?"

Three slammed doors, Lola thought. Tyson Graff at the hardware store. Tommy McSpadden's mother. Now this.

"It's not important, sweetheart. Mommy's just set a new record is all." Lola put the spaghetti pot in the cupboard and, just for the sheer hell of it, banged the door shut with as much force as she could muster. She hoped Pal could hear it in the bedroom. She doubted Pal cared.

———————

The hardware store owner remembered Lola, emerging from the store's dim interior as soon as she walked through the door the next day. Margaret wandered over to the popcorn machine and stood hopefully before it as the man approached. "You're looking for Tyson."

She hadn't said anything. "I am," she admitted.

He wore a green bib apron with his name stitched on it. "Carl." As before, the store was empty of customers. "He's not here."

Tyson must have made it clear he didn't want to talk to her again. Just as Dave had made it clear, when she'd forced herself after their encounter to call him and ask, that he wasn't going to come with her. "You're on your own on this one," he'd said.

She'd promised herself not to beg. "But it's a big story," she'd blurted anyway. Which, she thought, she shouldn't have had to point out. Most reporters she knew were like bird dogs on the hunt once they got even a whiff of story, let alone one of any size. Everything else—food, family, even sex—became secondary.

"Is that what this is about?" Dave had said. "Another feather in your cap?"

Lola expected questions like that from outsiders. She didn't think she'd have to explain to one of her own that it went beyond that. "Dammit, it's the human element. This war is more than Pentagon budgets and kill counts. But people want to ignore that. They can't when you put something like this next to their breakfast cereal in the morning."

"Put it on their phones, more likely," Dave said.

Lola took a moment to let the crack at their age difference pass, and bit back a dig of her own. *Coward*, she'd thought, glad yet again she hadn't slept with him. Cheating on her boyfriend was bad enough, but sex with a lazy reporter was its own special category of sin. The store owner spoke again, bringing her back to the task at hand.

"He quit."

"Excuse me?"

Carl picked up a wrench and sat it back down with more force than necessary. Lola was getting sick of everybody banging things around. "Up and quit. After I spoke up in court on his behalf and everything. Guess he didn't need me once they dropped that attempted murder charge."

Lola sensed a potential ally. "I read in the paper about what you did. That was really nice of you."

"He thought so, too. At the time."

Lola veered away from the subject. Best not to ask too soon about what she so desperately needed to know. Time to talk about the weather. "Hot out there."

"Too hot."

"How's the snowpack?" Even after five years, she still thrilled to the fact that she'd learned the lingo, knew that water—actually, everyone in this part of the world called it "moisture"—was an all-consuming topic, and that instead of rain it came in the form of high-country snows whose springmelt fed the rivers and creeks, enabling the irrigation that had made white settlement possible in the West.

"Below average. Again."

Lola whistled long and low. "Sorry to hear that. It's the same up in Montana, where I'm from."

"Saw your license plate. What brings you to Wyoming? Not Tyson."

Nice, she thought, that he'd led her back on topic. She affected an airy laugh. "No, not Tyson. Just visiting friends on my way to Yellowstone." She hurried on so that he wouldn't ask about the friends. "Any idea where I can find Tyson? He's the friend of a friend." Which was sort of true, given that he and Pal and served together.

The wrench banged against the counter again. "Try the Mint. Back to the scene of the crime, you might say."

"The scene of the crime," Lola murmured as she left the store. "That would be my specialty." She was back on the chase, slipping into the old well-oiled moves, shedding the confusion of the previous day with Dave. It felt familiar. It felt good.

TWENTY-ONE

IT WAS EITHER GUTSY or truly stupid on Tyson's part, returning to the bar where he'd gotten into so much trouble, Lola thought. She leaned toward the latter.

But The Mint presented problems of its own. It was one thing to bring Margaret along on interviews in a store, or at someone's house, or even on a picnic where she'd ended up in near flagrante delicto as her daughter—please God—had lain sleeping. But a bar. That was another matter, despite the fact that Lola had seen her fair share of toddlers in Montana's homespun bars, the kids' lips and cheeks stained scarlet from a steady succession of maraschino cherries as their parents got shitfaced beside them.

Lola stood with Margaret outside The Mint, the sidewalk radiating fire through her running shoes, glad that in deference to the unrelenting heat she'd worn shorts instead of jeans. What the hell, Lola thought. Chances are Tyson wouldn't be there, and that nobody else there would know where he was. Or, more likely, they'd know but wouldn't tell her. She'd be in and out of there in three minutes flat. Less. She'd convinced herself. Now she needed to persuade Margaret, who'd turned on her the narrow-eyed gaze she employed when she suspected her mother was about to do something that would not in any way be to her benefit. "We're going into this restaurant," Lola said. "It'll be nice and cool in there."

"But we just had lunch," Margaret said.

"This is a kind of restaurant that mostly serves things to drink. If we decide to stay, maybe you can have a nice cold pop," said Lola, choking out the last word. Pop was most emphatically on the forbidden list.

"It's a bar," Margaret said.

Lola picked her up and balanced her on her hip. "You're five years old. How do you know about bars?" She pushed open the windowless door and went in. The hardware store had been dim, but the Mint was frankly dark, its only illumination coming from a couple of weak lamps along the back bar. The back bar itself was a thing of beauty, ornately carved and inset with high mirrors, brassy with age. Lola had seen such back bars in the smallest of towns, each accompanied by its own story of being toted across the prairie in sections packed carefully into Conestoga wagons. She didn't much care whether the stories were true. The bars' exotic beauty deserved such fanciful tales. She stood to one side of the door, letting her eyes adjust.

A bartender in a white shirt and black bowtie—fancy duds for midday in a town like Thirty, Lola thought—polished the taps with a soft towel, politely ignoring her until she was ready. The usual old-timers took up the seats closest to the door. Even though it meant a farther walk to the restroom to empty their aging bladders, it gave them first peep at whoever walked in and thus a chance to comment on anything, or anyone, new in Thirty. They swiveled in their seats and fixed rheumy eyes upon Lola, and she knew that if she were to perch upon one of the barstools, one or the other of them would find a way to approach her and quiz her as to her identity, her business in Thirty, and any other questions triggered by their slow-firing synapses. And she might let them, might plant Margaret on a stool next to her and signal the bartender for—gawd—some pop, and gently prod the men toward talk of their own days coming home from war, and what it was like for them as compared to the recent run of misfortune among the returning Afghanistan veterans. She would have done exactly that, had she not spied at the far end of the bar two men, younger by decades than the others, with a nearly empty pitcher of beer between them.

"Thank you," she breathed to the journalism gods. She stepped to the bar. The bartender materialized before her.

"A new pitcher for those gentlemen," she said. Had she imagined the twitch in the corner of the bartender's mouth at the word "gentlemen?" "And a glass for me, along with a Coke with extra cherries for this young lady. We'll take it down there."

Nobody, thought Lola as she sauntered the length of the bar with Margaret squirming on her hip, tattooing her heels against Lola's thighs, would dare be rude in public to a woman with a child. Especially not someone who'd just bought them beer. Not even Tommy McSpadden and Tyson Graff.

———

The men's faces brightened when they saw the beer. Then they saw Lola. From the way it took them awhile to recognize her, she surmised the pitcher was not their first.

"You're that girl came by the hardware store," Tyson said.

"You know her?" McSpadden chimed in. "She came by my house, too. Made my mom all crazy."

"Your mom's crazy anyway."

"Ain't that a fact?"

"Woman," Lola said.

They gaped.

"Not girl. Woman. I'm the woman who just stood you a new pitcher of beer." Which arrived on cue, an inch of foam precisely even with the lip, sides beaded with moisture. The bartender came back with two fresh glasses for the men and one for Lola, all of them frosted from the freezer, and returned one last time with Margaret's Coke. Lola positioned Margaret on a stool and gave her a look. *I've bribed you and you know it*, it said. *Don't even think about any funny stuff.* Margaret plucked the first of a handful of cherries from the glass and popped it into her mouth and smiled her sweetest at the men before turning her attention to the paper straw striped like a barbershop pole.

Lola tilted the pitcher over each of the three glasses, filling the men's to the brim and hers about halfway. "Cheers," she said. They clinked, frowning.

"What are we drinking to?" As before, Tyson took the lead.

"That guy's recovery," Lola said. "What's his name again?"

"Oh," Tyson said. "Him." Which was as far as Lola got in her attempt to determine their victim's name.

"Nice break for you guys. Sounds like everything's going to work out okay," she said. She took a sip of her beer.

"Everything was gonna work out okay, anyway," Tyson said. Each time he spoke, he thrust his head forward. The cords in his neck leapt to prominence. His shoulder muscles bunched. Lola forced herself not to pull back.

"How's that?"

"Fucker started it. His fault, not ours."

That old story, Lola thought. Always somebody else's fault. Except that sometimes, it actually was. "What happened?"

Tommy McSpadden had already drained his glass. He reached for the pitcher but missed it.

"I'll pour," Lola said.

"Why do you want to know?" he asked her.

Dammit. She'd hoped to get to that part later. "I'm writing a story about it. About you. Not just you two," she added at the wariness rising fast in their faces.

"What are you, some kind of reporter? Are you new here?"

"I'm not from here," she said. "I write for a publication based … out East," she said, thinking fast. In these parts, New York could be an interview-killer. She hurried on. "Sounds like you all went through hell over there, what with Mike getting killed and everything."

Tyson's head jutted forward again. "Mike got himself killed. But Pal. She helped."

Lola poured beer so fast that some splashed onto the bar. The bartender approached with his rag. Her glance warned him away. Tyson called him back. "Let's get some shots over here. Schnapps."

Let's not, Lola thought. Beer was one thing. She needed at least some semblance of clear thinking on their part while she asked her questions. "Why don't you hold off on those shots a minute?" she said. The bartender nodded his approval.

She pulled out her notebook and pen. "Just to make sure I keep everything straight," she said. "You said Pal helped get Mike killed. How's that?"

Tyson hitched his stool forward. Tommy followed suit. They exchanged glances.

"You want a story?" Tyson said. Tommy grinned, lips wet with beer. "'Cause we got one will knock your socks off. Put that goddamn notebook down."

———————

It should have been an easy, even boring, patrol, they told her. The hairs on the back of Lola's neck stood up. Expecting anything to be easy, let alone boring, was a recipe for disaster in Afghanistan.

The village near the forward operating base had never posed a threat. Their task was to keep it that way, an example for other villages to follow. To that end, a small group of soldiers was assigned to observe a meeting between the elders of this particular village and another somewhat farther away. The Wyomingites drew the short straw. The meeting would take hours. Tea would flow freely. "Everybody take a piss before you leave," Tommy recalled Skiff saying. "Especially you, TB."

Lola wracked her brain for someone with those initials. She didn't want to interrupt, but had to. "Who's that?"

Tyson barked a laugh. "Pal. We all called her Thimble Bladder because she had to pee more than the rest of us."

"Not more," Tommy said. "But it was a bigger production when she did."

Lola felt a stab of sympathy for Pal, remembering her own days of desperately holding her water among groups of men in a barren country that offered precious little in the way of roadside shelter. And even if there had been a friendly boulder or shrub, it would have been too dangerous to step off the roads, which at least were swept intermittently for mines. Away from the roads, all bets were off. As her male companions lined up in front of the aging Russian jeeps in which the journalists traveled, turned their backs and unzipped, she

153

crouched behind the vehicle—only, more than once, to spy an Afghan driver flattened on the ground, peering beneath the jeep, hoping for a glimpse of foreign female ass.

"So, you went to the village," she urged. "Any problems along the way?"

"None. But the meeting went even longer than we expected. All afternoon, until almost dark."

Lola could imagine. Village councils were tribal affairs, marked by elaborate and time-consuming courtesies. To leave early would give unimaginable offense. She could see the soldiers, sitting cross-legged on the inevitable rug inside the simple mud hut, unable to hold the seemingly effortless knee-crouch of the Afghanis around them, stirring restlessly as the light outside dimmed.

"By the time we left, the stars were out."

Another memory kicked in, a rare good one. In a country where only the cities had widespread electricity, and even that unreliable, the night skies above Afghanistan were starlit in a way Lola only vaguely remembered from her small-town childhood. The Milky Way unfurled in a great shimmering ribbon across the heavens, the billion or so other stars in the sky mere accessories to its magnificence.

"Skiff had radioed back, letting them know we were on our way, and that everything was okay. They offered to send out someone to escort us, but he said we were fine. And we were. At least until the vehicle broke down. We knew they'd come for us soon. So we set out to meet them."

The stars lit the dirt track so brightly there was no need for head-lamps. The temperature plummeted at night, meaning that for once their heavy body armor was almost bearable. After the long day in the hut, the interpreter's steady drone broken only by pauses for another round of tea or a shared plate of greasy mutton, it felt good to be moving, and back among their own, free of the constant tension of the need to avoid inadvertent insults. They joshed among themselves, horsing around, pretending they were playing that old nursery school game, Lion Hunt. Except they made it a Taliban Hunt.

"I'm going Talib hunting!" Pal hissed, eyes shining in the dark. "I'm not afraid."

She led the way in a half crouch, rifle at the ready in one hand, the other shielding her eyes from the starlight as she scanned the surrounding rocks. "Talib? Are you there?" They all waited, chuckling during the long pause. "Nope!"

She and Mike jogged ahead, the others hurrying to catch up. "I'm going Talib hunting…" They disappeared around a bend in the path.

"Hey," Skiff called, his voice low. "Wait up."

Something rustled off to the side. Guns came up in unison, the men turning in a tight circle. Nothing. "Jesus Christ," Skiff said. "Those two fuckers better not be messing with us."

Lola glanced toward Margaret. She seemed engrossed in standing up her cherry stems in a sort of tipi shape, one that kept collapsing and required even more intense concentration. She gave no sign of having heard Tyson's language as he recounted Skiff's words.

They heard scrambling. A shout. A burst of gunfire.

"Motherfuck!" Skiff screamed. In deference to Margaret, Tyson whispered it, but the expression on his face gave no doubt as to the intensity of the moment. The soldiers, he said, rounded the corner at a sprint, nearly falling over the cloaked man who lay across the path before them, making slow swimming movements as his life leaked away into the dust.

"Got him!" Pal stood a little away from the man, breathless, doing a sort of jig. "Got our Talib."

"You got him, you mean," Mike said, his grin very white in his dark face. They bumped fists.

"What the fuck? What the fuck?" Skiff was the only one among the others who appeared capable of speech. Something baa'ed in the brush, an old familiar sound. The group bunched together, Pal and Mike joining the others. Sheep trotted into the clearing, stopping when they saw the soldiers, blowing and snorting, hooves shifting uneasily in the dust.

"Talib, my ass. You assholes shot a motherfucking shepherd. People get court-martialed for this shit."

The man moved again in the dirt. It seemed impossible. One side of his head was gone. Mike knelt over him. "Pretty sure this is a Talib."

The man's arm came up. Something flashed. Mike fell beside him. Pal screamed.

Skiff moaned. "Motherfuck. We are so fucking fucked."

TWENTY-TWO

"Now you know," Tyson said, "why we had to cook up that bullshit story about Mike falling asleep while he was on watch."

Tommy bobbed his head. "Had to."

With some effort, Lola lifted her hand to signal the bartender. "Whiskey," she said. "Jameson's, if you've got it. A double."

"All around?"

"Hell, yeah," Tommy and Tyson said in unison.

The Jameson's burned, doing exactly what it needed to do, focusing her thoughts on something other than the horror that had just been laid out before her. "Better to think Mike died falling asleep—"

"Yeah. As a, you know, mercy," Tommy said.

"To his family," Tyson added. The words had the air of rehearsal. They held the shot glasses over their beer mugs and released them with a splash, lifting mugs to their lips and canting their heads back, Adam's apples jerking until the shot glasses clinked against their teeth.

Lola was tempted to follow suit with her own whiskey, but sipped instead. "A mercy to you, too. That court-martial business. That's some scary shi—. Some scary stuff."

"It would have been on Pal." Tyson called for more shots and fresh mugs.

Lola decided that the wiser course was to go along. Even though she knew, and they clearly did, too, that the shooting of an unarmed civilian would have fallen on the whole group, and fallen harder still for their not reporting the true circumstances. She glanced at her blank notebook.

Tyson followed her gaze. "All of that was—what do you guys say? Off the record. That's it, right? Off the record."

Lola slapped some money on the bar. "That's exactly how you say it. It means I can't quote you on anything you just told me. So your asses are covered."

Let them think they had their secret, she thought. Now that she knew what had really happened, all she had to do was verify it elsewhere. She gathered up Margaret and bade them a distracted goodbye, already thinking of the new request for information she was going to file with the Department of Defense.

———

Pal was sitting on the porch steps when they pulled up to the house, lacing up her running shoes.

"Anybody want to come on a run with me? Lola?" It was the first time she'd made anything resembling a gesture of friendship. Earlier, Lola would have jumped at the chance. Even if it meant running, a direct contradiction of her opposition to all forms of exercise. Now, the idea of running with someone who'd killed an innocent man, and not only killed him but *for fun*, nauseated her. Lola had been in the villages, and she knew that widowhood could bring slow starvation for the man's wife and children.

"God, no," she said. Then, to soften it, added, "I can't leave Margaret alone."

"We can just run back and forth, so that we can see her on the porch. Besides, Bub and Jemalina are with her. Neither of them would let anyone get within three feet of that child. Come on." She looked Lola up and down, taking in her T-shirt and shorts and the running shoes Lola wore in place of her wintertime hiking boots. "You've got the right shoes."

"But I don't run in them," Lola protested. "I just wear them because they're comfortable. To walk in. Slowly."

Pal grabbed Lola's arm and pulled her away from the truck. "Just a little ways. It'll be good for you." She broke into a jog, still holding Lola's arm. Lola pulled back. Pal's grip loosened not at all. Lola stumbled, then found herself moving beside Pal in the slowest of shuffles. Her fists clenched. Who was this murderer, dragging her away from her child?

Pal let go just in time. "Let's pick it up."

Lola glanced back. As Pal had promised, she could still see Margaret, flanked by Jemalina and Bub, neither of them looking particularly happy with the situation. That makes three of us, Lola thought. They ran up a slight rise. Lola's breath came harder. Sweat ran into her eyes. It stung. Right about the time she thought her lungs would burst, they came to the top of the rise.

"We'll run along the ridgeline," Pal said. "Otherwise we won't be able to see Margaret."

Back on level ground, she picked up the pace yet again. Lola lengthened her own stride. If she was going to be this miserable, she thought, she might as well make the most of it. She pulled alongside Pal. "I don't know if your cousin told you," she gasped, "but I spent some time in Afghanistan, too. Years, actually. I'd love to compare notes." If her oxygen deprivation hadn't approached dangerous levels,

Lola would have held her breath awaiting Pal's response. As it turned out, it didn't matter. Pal turned her head and gave her a long look, then sprinted away, down the other side of the ridge, out of sight of Margaret, where she knew Lola wouldn't follow, kicking up her speed so that Lola couldn't catch her even if she'd tried.

––––––––

"Charlie?"

Lola pressed her cellphone tight against her cheek, wishing that, for all her ambivalence about marrying the man, she were in his arms instead of being separated by nearly six hundred miles. Charlie's most compelling appeal was his quiet, uncompromising strength, which was also the quality that left her most wary. When a potential threat—which was how she was starting to see Pal—presented itself, Charlie could be counted on to handle it effectively, without fanfare. But this time, Lola had brought the threat, if there was one, upon herself. And not just herself, but Margaret. Charlie had little patience with Lola's tendency to get herself in trouble, and Lola knew that if he thought the trouble might involve his daughter, he'd break speed limits all the way through Montana and Wyoming to get to Margaret. Lola lectured herself to play it cool in their conversation. But apparently she'd already given herself away in the single word she'd uttered.

"Lola. What's wrong?"

"Nothing. Why do you think something's wrong? All I did was say your name. For heaven's sake, Charlie." She kicked herself, a real physical kick, left heel to right shin, reminding herself too late not to blather, a sure sign of guilt.

"It's in your voice. And you didn't answer any of my messages last night. What's going on?"

"Nothing. Honestly. It's just—" The last few days caught up with her, the terrifying truck chase, the watery dalliance with Dave, the revelations about Pal, and all along, Pal's lies and avoidance. Lola turned her head and faked a sneeze and held her face to the hot wind, hoping it would dry her tears. She sneezed again, a real one this time. "This place is giving me allergies. So much dust."

Silence. Charlie knew better than to talk when someone was doing a fine job indicting herself.

Lola pasted a smile onto her face, hoping it would carry through in her voice. "How are you? How are things going with the new deputy?" It didn't work.

"Where were you yesterday? Why you didn't answer your phone?"

"It ran down. I misplaced my charger." A fine and believable excuse. Lola was always losing things. She was on her fifth phone charger.

"What about the car charger?"

Damn. Because Lola lost her charger so frequently, she kept a backup in the truck. "I didn't go anywhere yesterday. It seemed silly to run the truck just to charge the phone. Anyway, nothing much happened yesterday. I figured we'd just wait to talk to you today." Her voice was stronger now, skipping blithely from one lie to the next.

"Speaking of *we*, put Margaret on."

Lola waved to Margaret and held up the phone.

"Daddy!" Margaret charged toward her, Bub and Jemalina twin clouds of dust in her wake. Lola sidestepped Jemalina's beak and handed the phone to Margaret.

"Daddy, I miss you."

Charlie spoke for a long time. Margaret's face brightened by degrees. "We *are* having fun, Daddy. Mommy lets me have ice cream here. And I have a chicken! Can I bring her home with me?" Margaret, no fool, didn't give him a chance to answer the question. "And yesterday we went swimming! Me and Mommy and her friend, Dave."

Shit. Shit. *Shit.*

Lola didn't even have time to think of a good story before the phone landed back in her hand. She waited for Charlie to speak. He didn't. She waited some more. Gave up. "Dave's a reporter at the paper here. I'm, ah, sort of helping him out with a story."

"A story about swimming?"

Shit.

Lola's laugh was so weak as to barely qualify. "No, he told us about a swimming hole. He thought Margaret might like it. Then he offered to show it to us."

"Showed it to you yesterday? When you said you didn't go anywhere? And you're helping him out with a story?"

The question about a story was, Lola thought, a marginal improvement only in that it got them away from the topic of the swimming hole.

"Yeah." She'd gone monosyllabic way too late. Charlie's questions came so fast that she might as well have been sitting in the dingy interview room in the sheriff's office, with its foul carpet, gray-painted cinder-block walls and tiny opaque one-way window through which an unseen video camera peered.

"What kind of help? What story? How'd you meet up with a reporter, anyway? Something tells me you went looking, right? So whose story is it, anyway? His? Or yours? It's yours, isn't it? Which means you're working on your alleged furlough. Are you trying to get yourself fired? How do you plan to sell a Wyoming story to the *Daily Express*, anyway? Or is it even a story for the *Express*? Is that how you're getting around this? Freelancing? And what about Margaret? This is supposed to be a vacation for her, real mother-daughter time, isn't it? What sort of quality time is she getting if you're working? Goddammit, Lola." He'd asked all his other questions in the low monotone he'd perfected during his just-shy-of-a decade in law enforcement, but his voice broke on the final one. "Do I need to withdraw my question?"

Lola didn't have to ask which question. He meant his proposal. This time, the silence was hers. She'd resented his ultimatum. Now, she found out she didn't like having the option of marriage yanked away, either. He'd let her hear his anger. She fired back with a dose of her down frustration. "Dammit yourself, Charlie. Why couldn't we just go on the way we were?"

Charlie's words escaped on a long breath. "No matter what happens, we can never go back to the way things were."

TWENTY-THREE

LOLA WAITED UNTIL SHE was sure Margaret was asleep, breathing slow and easy beside her as the dog panted on the other side. She lay sandwiched and sweaty between them, wishing for her bed at home with Charlie's bulk curved protectively around her.

He and Margaret were prodigious sleepers, their slumber deep and impervious to interruption, a thing of wonder to Lola. At home, she'd lay awake for hour after restless hour, turning her head occasionally against Charlie's chest, inhaling his reassuring scent. Now, if she turned her head one way, she breathed in the cloying sweetness of candy—Margaret must have squirreled away her parade stash somewhere—while the other led to a mouthful of dog hair. She spit it out and checked the time on her phone. Two a.m. She tried to ease from the narrow bed without waking either of her companions. Margaret didn't move, not so much as blinking when Lola snapped on the light. Bub stood yawning but game in the unexpected overhead glare. Lola shook the kinks out of her arms and legs. "Go back to sleep, buddy. I'm just going to get some work done." She thought she might as well take advantage of being away from home. Charlie never woke during her occasional midnight forays into another room, where she'd tap furtively at her laptop until dawn, sneaking back into bed just before the alarm went off at five-thirty. But no matter how she tried to cover her tracks, he'd always find her out, prompting a lecture on the dangers of workaholism.

"How'd you know?" she'd say when he rolled his eyes in response to her standard denial. He'd point out the telltale ring of a coffee cup on an end table, the wadded up printouts in the trash can, a stack of inadequately concealed three-by-five cards tucked beneath a magazine. Lola, who used the cards to organize elements of her longer stories, wished she had them now. Instead, she tore pages from her reporter's notebook and labeled them in the abbreviated references she'd developed over the years. The first page: "Skiff, A'stan." It was all she needed, a signal to herself that the story would start with Skiff stumbling over the body on the rocky path, struggling to make sense of what had just happened, unable to stop Mike's quick scuffle, the slide of knife across tender flesh, the whoosh and gurgle of an escaping last breath. She lay the paper on the floor and selected a new page.

"Statistics, blah-blah-blah." The story's second section would feature the standard pull-back from the drama, putting it in context. How many U.S. troops had gone to Afghanistan since the beginning of the war; how many were there now, and how many of those were from Wyoming. How, statistically, Wyoming contributed more than its share of cannon fodder. Lola supposed that these days the more correct term would be IED fodder. She'd add a quick reminder for readers that without a military draft, kids from inner cities and rural areas comprised the bulk of recruits, and why. And, finally, the fact that tiny Thirty was off the charts when it came to the price paid for such default patriotism. She lay that sheet beside the first, and tore off another.

"Skiff, et al." It was crucial to get out of the statistics as quickly as possible and back to people, with some history about Skiff and his friends, along with a quick portrait of Thirty and the hard life choices it demanded. She'd throw in a few extra paragraphs about the reservation to bring Mike into the story. Maybe the principal had had his doubts about Mike's inclusion in so many of the white school's activities, but given the recruitment photo of everyone smiling together, the others seemed to have had no such qualms. She'd lead the reader into thinking, as Mike must have, that everything among them was hunky-dory. She lay the paper down beside the others. When she was done, she'd have a long line of papers, a visual aid that she'd shuffle according to which elements needed to be moved up, which revised, and which discarded altogether.

Next up, "PTSD," a section that would ground the reader in its complications. She wondered whether to introduce the topic so quickly, then realized that in her rudimentary outline, she had yet to mention Cody Dillon's suicide, or T-Squared's legal issues—the whole reason for doing the story. "For God's sake," she said. A week away from the job, and she was already losing her edge. Bub opened an eye and rolled onto his back, the stump of his missing leg tucked against his belly. She retrieved the second piece of paper, the one labeled "Statistics" and jotted a note to lead into the section with the riveting numbers from Thirty. She even penned some sample sentences: "Mike St. Clair, a Shoshone youth from the nearby Wind River Reservation, was the first to die, throat slashed nearly to the point of decapitation by an Afghani insurgent. Ranch kid Cody Dillon was next, dead by his own hand at the homecoming ceremony three months later. Within forty-eight hours, two more of the Wyoming soldiers there that night would find themselves in jail. They were among"—here, she left a series of dashes, awaiting the number to be filled in later—"U.S. troops to serve in Afghanistan this year . . ." There. That was better.

She checked the time again. An hour had passed. For sure, it had been more productive than the times at home when she heeded Charlie's admonishments and remained beside him in bed, occasionally using her phone to email herself thoughts about how to organize the story she'd write later that day. She turned back to her work and tried to close her mind to the memories of those languorous nights with Charlie. But it was harder to push away the inescapable realization that, given their most recent conversation, such times might be over.

————

Lola's phone woke her, buzzing with an email alert. The bed was empty. She picked up the phone. Her eyes were too unfocused to read the small-print email, but the time, in tall numbers, was clear. Eighty-thirty. Somehow she'd slept through breakfast. Pal must have fed Margaret, whose hunger during her waking hours was as focused as her nighttime sleep.

Lola stumbled into a kitchen empty but for some dishes in the sink and two flats of strawberries occupying most of the counter space. She decided not to look too closely at the dishes, for fear of seeing remnants of ravioli. She poured the inch of suspicious liquid left in the coffee pot into a mug and studied the strawberries. Each flat held a dozen pints. During the brief weeks when strawberries made their way to supermarkets in Montana, Charlie occasionally would pick some up to slice over their cereal. A pint lasted a few days. Lola reckoned there were weeks' worth of strawberries in the flats. Maybe Pal planned to freeze them. Apparently Margaret wasn't the only one in the house with a sweet tooth. Lola ate a strawberry and ventured out onto the porch. The sun, already up for hours, had heated the floorboards beyond barefoot comfort. Lola moved into the shady corner Margaret had claimed as her own.

"Morning, sleepy Mommy," Margaret said without looking up. She wielded pen and paper with fingertips stained red. Even if she'd had ravioli for breakfast, at least she'd balanced it out with some fresh fruit, Lola thought. Color flashed at the corner of Lola's vision. She lifted her gaze. Pal jogged along the ridgeline, running within sight of the house. Lola waved, letting Pal know she was on duty. Pal disappeared over the ridge without an answering wave. Lola cast a wary eye about for the chicken, then bent and planted a kiss on Margaret's head.

Margaret pulled away. "You're messing up my story." She held up a skinny sheet from one of Lola's reporter's notebooks, adorned with hieroglyphics.

"That's nice, honey," Lola said, her standard response to Margaret's incomprehensible doodles. She took a sip of the coffee, lukewarm and grainy with sediment, but providing the necessary shot of wakefulness that reminded her to look at her phone. A moment later, she clenched her hand against the urge to hurl it in to the yard. Only the likelihood that she'd have to fish around beneath the rattlesnake-infested sagebrush, while the chicken emerged from its hiding place to ice-pick its beak into her bare ankles, saved it from her rage. She turned on her heel, stalked into the kitchen, smacked the phone facedown on the counter and counted through five long breaths, turning her head against the cloying scent of strawberries. She turned the phone over and looked again at her email. Maybe she'd been mistaken. But no, there it was, the note from the Department of Defense informing her in convoluted governmentese that nonetheless conveyed a clear message: that the investigation into Mike's death remained classified information and as such was not subject to public scrutiny. Which meant that she did not have a description of the night's incident on the record. The repercussion escaped aloud—"No goddamn story." She glanced around to make sure Margaret had not followed her into the kitchen, and made a vow. "No goddamn way."

She'd get the story, even though it meant confronting the single remaining, and most determinedly elusive, witness: Pal. Who, as though summoned by Lola's very thoughts, reappeared on the ridgeline, a moving stick figure silhouetted by the sun. Lola stepped back into the kitchen and waited out of sight beside of the door. She heard Pal before she saw her, a pounding approach slowing to a reluctant walk, breath still ragged as she neared the porch. "Hey, kiddo," Pal said to Margaret. "Where's that killer chicken?"

"Over there. I think she's made a nest under the bushes." Good, Lola thought. Maybe the snakes would eat Jemalina's eggs and, while they were at it, chomp on the chicken, too. A single venomous bite should do the trick.

"What have you got there?"

"I'm drawing a story," Margaret said. "About a *sweet* chicken named Jemalina."

Pal produced the dry sound that passed as a laugh. "So you're a fiction writer."

"What?"

"Never mind. Can I see?" Lola heard the rustle of paper. "Hey, I didn't know you could write already."

"I can't," Margaret said, but Pal spoke over her. "Wait a minute. 'Skiff? A'stan'—I guess that means Afghanistan. What the hell? What is this? *Lola!*" She burst into the kitchen, incriminating paper in hand, Margaret's scribbles on one side, Lola's note on the other. Margaret followed close behind. "My story!"

"Your story, my ass. Your mother's, more like. Lola, what's this about?"

Lola backed up all the way to the counter and popped a whole strawberry into her mouth, giving herself a few seconds to come up with an explanation. She'd left her outline arranged on the bedroom floor. Margaret must have claimed one of the papers as her own. Lola spit the berry's leafy cap into her hand. "You wouldn't talk to me about Afghanistan. I thought Skiff might. It's been five years since I lived there. I wanted to see what it's like now, how things have changed." True enough. "So I wrote myself a reminder."

"You had to write yourself a note just to talk to somebody?"

"It was just a thought. Sometimes I write my thoughts down." Lola was deep in the weeds. She decided to see it as an opportunity. "I'd much rather talk to you about it."

"Hell will freeze over before I talk to anyone about that godforsaken place!" The veins in Pal's skull mapped blue lines beneath the blond furze covering her skull. They kinked and throbbed when Pal shouted. Lola looked away. When she looked back, Pal was gone.

TWENTY-FOUR

DINNER THAT NIGHT WAS as chilly as the array of cold cuts, cheese, and sliced peppers and tomatoes Lola had laid out. "It's too hot to cook," she said by way of explanation. Not that anyone demanded one. Her words dropped like stones into a black pool of silence. Ripples of bad feeling flowed to the edges of the room.

Delbert shoveled meat and whole tomato slices into his mouth as if to get that much closer to the point where he could leave. Pal didn't even bother with the pretense of pushing food around, glaring at it as though it had somehow given offense. Margaret was so obviously worried about the adults' bad mood that she forgot to "accidentally" select some pieces of forbidden cheese. Bub whined, padding back and forth across the room, finally stopping beside Pal's chair and resting his head on her thigh. Lola caught his eye. Traitor, she said wordlessly. He looked away.

Lola supposed it was just as well Pal opted for the silent treatment, given that the alternative might be some anatomically impossible suggestions about what Lola might do with any further questions about Afghanistan. She was going to have to pose those questions to somebody, though. She could appeal the DOD's denial, only to get turned down again months later—if she heard from them again at all. After two tries and two rebuffs, Tommy and Tyson were unlikely to be persuaded to go on the record, and Dave had made it clear he wasn't going to help. She tried to imagine a telephone call in which she'd tell InDepth.org that her story had fallen through. She'd have blown her first and almost certainly her last chance to write for one of the few organizations that paid freelancers real money for serious pieces. It was time to talk again with Skiff Loughry, at this point the single fraying thread upon which her story hung. She'd called him, seeking one last interview. "General stuff," she said. "Just to help me nail down some details." He'd agreed to meet her the next morning. Lola tried to take that as a hopeful sign. "Hope," at this point, being a word fast disappearing from her vocabulary.

She stabbed at a slice of tomato as though it were a DOD functionary. It obliged by squirting her in the eye. "Damn—darn it!" Margaret opened her mouth and closed it before she could request the obligatory quarter. Lola didn't much care that Pal was in yet another snit. And, although she felt sorry that Delbert was caught in the crossfire of malevolent emotion, she knew he'd handled worse in his life than quarreling women. But Margaret, who'd already endured so much on this trip, drooped wan and dispirited in her chair. Lola owed her at least the pretense of normalcy. She straightened and threw a shine into her voice.

"Where'd all those strawberries come from? And what are they for?"

Delbert's look was one of pure relief. Take *that*, Pal, Lola thought. I'm the one who extended your buddy a helping hand.

"Dolores Wadda." He paused to give Pal time for the smartassery that emerged whenever Dolores' name arose. Pal failed to oblige. Delbert soldiered on. "Said they were two-for-one at the market. They're full ripe now, going bad soon. She thought they'd be good for jam."

Lola had no idea how one made jam, and didn't want to know. "Don't they sell jam at the store?"

Delbert flashed a tooth or two. "Not like Pal's mother made. You've never tasted anything like it. Bet Pal will show you how."

Pal looked at Lola for the first time since their morning encounter, her own false brightness mirroring Lola's. "I'd love to. It's easy. I've got all of Mom's old jars and lids. I'll show you what to do and then get out of your way."

First the chicken. Now, strawberries. Lola knew that plenty of people around the world transmogrified fruit into jam, and that they still slaughtered their own dinner before they cooked it. Lola had made the mistake of petting a goat one morning in the courtyard of a guesthouse in Kabul, only to glance out a window shortly before mealtime to see it on its back, all four hooves pointing skyward, as men with knives carved her lunch from the carcass. She wasn't squeamish as to the source of her food. She just didn't want to be the middleman when it came to preparation. Her nascent plans snapped into focus.

"That sounds like fun," she said. To hell with you, Pal, said the smile that accompanied her words. "But we're leaving first thing in the morning."

"We are?" Margaret did not sound nearly as enthusiastic as Lola expected. "Why? Where are we going? Home? Jemalina's coming, right?"

Where indeed, Lola thought. Back to Montana, to face Charlie's anger and her own damnable ambivalence? She supposed she and Margaret could resume their vacation. The Tetons were only a few hours away. Rather than camping in the back of the truck, as they'd been doing, she could spring for a night in one of the lodges. She'd talk to Skiff on their way out of town, and work on the story in the comfort of the lodge. There. She had a plan, one that eliminated the strawberries from the equation. "We've taken up far too much of your time, already. Pal, you seem like you're feeling better."

Pal speared a slice of ham, swallowing it with obvious difficulty, and followed it with some cheese as though to underscore the tenuous fact of Lola's statement. Delbert nodded his approval. Given that Pal had lied to her about so many things, Lola felt justified in floating a fib of her own. "When I started this trip, I made some reservations in advance. We've got a motel room in the Tetons for tomorrow night. We'll leave first thing in the morning."

———

Lola spent much of the drive into town the next day explaining to Margaret that continuing their vacation didn't mean abandoning Jemalina. She steered with one hand, sliding the other beneath her thigh and crossing her fingers.

"We could pick her up on the way back," Lola said, trusting that Margaret was still too young to realize that vast chasm that yawned between "could" and "will." Not to mention that a trip back to the ranch from the Tetons would involve a monumental backtrack from the most direct route to Montana.

"Back from where?"

Lola explained. Again.

"What's Tetons?"

Mountains that look like titties, was all Lola could think of. She cast about in her memory for images from guidebooks and postcards. "A place with moose. And bears. It'll be fun."

Bub threw himself down in disgust, sensitive as always to deceit in her voice. Margaret's yawn echoed Bub's in theatricality. Bear were so plentiful around Magpie that Lola had taught her the "stop, drop, and protect your head" routine for grizzlies as soon as she could walk.

"I don't want to go on vacation. Vacation is boring," Margaret said. "I want to stay with Pal and Delbert and Jemalina."

Lola was in full agreement with Margaret's assessment of vacation. But she failed to see the charm in a hardscrabble, snake-infested ranch populated by a surly young woman and a psychotic fowl. "We're going on vacation," she said, in a tone meant to brook no argument. She'd forgotten that Margaret invariably opted for bargaining over defiance.

"Is there ice cream?"

Lola cursed herself for having set an unfortunate precedent on the trip. But the thought clearly appealed to Margaret, in a way that nothing else about their departure did. And Lola had yet to see the tourist destination that lacked an ice cream stand. "Of course there is. Lots and lots." It seemed to suffice. Lola knew her daughter at least as well as Margaret knew her mother. Quickly, before Margaret could speak again, she made clear that there would be no ice cream until they arrived at the Tetons; that they would not, no matter what, be paying a repeat visit to Thirty's ice cream parlor. "You'll have to make do with playing in the park again."

She'd arranged to meet Skiff there, away from the prying ears of patrons in a café or, God forbid, another bar. He was waiting when they pulled up, a solitary broad-shouldered figure shooting and sinking baskets on the baking courts along the park's west side. He posted a final lay-up and dribbled toward them. Lola's truck was the only vehicle in the park's lot, a fact that Lola noted aloud.

"My parents' place is only a few blocks away," he said. "I walked."

"In this heat?" Lola spoke over her shoulder as she arranged Margaret's toys and snacks on one of the tables in the shade, brushing away fallen cottonwood leaves so dry they crumbled at her touch.

Skiff dropped to one of the benches. "I'm still getting used to the fact that I can walk around in shorts and a T-shirt, without all of that body armor."

"I hear you," said Lola. It had taken her weeks after her return to feel comfortable with baring her arms and legs, to relax and enjoy the freedom of loose, light clothing. "Do you remember Skiff?" she asked Margaret.

"Hi, Spiff."

"Skiff. Here." Skiff bounced the ball toward Margaret. "That basket's a little far away for you, but you can kick this around like a soccer ball. Let me show you how. You want to use the inside of your foot."

The ball rolled toward Margaret. She stuck out her tongue in concentration and aimed a savage kick. The ball flew past Skiff.

"Gooooaaaalllllllllll!" He held up his arms. Margaret awarded him with a grin.

"Pretty good for a rookie," he said. "But you're going to want to practice. Try kicking it around in big circles. We'll watch you. Looks like your dog wants to help." He blotted his forehead on his sleeve. Damp patched his shirt. A metal water bottle sat on the picnic table. Ice clinked within as he drained it in two long, gurgling pulls. The cottonwoods creaked and rattled in the useless wind. A car crawled past, its elderly driver hunched over the wheel. A pickup revved impatiently behind it. Despite windows cranked closed to keep the air conditioning in, Lola heard the deep thump of a bass beat. Inside, kids in cowboy hats jerked their heads to the rhythm of rap. Someday, Lola supposed, she'd get used to that. Thunks sounded a backbeat as Margaret whacked the ball again and again with her right foot. "Try one foot and then the other," Skiff called. He turned back to Lola. "What'd you want to talk to me about? As if I couldn't guess."

The ball rolled to a stop against Lola's leg. She picked it up and threw it toward the middle of the park. "Stay away from the street," she told Margaret. She knotted her hands together before responding to Skiff.

"About what happened in Afghanistan."

"I already told you."

"No. About what really happened."

———————

She laid it all out, just as T-Squared had in the bar, the interminable hours in the village, the trek through the darkness after the vehicle broke down. The Talib hunt. The shepherd. Mike. She stopped.

Skiff's face twisted. "Where'd you get this? You must have talked to Tommy and Tyson."

Lola sliced the air with her hand. "I can't reveal my sources." Her automatic response, silly given that only three other people knew what had really happened. Still, Lola thought it was interesting he hadn't assumed the information had come from Pal.

Skiff called Margaret to him. He patted his lap. She hopped onto it and he wrapped his arms around her. Lola tensed. He noticed.

"Don't worry," he said. "I won't hurt her. This little girl; *big* girl, I mean"—Margaret beamed up at him—"helps me remember the world isn't all black darkness." Margaret wrapped her arms around his neck and kissed his cheek. He released her. "Maybe," he said, "if that poor shepherd had had a child with him, she'd have held off. Captured him instead of shot him."

"Maybe the child would have gotten killed, too," she said. "You can't go there." Even though she knew he would. He was going to spend the

177

rest of his life on what-ifs, Lola thought. She had a few what-ifs of her own. "Nobody's told me anything on the record," she said.

"And I won't, either," he said. "Try to see it from where I sit."

Lola *could* see it, and what she saw was that, as leader of the group, his ass was on the line. Which, to her surprise, he acknowledged.

"She may have shot him, but I'm the one responsible. No matter how safe the situation, there was no excuse for dropping discipline. If I'd kept everybody in line, Mike would be alive, and maybe Cody, too. And then there's Pal. If this comes out, she'll be court-martialed. We all will, for the thing happening in the first place, and for covering it up. But they'll come down hardest on her. They'll want to show that they're not going soft on her because she's a woman."

"I don't get it. Why protect someone everybody hates? Even you. You told me she was trouble. And you were right. She's the one who caused this, and she's the one who gets off scot-free."

"You know why." He looked at her a long time, all patience.

Lola shook her head. "I don't know."

"Pal's a pain in the ass, but she's one of us. You know? I know that you do. You reporters are the same way. A tribe. You stick up for your own, no matter what."

Lola thought of Ahmed, her fixer. He hadn't been a reporter, but a translator. But he worked with the journalists every day, risking his own life alongside them. Lola had thought their bond was just as strong. That, had she seen danger heading Ahmed's way, she'd have thrown herself in its path. And then Ahmed had tried to kill her, to kill them all. Had Ahmed survived, would Lola have protected him just as Skiff now stood up for Pal?

"I don't know," she said, as much to herself as to him.

"I do," he said. "No question."

Lola envied his certainty. Admired the fact that despite everything, he'd managed to hang on to it. Yet the ass-covering aspect nagged at her. She said as much.

"No question that I come out better by keeping it quiet. All of us do. But it's not as though nobody's been punished. Look at us. Two dead and two more fucked up. How long do you think it'll be before those two idiots do something else that lands them in jail? They won't get off so easy the next time. And Pal. I saw her that day at the parade. She was a mess. Do you really think she's not paying for what she did?"

Sympathy tugged at Lola. She pulled back against it. "You're doing okay," she said before she could stop herself.

He looked away. When he turned back, his eyes were full of tears. He reminded Lola of Margaret, who cried on only the rarest occasions, managing each time to break her mother's heart. Skiff, not yet twenty, had seen two friends die before his eyes and bore the weight of knowing it was at least partly his fault.

"Am I?" he said. "Do you think I'm doing okay?" He folded his arms on the table and put his head on them. His shoulders heaved. His muffled voice reached her. "Sorry. I never do this."

Lola's hand hovered over his shoulders. She had a rule when people cried during interviews. It happened. People who'd lost children or spouses, their jobs to the recession, their homes in some sort of natural disaster. Victims of war, of injustice, of damnable circumstance. She always gave them a few respectful moments to collect themselves before resuming her questions as though nothing had happened. That way, everybody kept his dignity. Skiff's shoulders knotted with the effort of withholding his grief. Rusted sobs reached her. She let her hand fall on his back. Held it there. Gave it some pressure, steadying him the way she would a spooked horse.

"Take your time," she said. "We've got all day." Even though she didn't. Margaret had tired of the ball. She would soon run out of patience.

Skiff raised his head. He rubbed his face on his sleeve, a ghost of his earlier motion when the moisture on his face had been the healthy sweat of play. "You won't tell?" he said.

Lola's hand fell away from his back. "It's not a matter of won't," she said. "I can't. Nobody's said anything on the record."

A smile wobbled at the edges of his lips. "That's good, right? Not for you, I mean. But for us, that's good."

"You know what I think is good?" Lola said. "The truth. I know you think the way you're handling this is best. And I get it. Truly, I do. You want to protect your men—and woman. That's understandable. But in the long run, it never works. The truth always finds a way out, and the longer it takes, the worse the consequences." How many times in her life had she given that little speech? Sometimes, it even worked. Not this time, though.

"Hand to God, if it were just me, I'd do it. Get this shit off my chest, and out in the open. Make up for what Pal did to that guy, and for what that guy did to Mike. Even though nothing will make up for it. But what do you think that would do to Mike's grandfather? He and Pal are still close. What'll he do if he finds out she got his grandson killed? I can't do it. I just can't." He stuck out his hand. "No hard feelings?"

Lola remembered his previous handshake. She flexed her fingers and took it. As before, he stopped just short of breaking bones. "No hard feelings," she lied.

He dropped her hand and tugged gently at one of Margaret's braids. "Thanks for brightening my day. You're going to make a heckuva soccer player." He bent and picked up the basketball and tucked it under his arm and started to walk away. "Bye, Margaret."

She lifted her hand. "Bye, Spiff."

Lola watched her story walk away with Skiff. She wanted to call him back; make a final tearful plea. Even though she never cried, she reminded herself, as she rubbed the heel of her hand against the damning moisture in her eyes.

As if he'd heard her thoughts, Skiff stopped and turned. "Sorry I can't help with your story," he called to Lola.

"There is no story." Lola spoke as much to herself as to Skiff. Saying it made it real as the pain that accompanied the words. She tried it again. "There is no story." She wondered how many times she'd have to say it before the ache subsided. "There is no story," she whispered. Pain, three; Lola Wicks, zip. It was going to take awhile.

"Mommy?" A warm hand found its way into hers. Bub nosed at her leg, nudging her toward the truck. "Now what, Mommy?"

Lola turned her face into the hot wind. Let it go, she told herself. The story was never part of the original plan. This was supposed to be her time with Margaret, but so far she'd done exactly what Charlie and Jan and everyone else who knew her well had feared. She'd been unable to let work go. Now it was time to—what did people in these parts like to say? Cowboy up.

The hurt still throbbed within when she looked down at Margaret, but her eyes were dry. "We're going on vacation. And it's going to be fun, dammit."

TWENTY-FIVE

THE TETONS, AS LOLA described them on her way out of town, were a mountain paradise. She owed Margaret that much, she thought, remembering her earlier and transparent lack of enthusiasm.

Margaret had seen moose in Glacier, but nothing like the profusion of moose that roamed the Tetons, Lola said. "Whole herds of them!" Did moose travel in herds? She was pretty sure they didn't. "Whole families," she amended. "But we have to be careful not to get close. The mommies get mad if people scare their babies, and a mommy moose is a whole lot of mad."

"Like a mommy grizzly!"

"Close," said Lola. She'd encountered her share of grizzlies, but always at a comfortable distance and never with cubs, a record she hoped to maintain. She'd heard the stories. "I don't think anything in the world is as scary as a mommy grizzly."

"You, Mommy. When you're mad. Like when you were mad at the bad truck." Lola glanced in the rearview mirror. Margaret's face went from sly to somber at the memory of the truck. Lola had never discussed it with her after that night. She assigned herself another demerit, and belatedly tried to remedy the situation.

"Do you still think about the truck?"

"Sometimes." Margaret's tone was matter-of-fact. "Do you know what I'm thinking now?"

"No idea."

"That I'm hungry."

Lola far preferred hunger to lingering trauma, the former being far more easily remedied. But Thirty was well behind them, and the next town was nearly forty-five minutes away. Her own stomach growled. A sign flashed past, indicating one of the secondary reservation roads. Lola checked her map. Just as she'd thought, the road angled across the reservation, a shortcut of sorts to the two-lane highway that would take them to the Tetons. The gravel surface would make for a longer trip, but the road also passed by the reservation's convenience store. Lola flicked her turn signal and took it. "Lunch, coming right up," she promised Margaret.

When they got to the store, though, she realized lunch was more easily said than done. "Don't even think about it," she told Margaret as the girl lingered in front of the refrigerated cases of sugary pop. Lola walked the aisles, rejecting one thing after another. The plastic-wrapped sandwiches made of squishy white bread and processed meat, their stamped dates past due. The fried chicken slowly fossilizing beneath orange heat lights. The shelves of off-brand candy and chips. Yogurt—full fat, and loaded with fruit swimming in corn syrup—actually rated a moment's consideration. But the store was out of plastic spoons. She finally settled on a couple of blackened bananas and apples fast going mushy, pointedly ignoring Margaret's scowl and handing the clerk a twenty.

"Do you mind taking your change in ones?" the clerk asked. She showed Lola the change drawer, the trays for larger bills empty. The dollar bills were limp with use, as though their previous owners had fondled them one last time before reluctantly handing them over.

"I feel guilty taking them," Lola blurted. Then worried she'd given offense by implying she could spare them.

The young woman pointed with her lips to a jar on the counter. "You could put some in there. Every little bit helps."

The jar bore a handful of change and a few bills. A Xeroxed photo and hand-printed notice sought donations for Patrick Sounding Sides.

Lola retrieved a dollar from her wallet. "Who's that?"

The clerk slammed the drawer shut. The sound echoed in the empty store. "The guy got beat up by those soldiers. He's home now, but he still needs round-the-clock care. We're trying to help out his family."

Time stopped. The pain that had hovered above Lola, stubborn as a vulture over a dying animal, flew away even as her story coasted in for a landing, bright with renewed promise. Lola ducked to hide her inappropriate smile and fumbled with her wallet, extracting every bill. She dropped them into the jar, making sure the clerk saw. "Any chance," she said, "you know how to get in touch with his family?"

———————

By the time she turned off the gravel road onto the two-track that led to Patrick Sounding Sides's home, Margaret was in full revolt. Her usual MO when upset was to sulk, arms folded, lower lip outthrust, her scowling silence both epic and eloquent. Bub squeezed himself into the safe place beneath the sofa when Margaret was in one of her moods. Charlie, the very definition of calm and competence, wrung his hands and pleaded with her. Lola, after lecturing Charlie on the importance of ignoring such manipulative behavior, usually lost her temper and yelled. On this day, however, she would have preferred the sulk.

Because Margaret, never one for a tantrum, decided to give it a try. She threw back her head and screamed to the heavens. Her sneakered feet beat a drum solo on the back of Lola's seat. She flailed about with her fists, catching Bub on the ear. He yelped and dove for the floor, and did his level best to insert himself into the space beneath the passenger seat, managing only to hide his nose and front paws. Occasionally, words emerged from the din.

"Home!" "Jemalina!" "Daddy!" "Now!"

Lola caught her drift. In fact, with the exception of Jemalina, she shared Margaret's sentiments. Her hands shook on the wheel. She wished Charlie were there to deal with Margaret's tantrum. Maybe he'd know what to do. Even if he didn't, she'd be able to take comfort in their shared helplessness. Guilt sat like a boulder in her stomach. She'd turned what could have been a perfectly fine vacation into nothing but misery for Margaret, who until now had spent uncomplaining days playing quietly in the heat as her mother elicited tales of horror and death, punctuated by an unforgiveable amount of curses, from a series of strangers. Lola had been such an unsatisfactory companion that a psychotic chicken apparently was preferable. The truck passed a side road. "Dammit," she muttered. Although, she could have shouted without being heard. "I think that was our turn." She hit the brakes. Then she took a good look around. Nobody else was on the road. No houses nearby. Not even a wayward deer. No one to hear the sounds of a child screaming bloody murder. She pulled to the shoulder and turned off the ignition and stared straight ahead.

Margaret gasped for air. There was a brief, blessed moment of silence. The cessation of motion seemed to have caught Margaret unaware. Lola spoke quickly, quietly, without turning. "Go ahead," she said. "Take all the time you like. We'll just sit here until you're done."

Margaret obliged. Lola hadn't thought it possible for her to scream louder. She'd been wrong. She counted silently. When I get to one hundred, she told herself, I'll say something. Or do something. She had no idea what. At twenty-five, Margaret gulped another breath and Lola's hopes soared. At twenty-six, the scream re-emerged, stronger than ever. At fifty, she was still going strong. Lola put her hand on the passenger seat. It vibrated with Bub's trembling. Margaret breathed again at seventy-five. Lola closed her eyes and prayed. She'd grown up Catholic, but couldn't remember the patron saint of parents. St. Joseph, maybe? He'd married Mary, knowing she was pregnant with what he could only have assumed was another man's child. Would he have been so quick to marry her if he'd witnessed a temper tantrum the likes of which Margaret was throwing? Lola's prayer took her to ninety-eight. When Margaret ... just ... stopped.

The wind reasserted itself, howling hot past the open window as if to remind Margaret that, whatever it lacked in volume, it more than made up for in staying power. Bub crawled out from under the seat, staying as far as possible from Margaret, plastering his body against the dashboard, ears flat against his head as if to emphasize the pain of the recent aural assault. Lola said nothing at all. She started the engine and took the turn that would lead them to Patrick Sounding Sides's house.

————

Lola parked next to a truck on blocks, one of several in the yard. The Sounding Sides were like many reservation families in their reluctance to discard anything that might someday prove useful. The disabled trucks had been stripped of tires and bumpers and even their bench seats, one of which sat against the side of the house, its innards erupting through gashes in the vinyl. Still, its spot in the shade made it an inviting prospect, and Lola imagined family members taking their ease there in evening's cool, maybe sharing a cigarette and an illicit beer, watching the sun set the sky afire before it sank behind the Winds. She unbuckled Margaret from her booster seat. Margaret, usually a wriggling eel of a child, lay limp in her arms, flushed and spent from her outburst. Bub, after taking care of his business, stayed so close his nose bumped Lola's ankles, a cold wet shock every few seconds.

Lola stood some distance from the front door, in clear view should anyone choose to move aside the towels that blocked the living room window. Indian people didn't knock. The home's occupants would have heard her truck's approach, the slam of its door. Lola waited. A towel twitched. The door opened. Bub whined. A woman clung to the doorjamb as though fearful that if she let go, she'd slide to the floor, collapsing into exhaustion so complete that Margaret could pitch another tantrum without notice. Margaret's fury had fled, though. "Oh, Mommy," she whispered.

Lola let go of Margaret's hand and hurried to the woman, taking her elbow. "I think you need to sit down," she said. The woman leaned heavily on Lola. Patrick Sounding Sides's mother, probably.

"You're the whitelady from the store. Mona called. Said someone was coming." Her voice came out in a rasp. Her hair hung rough and matted, as though she arose from too-short bouts of sleep without brushing it. The house was dark and ferociously hot. It smelled of rubbing alcohol and urine and unwashed humans, a combination Lola associated with third-world hospitals. She made out a love seat covered by a star quilt and, across the room, a single bed with a kitchen chair beside it. Another star quilt covered the unmoving form in the bed. Lola led the woman to the love seat and eased her onto it. Bub draped himself across the woman's feet. Margaret clambered up beside her and stroked the back of her hand, her gaze fixed on the woman's face. Lola's heart swelled with love and pride and tenderness. "Are you sick?" asked Margaret.

The woman looked at her with uncomprehending eyes.

"I think she's just worn out," Lola said. "You stay here with her." Lola went into the kitchen and found a glass and filled it with tap water, hoping that the water on the Wind River Reservation was safer than that on some of Montana's reservations, where contamination from all manner of causes—usually at the hands of outsiders—had forced some people to drink bottled water for years. A washcloth lay on the counter. Lola lifted it to her face and sniffed. It was clean. She ran cold water over it, wrung it out, and brought it and the water glass to the woman in the chair.

"I'm going to put a cold cloth on your head," she said. The woman nodded. Lola lay the cloth on her forehead and held the glass to her lips. She sipped, and turned her head aside and closed her eyes.

"I thought someone was coming to help you." Lola tried to keep the anger from her voice. The man in the bed likely needed round-the-clock home health care. Yet he'd been returned to a remote reservation and left to the ministrations of well-meaning but untrained amateurs. But the woman disabused her of that notion.

"We got help. All kinds of help. Both my sisters are nurses. They've been here every minute they're not at their jobs."

"Then why—?" Lola didn't know how to finish the sentence. Why was the woman such a wreck? Was she a druggie, filching her son's medications? A loathsome scenario, but hardly unique. But no, if her sisters were nurses, they'd have been alert to that particular problem, and would have taken steps to fend it off.

The woman's whisper drifted toward her. "Can't sleep. Not when he was in the hospital, not since he's come home. Afraid to close my eyes. Afraid—" As though pulled by her own words, the woman put a hand on the love seat's arm, levered herself upward and tottered toward the chair by the bed. Lola and Margaret and Bub followed close. The woman put her ear to the mouth of the man in the bed. Relief bathed her face. Lola understood then. The woman was afraid that if she relaxed her vigilance long enough to get the sleep she so badly needed, her son would relax his tenuous hold on life, let it slide from his fingers and fly out the window before his mother could rise and snatch it back.

The man stirred. "Ma. You look like hell."

Lola stepped back at the surprising strength in his voice. It seemed to flow directly into his mother's body. The woman straightened and ran a hand through her hair. She managed a smile. "Maybe I should bring you a mirror. You're no movie star yourself."

His head moved slowly from side to side. "Maybe not. Who's this?"

Lola took a breath. She had no idea how long he'd be lucid. Or when his, or his mother's, patience would wear thin. And whether they, like everyone else, would show her the door the minute she stated her mission. But it had to be done.

"I'm Lola Wicks. This is my little girl, Margaret. I'm a newspaper reporter. I'm here to write about all the people from Thirty who went over to Afghanistan. Mostly, I'm writing about Mike St. Clair and how his death affected everybody else."

A laugh rattled in Patrick's chest. It turned into a wracking cough. His mother slipped a hand beneath his shoulders and strained to raise his torso. Lola hurried to the other side of the bed to help her. Patrick's body, like his voice, was unexpectedly robust. Lola guessed he'd inflicted some damage on T-Squared until the two-against-one odds had finally triumphed. Patrick caught his breath and nodded. Lola and his mother eased him back onto the pillow.

"Why write about how it affected everybody else? Looks like it affected Mike most of all."

"Yes. But nobody will talk to me about that on the record. They don't want the story to come out because of the shame to his grandfather."

Patrick pushed himself up unaided, propelled, it seemed, by fury. "Shame?" he shouted.

His mother put a thin hand to his shoulder to push him back. "No, Patrick, no," she whimpered.

He spoke past her. "The only shame is on those bastards for how they treated Mike."

TWENTY-SIX

Mrs. Sounding Sides moved so close that Lola was forced to step back, and then again, the woman herding her toward the door as efficiently as Bub maneuvered Margaret away from any piece of food he deemed within his reach. "I'm sorry. You seem like a nice lady. But you should go. He's upset."

Patrick's voice snubbed both women up short. "Ma. No. I want to talk to her."

Lola held her breath. By rights, his permission was all she needed. But she'd spent too many years amid the Blackfeet to easily disregard his mother's opinion. And, as a practical matter, given that she and Patrick couldn't slip outside for a private chat, the interview would go more smoothly if his mother agreed.

Mrs. Sounding Sides took her son's hand. He covered it with his other hand, pain creasing his face at the effort. "It's okay. I want to do this."

Lola allowed herself a breath. "I won't take long. I promise. You can sit here and listen if you like. But I want you to do one thing for me, as long as it's all right with both of you." Now she needed the son's permission to help his mother. "When I'm done—or even while I'm talking with him, if you like—I want you to lie down on that love seat. You can go to sleep now or wait until I'm done talking with him. I'll sit right beside him until your sisters or somebody else comes. I won't go to sleep and I won't ask him any more questions after I'm done. I'll just sit with him. And Margaret will sit with you. You have got to get some sleep or you won't be any good to your son."

Even as she spoke, Lola wondered at her own words. Despite the surprise that had turned out to be Margaret, she had never thought of herself as anyone's caretaker. But ever since she'd arrived in Wyoming, she seemed to be helping people care for themselves against their will.

The woman looked to her son. "Go ahead, Ma. You can lie down right now. If she asks me anything I don't like, I just won't answer."

Mrs. Sounding Sides let Margaret lead her to the love seat. "I'll sit by you like Mommy sits by your little boy," Margaret said. Lola thought the woman might cry. Instead she toppled sideways onto the love seat, eyes closed and mouth slack before her head hit the arm. Margaret fit herself into the curve of the woman's torso and stroked her head and crooned to her, much as she did to Bub at their mutual bedtime. Lola felt a cracking sensation in her heart as it expanded to accommodate another surge of the love and guilt her child provoked.

"Well?" Patrick waited. He offered a polite smile, mostly gums, the upper teeth along one side of his mouth knocked out. His nose skewed to one side. His left eye drooped. Broken occipital bone, Lola thought. His hands lay atop the quilt, backs still bruised, fingers fat and mottled as salamis. They'd stomped his hands, then, once they'd gotten him down. His right arm was in a cast past the elbow. Lola imagined those same booted feet coming down on the vulnerable bones of the forearm, the fragile radius snapping beneath a single blow, the ulna demanding concentrated effort. She thought back to the bow-tied bartender, so narrow of shoulder and hip, no bulk to leverage one drink-strengthened man away from Patrick, let alone two.

Lola clicked the recording app on her phone, held her pen above her notebook, and posed to Patrick the same question she'd asked everyone else:

"What happened over there?"

————————

"All I know is from Mike's texts," Patrick began. He ran his tongue over cracked lips. Lola put down her notebook and held the glass of water to his mouth. A few drops dribbled through the scant stubble on his chin. Lola found the washcloth she'd gotten for his mother and used it to blot them away. "I saved them all. They're on my phone. There." He lifted the hand in the cast and waved it toward a nightstand on the other side of the bed. Lola reached across him and picked it up.

"Go ahead," he said. "You can look."

She hit the text icon and started scrolling backward. Down, down and down. In the six months he'd been in Afghanistan, Mike St. Clair had sent his friend hundreds of texts. Lola finally reached the beginning. The first few were lighthearted. "Yo, bro check out this shit. We gettin' it done." A photo of Mike and Pal in fatigues and helmets, posing with rifles aimed from the waist, wide smiles on their faces. More like that. Lots more.

"Back from 1st patrol not dead yet." Mike standing atop a Stryker, fists raised high in triumph.

"Roughin' it in the Stan." The crew lounging in lawn chairs back at the base, throwing approximations of what people in Wyoming believed to be gang signs.

Lola remembered her own early days in Afghanistan, the seductive lull granted a newbie, cruising through the streets of Kabul with her driver and Ahmed, learning the lay of the land, snapping feature photos of the winsome children, the azure blurs that represented women hurrying past in burqas, and the magnificent wreck of the old king's palace, its soaring domes reduced by shelling to ribby metal struts. Easy days. Tourist days, she'd later think disdainfully, days before the real work began.

Mike apparently encountered real work about a month in. "Firefight today 2 dead." Lucky guy, Lola thought, that the first casualties his unit experienced came in a firefight, nice clean bullet wounds, nothing like what inevitably awaited. The inevitable arrived all too soon, as Mike noted in a text two weeks later.

"IED. Guy's legs gone. Fuck."

"Which ones you looking at?"

Lola jumped at the sound of Patrick's voice. She'd been so immersed in Mike's account she'd forgotten he was there. She held the phone before his face so he could see. He lisped through the gap in his teeth. "Fuck those. Go to the last ones."

Lola looked toward the love seat. Mike's mother slumbered on with Margaret—the child who'd recently declared herself too old for naps—tucked in beside her, her breathing rhythmic and peaceful, no doubt worn out from her tantrum. Bub sat beside the love seat on full alert, ears up, eyes intent. Lola imagined the same trembling intensity in Patrick's mother when she watched over her son. No wonder she was so exhausted. Lola scrolled back up through the texts until she reached the final few.

"Here we go with the NDN shit again," read one. "U know the drill." NDN being shorthand for Indian, Lola knew. And, "Dude they all on her like dogs. Tryin' to hold 'em back."

"What the hell does that mean?" said Lola.

"Shit." Patrick turned it into two long syllables. "What do you think? Giving him grief about being Indian. And pissed off Pal wouldn't give it up."

"Give what up?" Even though she knew, her stomach already turning.

"What do you think? Them boys wanted some snatch."

"But." Lola heard the stupidity of her words as soon as they slipped from her mouth. "They were his friends. And hers."

"Bet that's what they told her, too. Probably said she owed it to them. Friends with benefits."

Lola could see it. Pal and Mike, hanging on each other back at the base. The weeks sliding by in long stretches of boredom and increments of blind terror. Everybody young and healthy and horny, looking for release from the boredom, and comfort from the fear. Mike had gotten his. Why shouldn't they get theirs? She said as much to Patrick. "Was that what was going on? Share and share alike?"

"What are you talking about? Mike didn't have anything to share. He was as hard up as the rest of 'em. Guess you didn't read all his texts."

Lola was just as glad she hadn't. What she knew about the young male mind was bad enough. She didn't need her worst suspicions confirmed. But her mind snagged on one thing Patrick had said. "I thought she and Mike—"

His chest rattled with that awful wet cough. He pushed himself up on his good elbow before Lola could help him. She snagged a tissue from a box on the nightstand and handed it to him. He held it to his mouth and let it fall when the coughing stopped. The floor beside the bed was a snowfield of crumpled tissues. He lay back and drew a ragged breath. "Everybody thought that. Because no way an

Indian boy and whitegirl can just be friends, right? But that was the deal. They grew up together. Brother and sister, more like."

Lola puzzled awhile. So—at least according to Mike—the other guys harassed Pal. Mike was trying to fend them off. Which jibed not one bit with what Skiff and T-squared had told her. "I got the feeling those other guys didn't much like Pal," she ventured.

His gap-toothed grin underscored the ugliness of his words. "So? Don't have to like a girl to fuck her."

Or a guy, Lola thought, remembering some of her own more pragmatic encounters. Patrick closed his eyes. Lola rued her promise to keep the interview brief. "What does any of that have to do with how Mike died? Lots of folks go racial without anybody ending up dead."

His twitch could have been a shrug. "No clue. That text? That was last thing I got from him."

Lola checked the text again. It was dated a few days before Mike's death. Patrick's breath escaped in a sigh that could have been a light snore. Her time was running out. She touched her fingertips to the back of his hand. "What happened in the bar?"

He spoke without opening his eyes. "Was just having a cold beer in an air-conditioned bar. Can't do it on the rez, you know."

Lola knew the Blackfeet reservation was unusual in selling alcohol. Wind River apparently was dry.

"Those two guys came in, already likkered up by the sound of them. Bartender told them to keep it down. But they just moved down to the other end of the bar, where I was. I didn't say anything. Didn't look at them."

Rule Number One for an Indian guy in a whiteman bar, Lola knew. Eyes front. Don't engage. Sort of like being a woman in any bar.

"But they started right in on me. 'Just got away from all those sand niggers and now here we are sittin' next to a prairie nigger. What the fuck?'"

"What the fuck, indeed," Lola murmured.

"Yeah. So I turned around and told 'em that one of those so-called prairie niggers, Mike St. Clair, died for his country. They started laughing. Said Mike was nothing but a coward. That's when I hit them."

"Them?"

"Tommy. Then Tyson. They were likkered up, like I said. Moving kind of slow. At first."

Lola imagined the surprise and outrage in their faces as the punches landed, their heads snapping back. She thought of how Tyson bunched his shoulders when he spoke, could imagine those muscles flexing as he began the windmill that would take Patrick down, could see Tommy jumping in, all aflame at the indignity of being hit by someone he considered beneath him.

"Who finally got them off you?"

"Sheriff's deputy. Bartender wasn't any good, nor those old guys who hang out there every day, neither."

Lola had seen the sheriff's office, a couple of blocks from the bar; calculated the time it would have taken the bartender to call 9-1-1 and a dispatcher to fetch a deputy. Only a few minutes. But more than enough time for near-lethal damage. "Jesus," she said.

Patrick said nothing beyond another long, slow breath. Lola knew they were done.

She thought back over what he'd said. If the two had hurled the "prairie nigger" epithet at Patrick at home, precious little would have stopped them from using it against Mike in Afghanistan, especially if he'd been sticking up for Pal. Maybe they'd all been friends when they started, but Lola knew from her own experience among the foreign correspondents that friendships had a way of going sour amid Afghanistan's strains. They might have been a single united tribe when outsiders threatened, but among themselves, divisions ran deep. So there'd been some unpleasantness over there, which unfortunately probably wasn't all that different from the unpleasantness Mike had faced for much of his life at home.

Patrick's information added nuance to the story, showing the stress of war. It didn't shed any new light on how Mike St. Clair died. But it left Lola with still more questions, ones that—given that she'd had her last shot at Skiff—left only Pal.

TWENTY-SEVEN

LOLA WAITED UNTIL IT was nearly dark to return to the ranch. She treated Margaret to a substantial meal in town, followed by ice cream, by way of apology for yet again abandoning their vacation. Margaret didn't seem to mind, bouncing in her booster seat.

"I get to see Jemalina! And Pal and Delbert. Faster, Mommy."

She seemed to have forgotten about the bad truck. Lola hadn't. The ride to the ranch in the near-dark was too reminiscent of the encounter. Yet she drove slowly, taking time to formulate a plan for approaching Pal. She'd have the element of surprise, given that Pal wasn't expecting them. That was good. Lola usually soft-pedaled her interviews with most people, starting with the safe stuff, edging so innocuously into dangerous territory that by the time they realized that the nature of her questions had changed, they'd already answered enough of the crucial ones. That approach, she suspected, wouldn't work with Pal, not with her fists-up approach to even an innocent "How are you?" Lola would hit her hard with all the information she'd gleaned, without letting on that so far, no one who'd been there the night Mike was killed had gone on the record. All she had were second-hand accounts, as inadmissible in a story as they were in court.

The ranch, nestled within its sagebrush-dotted bowl, looked almost welcoming as Lola pulled up. *I've been in Wyoming too long if this place looks good to me*, she thought. Long enough to appreciate the way Pal's family had tucked the house below the ridges, sheltered from the screaming winds, which were annoying enough in summer but must have been punishing and potentially deadly in winter's subzero fury. Long enough to take note of the fact that, despite its haphazard add-ons and indifference to paint, the house was solidly constructed, unlike the decrepit-upon-arrival bungalows that the Bureau of Indians Affairs had assigned to the reservation to replace the tribes' practical and serviceable lodges. Long enough to have studied its layout, the proximity of house to calving shed, a sign that the ranchers cared enough about their livestock to give them a strong start in life. The house faced east, catching the morning sunlight. Lola wondered if the Joneses had copied the tradition of their Arapaho and Eastern Shoshone neighbors. But someone—Lola decided to credit the first woman who lived there—had also insisted upon a big window facing west, over the kitchen sink, to allow a ranch wife moving slowly through the end of her day's labor the luxury of the evening alpenglow highlighting the peaks of the Winds. She herself had often halted, the dish in her hand only half-scrubbed, to watch as the sinking sun filled the sky with flame.

She sat in the truck, delaying the inevitable confrontation with Pal, watching as Margaret and Bub ran for the door, Bub swerving away toward safety as Jemalina made a beeline for Margaret. Not once, Lola thought as she hefted their bags and trudged behind them to the house, had the chicken pecked Margaret, despite the child's increasing demands upon its attention. Margaret flung open the door and disappeared inside, returning a moment later.

"She's not here."

Lola hefted Margaret. The sun still wobbled atop the peaks, but much of the kitchen already lay in darkness. Lola flipped the switch and pointed to the bare space beside the door. "Her shoes are gone. About time she figured out not to run in the heat of day."

"I want to stay up until she gets back."

"Not a chance." Lola carried Margaret back to the bedroom. There would be no distractions when she talked to Pal, Lola decided.

Margaret's eyebrows met above her nose. Her lower lip pooched out. She crossed her arms over her chest.

Lola braced herself for another tantrum. Heaven help her if Margaret were entering a new phase, one that involved regular detonations. A creaking sound came from beneath the bed. Lola bit her lip to hide a smile. For the first time, she gave thanks for the chicken's presence. "You," she said to Margaret. "In bed. Now." She bent and looked under the bed. "And you, out of the house," she said to the chicken nesting contentedly on a folded towel that had somehow found its way beneath the bed. She clapped her hands at the edge of the bed, dodging the chicken's feint toward her ankles as it beat a flapping retreat.

She pressed her lips to Margaret's forehead and told Bub to stay. In the kitchen, she fetched the bourbon bottle and two glasses and went out onto the porch to wait for Pal.

———————

Lola had thought to surprise Pal. Instead, Pal turned the tables.

"Hey."

The voice reached her as she stepped onto the porch.

"Jesus Christ!" Lola jumped, dropping the bottle and glasses. Pal reached from the shadows to rescue the bottle. The glasses rolled somehow intact from the floorboards into the dirt.

"Leave them," said Pal. "We don't need them." She sat down on the step, unscrewed the bottle cap, took a pull, and held it up to Lola, who caught a whiff of sweat and dust.

Lola took the bottle. "You scared the crap out of me. Where'd you come from?" She lifted the bottle to her lips and tried not to make a face. She'd never developed a taste for bourbon's sweetness.

"From my run. Saw your truck and decided to wait out here for you. What brings you back? The Tetons not enough fun for you?"

Lola took a minute to appreciate the fact that Pal was doing to her just what she'd hoped to do with Pal, needling her, keeping her off balance. Pal knew good and well the Tetons weren't a day trip. Lola decided not to answer. She lowered herself to the step beside Pal and tucked her feet up beside her. "Aren't you worried about snakes, sitting down here like this?"

Pal lifted a shoulder. "Not really. You can hear them coming."

"How's that?"

"Listen. What do you hear?"

Lola heard what she always did. The wind, reduced to a sweet susurration, mild-mannered in the evening compared to its daytime shriek. Jemalina, high-stepping around the yard, head bobbing low to snag an occasional grub, burbling contentedly deep in her throat. "The wind. That stupid chicken."

"That's good. A snake, it makes a scritchy sort of sound. Not like either of those two. We're fine."

Lola was unprepared to concede the point. "Seems like, by the time you heard it, it'd be way too close."

"All you have to do is sit still and wait for it to go away."

Lola was disinclined to sit still and wait for a snake to do anything. Pal took the bottle back. Enough dilly-dallying, Lola thought. "So," she said.

Pal put the bottle down and waited.

"You know I'm a reporter. Just like your cousin."

A nod.

"And seeing that guy shoot himself at the airport, then hearing about your friend Mike getting killed over there, well, it made me think."

"About what?" The warning in Pal's voice could not have been more clear. Lola had no business thinking anything, it said.

"That it makes for a story. A story about the toll war takes. Not just in lives, but in psyches. Look at the six of you. Two dead and the rest of you all messed up."

Pal's teeth flashed. "I'm not messed up." She held the bottle high in an exaggerated preview of her next drink. Lola decided she was being ironic.

"I've been talking to people around town for the story."

Pal had been slouched against a porch support, but she sat up so quickly the bottle tilted. She grabbed it before any bourbon spilled. Not drunk yet; in fact, a long way from it.

"What people?"

Jemalina raised her head and cocked it. The alpenglow was gone, the Winds distinguishable only by their deeper black against the charcoal sky. Lola couldn't see the chicken's yellow eyes but imagined them trained on the porch, attentive to the change in atmosphere.

"I talked to some folks at the Fourth of July picnic. The high school principal, too. What's his name again?" She supplied her own answer, and ticked off more names, letting Pal know—in case she was tempted to lie yet again—that she already knew quite a lot about what had happened in Afghanistan. "Those two guys who got arrested, I talked to them, too. Tommy McSpadden and Tyson Graff. And your friend from the parade. Skiff."

"*What?*"

Lola continued inexorably. "I contacted the DOD, too."

Pal was on her feet, breathing hard, holding on to the porch railing for support. "Oh, God. Please, no. Please tell me you didn't do any of that. Especially Defense." Her voice shook, the words running together.

"As a matter of fact I did. I wanted to get the straight story." No reason for Pal to know that DOD would probably never come through with useful information.

Pal's arm flew up. The bottle smashed against the porch support. Lola ducked bourbon and flying glass. Jemalina disappeared squawking into the darkness. The neck of the bottle slid from Pal's fingers. It hit the porch and rolled, coming to a lopsided stop against the toe of Lola's running shoe.

"You fool," Pal said. "You've just killed us all."

———————

Lola retreated to the kitchen, snapping on lights, and returned with a broom and dustpan. She left the door open so that the yellow light spilled across the porch. Pal stepped away from its reach. Lola followed, thrusting the broom at her, trying to quash the thought that Pal might use it as a weapon. On the other hand, there was the snake-killing shovel, closer at hand and far more treacherous. If Pal hadn't gone for that, Lola was probably safe.

"Clean up your mess," she ordered Pal. "I don't want Margaret or Bub or even that damn chicken cutting its feet on the glass." Ordering Pal around had worked before. Not this time.

"You take that goddamn broomstick and shove it up your ass. I've got to get out of here. And if you're smart, you will too if you care even the slightest bit about that little girl of yours. Which I'm not sure you do." Pal shoved past Lola into the kitchen and headed for her bedroom. Lola followed close behind. Something bumped the back of her legs. She turned. Bub, alert to trouble. He followed her into Pal's bedroom.

Pal's Army duffel was on the bed. She yanked open dresser drawers, randomly pulling out underwear and T-shirts and socks and jeans, flinging them toward the bag.

"Hold on," said Lola. "What are you doing? Where are you going? And why do we have to get out of here?"

Pal wadded up the clothes and shoved them into the bag. She zipped it shut with shaking hands and headed for the door. Lola blocked it. Pal's chin jutted. "Move."

"No. Not until you tell me what's going on. You tell me I'm somehow going to get us killed. That Margaret is in danger. My child! But you won't tell me why."

Pal began to shake all over, teeth clicking together audibly.

"I've been here for almost two weeks," Lola said. "Stuck out on this damn ranch instead of going on the vacation I'd planned." In the process of whipping herself into high indignation, Lola shoved aside her own ambivalence about the vacation, not to mention the usefulness of staying at the ranch as she pursued her story. "Cleaning. Doing your stinking laundry. Cooking—at least to the best of my ability. Making sure you don't finally cut your wrist instead of your arm. What's that about, anyway? So, no. You are not going to leave this house without telling me what's going on. Right now."

She wrapped her hands around Pal's thin wrists, forcing her to drop the duffel. She dragged Pal into the kitchen and sat her down hard on a straight chair. "Talk, goddammit. I don't care if it's on the record or not. Just tell me what the hell is going on."

Pal crumpled before her, fell right out of the chair onto the floor and curled wailing into a ball.

"I can't. I can't. I can't."

———

"I'm so sorry," Lola said for about the fiftieth time. Even though she didn't yet know what she was sorry for. She stood at the stove over a saucepan of milk, stirring so it wouldn't burn, something she'd learned in the past week. Pinpoint bubbles rose to its surface. Lola turned off the flame and poured the milk into two mugs—by this point she was nearly as shaken as Pal—and added honey and, after a moment's thought, healthy slugs of bourbon from a new bottle from Pal's stash. Lola placed the mugs on the table and eased Pal from the floor back into the chair and sat down across from her. "Drink this. It'll help. Take all the time you need."

Pal sipped. "I'm sorry," Lola said yet again. She took the movement of Pal's head as, if not exactly a nod, at least acknowledgment. Pal's hands shook. Some of the milk in her mug splashed onto the edge of the table. Bub hopped up on his single back leg, braced his forepaws against the table for balance, and cleaned it up, sneezing at the whiskey. If Pal was still shaking, Lola decided, it was too soon to expect her to talk. She took the lead.

"Here's what people have told me," she began. She took a soothing swallow of milk and outlined all the different stories. That an insurgent had slit Mike's throat as he slumbered while on watch, and that Skiff had slain the insurgent, saving them all. That Pal and Mike had led the silly Talib hunt, culminating in the shooting of the shepherd.

That the shepherd, believed dead, had slashed Mike's throat in a final futile blow, and that the asleep-on-watch story had been concocted to save everyone's collective asses. That Pal and Mike were sleeping together. That Pal and Mike weren't sleeping together. That, regardless, the other guys had started harassing Pal. And that Mike had come in for his share of racial taunts.

"You got that right." Pal's voice emerged unexpectedly. Lola drained the last of her milk. "It was sand nigger this, raghead that when we were out on patrol for hajis. And then, back at the base, prairie nigger for Mike. All a big joke, of course. 'Hey, Mike, better not walk around in your civvies. Ain't nobody here can tell a sand nigger from a prairie nigger.'"

"How'd he handle it?"

Pal searched for the right word. "Dignified," she said. "He'd say something like 'Uncool,' and leave it at that. One against four. Not much he could do, right?"

At least he stood up for himself, Lola thought. But according to Patrick, Mike hadn't been the only one getting shit. She reminded Pal that Patrick had mentioned as much. "He said Mike told him they were on your case, too."

That long shudder again, starting at Pal's shaven head. Her calves knocked against the chair legs. Lola rose and turned off the light and came back to the table. "Now you can't see me. So just act like I'm not here," she said. "Were you sleeping with Mike or not?"

"God." The word came out on a fast-checked sob. "No. Never."

"But they thought you were."

"Of course." Generations, entire centuries, of bitterness in the words, the only assumption, ever, no matter the culture or country, between a man and a woman of different colors.

207

"What would they say?" Easier to start with the words. Please, God, Lola thought, let it have been limited to words.

"The usual."

Lola had gotten her share of the usual, but imagined the color aspect made for a different sort of usual. "Such as?"

"You know. 'Must be getting tired of that ol' greasy dark meat. Try some white meat.'"

"Classy."

"Or, 'He's had his turn. When's mine?'"

"As though they had a right to you."

Pal talked right over her, on a roll now, a festering wound lanced, the purulence spilling out. "'I hear them Indian boys got little dicks. How 'bout a real man? You won't walk right for days.' Tyson pulled it out once. Waited for me behind the latrine. Called me back, said he had something to show me. 'Suck on this,' he said. Like I was one of those goddamned Porta-Potty hotties. Thank God somebody came along with a case of the runs."

So it had crossed the line into action. Lola wished she'd poured a little more bourbon into her milk.

"Did you tell anybody?"

Pal's laugh was worse than anything she'd said. "I can read," she said when she finally stopped.

Lola knew what she meant. The issue of sexual assault in the military was finally getting traction in the press. Unfortunately, most of the stories had to do with the disastrous consequences to the women who reported assaults. Pal, like Mike, had opted to suffer in silence. At least, thought Lola, she and Mike had each other. Until they didn't.

One last time, she posed the question.

"How did Mike die?"

TWENTY-EIGHT

THERE WAS NOT ENOUGH sweetened warm milk in the world to ease Pal's next words. They should have been drinking gall, Lola thought. Hemlock. Something that would have vanquished forever the images that Pal's story seared into her brain.

The soldiers left the village late. The vehicle coughed to a halt. It was protocol to wait for the replacement vehicle. Nobody was to be out on foot after dark. Skiff radioed in, standing apart from the others. "I think he told them not to come. Or maybe he told them the meeting was running late and he'd call when we were done. Either way, there was no vehicle," Pal said. "But he said one was coming and that we were to go meet it. So we set out. Leaving a vehicle that for all I know wasn't even broken."

As Pal spoke, Lola could hear their heavy footsteps in the dust, the clinking of metal gear. Far in the distance, the rising keen of wolves. Overhead, the dizzying swath of stars. Maybe the stars distracted Pal. Maybe she was gazing upon them, marveling as Lola so often had, not realizing that T-squared had come up on either side of her until they seized her arms.

"Hey. Knock it off." Wrenching herself free. A few blessed, sprinting steps. Hands grabbing at her clothing, her head, the damnable military bun coming loose, her rope of hair perfect for pulling her back into their grasp. Skiff looming before her. "Time for you to be a pal, Pal." A quicksilver flash in the darkness. A knife, held to her throat. No one to hear her screams.

Mike, launching himself at Skiff from behind. Skiff turning. The knife.

"Holy fuck, man." This from T-squared. One or the other. Maybe both. "What are we gonna do?"

Skiff, dropping the knife. "We'll deal with that later. Right now, we're gonna deal with this." And so they did.

Rising at leisure. Stretching. Laughing. Leaving Pal in the dirt where they'd held her down, the cold stars wheeling spectacular and unfeeling overhead. "Hey." Skiff held up his hand. "What's that?"

An unmusical bell. A pattering of hoofed footsteps. The sheep first, then the shepherd. Shots. Skiff slung his gun back over his shoulder and retrieved his knife from where it lay beside Mike. He wiped its handle on the shepherd's robe, then tossed it down beside the corpse. He took Mike's knife, identical to his own, and stuck it in the sheath on his belt. "Too bad. This guy grabbed Mike's own knife and killed him with it. What a shame. That settles that. Get her away from him."

Pal had crawled to Mike. She lay across his body. Skiff raised his chin toward T-squared. They hauled her to her feet. Tommy waggled his tongue at her. "Was it as good for you as it was for me?"

She pulled away. This time, they let her go. But Skiff's whisper followed. "Karma's a bitch, huh?"

The milk in Lola's mug had gone cold. She moved her hands helplessly. She felt as though she should say something, but she didn't know what. Nothing, it turned out.

"That's not all," said Pal. "When we got back—" She stopped.

"You told someone," Lola guessed. It was one thing to keep your mouth shut about harassment, to hope it would go away, to know that even if it didn't, it would be brushed aside as whining. But this was different. Murder. Rape.

She couldn't see Pal in the dark room. But Pal's tone was thick with pity for Lola's cluelessness. "No. Oh, no. I did not tell."

She'd moved zombielike through her first twenty-four hours back, deviating from her normal routines only to duck into a latrine with a pair of scissors, emerging with her hair hacked short, finishing the job later in the shower with a razor. It would be the last shower she took for weeks. Everybody took her behavior as shock over Mike's death. Even people who'd sneered openly at her presumed relationship with Mike showed her some deference. They mumbled their "Sorry's" and bestowed awkward shoulder pats and hugs. The hypocrisy of their verbal sympathy nauseated her. The physical contact was unbearable. There was the ceremony. Mike's boots and rifle, the helmet atop it. Taps. Skiff eased into the space next to her. "He was your family," he said. Skiff, master of the obvious. "He and his grandfather were all you had after your parents died. Except for some folks up in Montana, am I right?"

Pal dug her fingernails into her palms until the skin broke, trying to stop trembling at his proximity.

"Shame if anything happened to old Delbert."

She lost her battle with the shakes then. She whirled to face him. "You wouldn't."

His smile was wide and easy. "Not unless I have to."

Somehow she choked out the words. "You'll never have to."

211

"This is bullshit!" Fur brushed Lola's legs. Bub must have been with Pal as she laid out her story. Now he rushed to Lola's side. "You can't let him get away with that."

"I can. Or at least I could until you showed up, snooping around, stirring up trouble. What are you going to do when he shows up here? When did you contact the DOD? Does he know that you did?"

Lola stood and moved away from the barrage of questions. "Do you mind if I turn the light back on? Close your eyes." The dark was fine for listening, but it left her muzzy-headed, uncertain of how to proceed. She squinted against the sudden glare of light. "I'm going to heat up some more milk."

"Here." Pal held out the bourbon bottle.

Lola shook her head. She needed to focus. She scrubbed the crust of old milk from the pan, poured in fresh, and sat the pan atop the flame, forcing herself not to stir in the honey while the milk was still cold, anxious for the comfort of warmth and sweetness. The flats of strawberries sat untouched on the counter. She selected a berry and bit into it, looking out the window over the sink. The darkness was less than complete. Dawn came early to the abbreviated nights of summer, first faint light at four-thirty, sunup well before six. They'd talked through the night. Lola wondered if she should put on coffee, or hold out hope of catching an hour or two of sleep before Margaret arose. She tried to retrieve her train of thought.

"I called the DOD last week. I only asked about Mike's death. Nothing else, because I didn't know about anything else. I followed up with an email, because they asked for one. I don't expect to hear back from them anytime soon, and when I do, I don't expect to get anything useful. So you've got nothing to worry about."

Lola might not have been done drinking, but Pal had no such reticence, head canted back, bottle gurgling. "Ahhhh, God." She coughed. "Doesn't matter. Skiff's connected. Sooner or later, he'll hear."

"What do you mean? Does he have an uncle who's a general, or something like that?"

"He's one of those Osbornes."

Damn Thirty and its incomprehensible genealogy. The milk burned Lola's tongue. She took a cooling breath and awaited an explanation. None came. It seemed never to occur to anyone in the area that outsiders might not be acquainted with every detail of their history. "The Osbornes?"

"Shirttail relative, anyhow."

Lola was glad Margaret was asleep. If this went on much longer, her quarter fund would expand exponentially. "Who the hell are they?"

"One of the Osbornes was the doctor who did the autopsy on Big Nose George."

"Oh, Jesus Christ. Just get to the point."

Some life crept back into Pal's eyes. "George was a cattle rustler back in the day. They finally put him in jail, but he got lynched after an escape attempt."

Lola couldn't see why a doctor who'd did an autopsy a century earlier had any meaningful bearing on Skiff's alleged ruthlessness, and said as much. "Sounds like Dr. Osborne was just doing his job."

"Oh, he did his job, all right. Opened George up, looked around inside, and then skinned him out."

Lola wished she hadn't been so quick to reject the bourbon. "Jesus," she said again.

"But he wasn't done yet. Had the hide tanned, down in Denver. Made a pair of shoes out of it."

"Please tell me he never wore them," Lola said.

"Not only wore them. Sported them at his inauguration when he was elected governor."

Lola wondered when the barbarism of humans would cease to horrify. Pal apparently had long ago come to accept it. "That's what we're dealing with here," she said. "The spawn of a guy who wore man-hide shoes. When he comes after us, we'll be lucky if he just kills us and leaves it at that."

For the first time since she'd met Pal, Lola finally agreed with something she'd said. "You've got guns," Lola said. "This is a ranch. And you were in the Army. You have to have guns." Then regretted her words. She needed Pal to think she was calm, controlled. Not panicked, grabbing at guns to man—or, in this case, woman—the ramparts. But Margaret was sleeping just down the hallway. She wanted a gun between Margaret and whatever danger might come her way.

Pal's answer made her question moot. "Nope."

Lola's voice rose. So much for control. "How is that possible?"

"Delbert took them. Said he was worried I might use them against myself. Pissed me off. But you know how it is. You can't argue with an elder."

Lola knew what she meant, but she thought she goddamn well might argue with an elder after all, starting first thing in the morning when Delbert showed up with his doughnuts. Well. Not argue. That was impermissible under any circumstances. But she could ask, ever so politely, that he return them. She'd promise to keep them out of Pal's hands. Unless Skiff showed up. Then she'd give Pal as many guns as she could handle. Her chest was tight. She gasped for breath.

"Hey." Concern was a new emotion for Pal, as far as Lola could tell. "Are you all right? Put your head between your legs. Take deep breaths."

Lola bent double. "I. Can't." The band squeezed tighter around her lungs.

"Easy. Slower. On my count. Breathe in—one thousand one. Breathe out—one-thousand two. Like that. Better? Good. Here. Drink your milk."

Lola pushed herself up and drank. She was glad she'd heard the bottle glugging above her, and so was braced for the whiskey bite. There was, she estimated, very little milk left in her nearly full mug. She drank deep. Then made a pronouncement.

"This is fucking ridiculous."

————

Lola pushed the mug away. "Just look at us. A couple of crazy women. Drinking. Talking about guns. Scared out of our gourds."

"With good reason, I'd say."

"Crap." Lola tried to project a bravado she did not wholly feel. At least, not yet. But she'd spent years chanting the "fake it till you make it" adage under her breath in tense situations. Time to resurrect her old coping skill. "We don't need guns," she said.

Pal looked appropriately skeptical. "How's that?"

"For starters, it's just stupid. What are we going to do, tote them with us every minute of the day in case he shows up while I'm in the bathroom or something? Or you're out on one of your runs? I can't quite see you jogging down the road with a rifle bouncing around on your back."

"You'd be surprised," Pal said.

Lola spoke over her. "We've got something better than guns."

"What's that?"

"My story. Hear me out." Lola talked fast, trying to forestall Pal's objection. If she ran a story, put it out there in public what had happened, then Skiff couldn't come after any of them. "Not you. Not Delbert. Not me. And not—" She stopped, unable to voice the possibility that anything could happen to Margaret. "He won't dare. If anything happened to any of us, you'd be on the record as having said he'd threatened you. They'd know right away to go after him."

Pal's lips pursed. "Lot of good that'll do me if I'm dead. And what's this 'on the record' stuff?"

Lola had hoped Pal wouldn't pick up on that so fast. She wanted her to get used to the idea, buy into it, before she laid out the ground rules. "It would be best if you let me use your name. News organizations usually don't name rape victims without specific permission. So I don't absolutely have to use it. But it's a stronger story if you put your name to it. And you'll have to report the rape to the DOD. There's no way around that. Otherwise, it's just your word against his."

Lola had seen storms breaking over Glacier, home of epic weather patterns, that held less menace than Pal's countenance. "And my word's not good enough?"

"For something of this magnitude? Where we name him? No. I'm sorry, but it's not. If you were both civilians, we'd want a police report. Something we could point to, show readers. An official account of what happened, right there in black and white, saying you're willing to stand up and say in public that this happened. Again, they black out victims' names. But something about that official document lends weight to everything."

The storm broke, instantaneous, daunting.

"No. Fucking. Way. You know how the DOD treats women who've been ... You've read the stories."

Lola trod carefully. "People will want proof. As much proof as they can have without a trial. Something that shows you're not—"

Pal supplied the words. "Making shit up?"

"Well."

"That's what you mean, isn't it? Do you think I'm making shit up?

Lola's words came even more slowly. "This is, what—the third version? Fourth?—I've heard of Mike's death. I'm going to have to lay out all of those other versions in the story. If people believe your story, it'll show how far those guys went to discredit you."

Pal's mouth opened and closed without sound. Her eyes went blank. She stood and backed across the room, her movements robotic. Bub's hackles rose. Pal found words. "Do you believe me?"

Lola's gut insisted Pal was telling the truth. She tried to bring her brain to bear. Pal had lied about knowing Cody Dillon. What else had she lied about? She started to ask for an explanation, something to back up her gut. Which was always right. But what if it wasn't this time? She couldn't afford to be wrong on a story of this magnitude. But she'd waited too long to answer, leaving an opening big enough for Pal to drive a semi-trailer through.

Which Pal did, in effect, standing on the accelerator with both feet. "You don't believe me. Get the hell out of my house. Take your brat and go. Right now. *No!*" She screamed as Lola started to speak. "Not another word from you!" Her face changed. Her gaze shifted past Lola.

"Mommy?"

Margaret stood in the hallway, sleep and fear at war in her eyes, thumb in her mouth, a return to the comfort of babyhood. "What's wrong?"

Lola ran to her. "Nothing is wrong," she murmured, wrapping the child tight in her arms. She was glad she hadn't unpacked their bags after they'd returned the previous night. "We're just going to hit the road a little early, that's all. You're going to sleep in your booster seat and when you wake up, we'll be almost to where we're going."

Wherever that turns out to be, she thought, as she hastened with Margaret to the truck, Bub at her heels, without a backward glance toward Pal.

TWENTY-NINE

LOLA SECOND-GUESSED HERSELF ALL the way to town.

She'd done the right thing. She was sure of it. But she wondered if she could have handled things differently, in a way that would have made Pal return to the table, pull out a chair, sit down and start spilling her guts. On the record. Along with a completed incident report to file with DOD. Lola knew that in rape cases, as in no other crime, readers liked that piece of paper. People were quick to denigrate sex crimes as "he said-she said" cases, conveniently ignoring the fact that so many others—muggings, burglaries, and the like—were, too. Yet nobody raised an eyebrow when those victims came forward.

Pal's fury lent credence to her account. Or did it? One of the things Charlie and Lola agreed on was that the bigger the lie, the more towering the indignation. It was a source of frustration for both of them that jurors were inclined to be taken in by theatrical, sobbing denials, while they looked askance at the man who sat quietly, saying, "No, of course I didn't do it," so secure in his own innocence that it never occurred to him that others might see his very calm as suspicious.

Still. The hard knot of uncertainty took up stubborn lodging in Lola's gut. If Pal were lying—again—Lola didn't dare go ahead with the story. "So much for ever snagging another assignment from In-Depth," she muttered. But if Pal were telling the truth, Lola would have to write the story quickly. It would be an about-face from the Skiff-As-Hero version she'd already outlined. Skiff-As-Villain was the one part of Pal's account that gave Lola pause. He'd been the soul of earnestness in each of her encounters with him. He'd even cried in front of her. Most important, Margaret liked him. "I just can't see it," Lola said aloud, convincing herself that she'd done the right thing by pushing Pal to file the paperwork that would bolster her case.

She'd give Pal a couple of days to think things over, she thought. This time, she'd really, truly head to the Tetons. Spend a day or two, before making the long detour back to Pal's on the way home. She'd check in, see if Pal changed her mind. She might even try to talk to Skiff yet again, to watch his reaction more carefully as she questioned him, without letting on that she'd talked to Pal, or what Pal had said. She felt marginally better. She had a plan. Now, to deal with the fact that she faced about three more hours of driving and a day of sightseeing, after a sleepless night. Coffee, she thought. And—she glanced at the dashboard gauges—gas. Margaret stirred as the truck slowed on the approach to town. A glance in the rearview mirror showed the slow surprise on her daughter's face at finding herself in her booster seat instead of bed, the confusion at her recollection of their abrupt departure. Margaret's lip trembled.

"I'm going to stop and get some gas, and some coffee," Lola said. "Or, maybe we can go to the café for a nice breakfast. Would you like that?" Thirty's outbuildings appeared. The gas station was on the edge of town. Lola pulled in and braked beside the pumps. Another pickup sat at a second set of pumps. Lola fumbled in her pocket for her credit card. She'd thought that staying at Pal's would save money, but she'd spent far more on gas than she'd expected, running back and forth from the ranch to town every day. At least gas was cheaper in Wyoming than Montana, a testament to the state's plentiful oil refineries.

"Mommy." Margaret's voice was urgent.

"Don't worry, honey," she said. "We'll go inside as soon as I'm done with the gas. I'll get my coffee and you can use the bathroom."

"No, Mommy." Lola glanced again in the mirror. Margaret pointed a shaking finger. "Mommy. Look."

Lola looked. She saw the store. A few cars parked in front of it. The other set of pumps. The truck at the pumps. *The truck.*

Silver and burly. A long scrape down the passenger side door. Bits of red paint embedded in it. The bastard hadn't even bothered to wash it off. Lola's first impulse was to rush inside the store and confront him. March him down to the sheriff's office herself. Which she knew was ridiculous. She took note of the other truck's license number. Chanted it to herself. Started her own truck. Glided away from the pumps.

"Mommy, where are we going?"

Lola pulled up to the curb across from the gas station. She opened the glove compartment and retrieved a reporter's notebook and pen from the stash that lived there and wrote down the license number. "We're going to sit right here and watch to see who comes out of that store. And then we're going to call the sheriff and have him arrest his a—um, rear end."

Margaret pressed her nose to the window. Bub stretched across her, adding a wet round circle to the glass. Lola rolled her own window down and held her phone at the ready. Her plan to was snap a photo, and then call 9-1-1. On the off chance the truck didn't belong to the driver, she wanted the photo for evidence. The store's door swung open. A beefy man in a cowboy hat emerged, a super-sized soft drink cup in his hand. Lola clicked the camera. The truck's driver, Lola remembered, had been a big guy, like his truck. But he'd worn a ball cap. A lot of people changed hats, depending on the day, Lola thought. Maybe not this one, though. He got into a car at the far end of the parking lot and drove away. Lola's breath came out in a whoosh.

"Not him, Mommy."

"No."

Lola erased the photo. The door opened again, letting out two men, one behind the other. Lola and Margaret sat up straighter. Bub whined.

"Oh." Margaret's voice went flat. "It's just Spiff."

On any other day—and especially on this day, given the questions Pal had raised—Lola would have hailed him. But she had to find out who was driving that truck. His big body blocked her view. Lola craned her neck, trying to see around him. Then she stopped trying.

Skiff got into the silver truck, started it with a roar, and drove away.

———

Lola drove fast, carelessly, the speedometer needle creeping into the danger zone. A deer she never saw made a desperate leap that constituted the difference between life and road kill and then stood trembling, looking at the vanishing red blur that had come out of nowhere.

Lola's thoughts slammed like blows. It hadn't been, as the deputy sheriff had suggested, some random creep on the road that night, intent upon scaring her or worse. It was Skiff. He'd known it was her, would have recognized her truck by its color and make alone, not to mention the damning Montana plates. He'd meant to scare her. Maybe scare her into leaving Wyoming. Scare her off the story. Which meant that, of all the versions of the story she'd heard, Pal's had been true.

Pal. Who was alone at the ranch. Lola looked in the rearview mirror. No silver truck. She stomped the accelerator harder. It already strained against the floor. They were almost to the ranch. Lola braked hard for the turn onto the gravel road, spraying grit in a great cloud behind her, obliterating the vista in the rearview mirror. If the silver truck crept up behind her, she'd have no way of knowing. Lola stomped the brakes on the final downhill to the house, steering to the very edge of the porch, trying to reassure herself that it meant nothing at all that there were no signs of life at the ranch. No smoke from the chimney, no lights shining from the window. Just Jemalina, scratching stupidly for grubs, as though this day was like any other.

Lola fumbled at the straps and buckles on Margaret's booster seat, torn between the desire to rush into the house and warn Pal, and the absolute necessity of not leaving her child alone. "Ow, Mommy," Margaret protested as Lola dragged her from her seat, hoisted her beneath one arm, and ran heavily toward the house, fending off Jemalina's predictable assault with a sideways kick that nearly threw her off balance. She took the porch steps in a single leap and reached for the door. It was locked. Lola stared stupidly, trying to imagine the last time she'd encountered a locked door in the five years she'd lived in the West. Something else was off. Her ankle registered a sharp pain. She'd foolishly taken her eye off the chicken.

"That does it," she said, and reached for the shovel by the front door. It wasn't there. Lola put Margaret down and pounded two-fisted on the door with all the fervor she'd intended to aim at Jemalina. "Pal! Pal!"

Margaret began to cry. Bub added his voice to the din.

The door opened. The noise stopped. Pal stood within, holding the shovel like a baseball bat, business end up, cocked above her head and ready to swing.

"Whoa." Lola moved back fast, well out of shovel range. Margaret, Jemalina and Bub positioned themselves somewhere in the middle of the yard.

"What the ... *heck* are you doing back here?"

Lola noted the verbal adjustment and thought that, despite all appearances to the contrary, Pal had actually paid attention to something she'd said. That probably required some effort on Pal's part. What Lola was about to do required more.

"I came back to apologize. And to make sure you're all right."

The shovel lowered a millimeter. Lola took a step forward. It went up again, blade catching the sunlight, its razor edge flashing an unmistakable warning. Lola froze.

"Apologize for what? And why make sure I'm all right?"

"For doubting you."

Pal's arms quivered. All that running wasn't doing a damn thing for her biceps, Lola thought. It had been awhile since she'd toted a heavy rifle for a good part of each day. The shovel had to be getting heavy.

"What brought on that revelation?"

Margaret's high thin voice reached the porch. "We saw Spiff."

"Who?"

"You know who," Lola said.

"*Where?*" Pal hoisted the shovel higher, cocked her arms afresh.

Lola made her voice low and steady, at odds with what she felt. "In town. He didn't see us. Didn't follow us. Believe me, I checked."

The shovel came down with a thump. Lola looked at the gash in the floor and imagined a similar wound in her head. She wouldn't relax until Pal let go of it altogether. "Why don't you set that aside? We can talk about this over coffee. Margaret, you can play with Jemalina now. Stay on the porch, though. And get in here lickety-split if you see anybody coming."

Pal stood aside. Lola crossed into the kitchen, back muscles tensed against the possibility Pal might change her mind. But Pal leaned the shovel against the wall and pointed to the coffeepot. "I just made fresh." She stood with arms folded while Lola poured herself a cup.

Lola looked at her over the rim of her mug. "What's with the shovel? The door being locked?"

Pal snorted. "You first. What's with *Spiff*?"

THIRTY

"IF I'D HAD ANY idea it was him that night, I'd never have doubted you," Lola said when she'd finished telling Pal about the truck chase. She spoke past a mouthful of strawberries.

Pal waved off the offer of a berry, and picked at the scars on her forearm. "Why didn't you tell me about it? That's some scary shit."

"You didn't exactly invite conversation." But since she appeared to be doing so now, Lola chanced another question. "What's with those?" She pointed at the scars.

Pal put her finger on the first one, the older whitened scar faint beneath the new, still-healing slash that X'ed it out. "Tommy McSpadden."

She moved her finger to the next. "Tyson Graff. Although, those two assholes being bonded out of jail makes me think I crossed them off too soon. Anyway." She moved her finger to the next. "Cody Dillon. At least he felt bad about it."

Lola forced the question through lips that felt frozen. Pal, scarring herself for each of her attackers, and then cutting herself again in a sort of triumph when God or the Creator or whatever you wanted to call a higher power dished out retribution. "What do you mean?"

"When he shot himself. He couldn't face his father, knowing what he'd done. And shouting, 'It's a lie,' the way he did. I almost feel bad that he's dead. But not really."

"It's *a lie*," Lola breathed. "Not, 'It's alive.'"

"What?"

"Never mind. What's that last one?" Even though she knew, mouthing the words along with Pal as she spoke them.

"Skiff. He's the last one to have gotten away with it." She dug her fingers into the line of scar tissue, reddening the skin around it. "And he's the one who caused it all. Without him, the rest would never have had the nerve."

Lola reached across the table and pulled Pal's hand away from the scar and held it in her own. "He's not going to get away with it anymore. You and I are going to talk, and I'm going to take notes like a fiend. And then you're going to call the DOD, aren't you? I'll sit right here with you while you do it."

She didn't know why she was so sure; wondered, as the words left her mouth, if once again she'd pushed Pal too far. But she must have sensed some shift in the woman, some new determination that stiffened her shoulders and lifted her chin and produced the first real smile she'd seen on Pal's face since that ghastly facsimile the day Cody had shot himself.

"Some reporter you are," Pal said. "Where's your notebook?" Then laughed outright as Lola dug through the pockets of her cargo shorts to produce the most basic tools of her trade.

———

Within an hour, Lola's hand felt clenched in a permanent cramp around her pen. She recorded the conversation on her phone but, always wary of technology, took handwritten notes as Pal talked herself hoarse.

They started easy, the way she usually did with her interviews, lingering over the innocuous stuff, comparing their own first impressions of Afghanistan. "Lucky," Pal said wistfully when Lola told of her travels around Kabul and beyond, accompanied only by her driver and fixer, her hair tucked beneath a shawl-like duppata. The arrangement that had seemed so limiting to Lola represented unimaginable freedom to Pal, who went nowhere without a full contingent of fellow soldiers, their appearance rendered appalling by helmets, blank-lensed sunglasses, robotic-looking body armor and of course the warning presence of rifles held at the ready. "Can you imagine wanting to talk to anyone who looked like that?" Pal said. "They'd see us coming and run. Which of course made everyone think they were up to something. Me, I think they were just scared shitless."

Which gave Lola an opening to talk of the one advantage to being a woman, the fact that, unlike the male journalists, people often invited her into their homes, there being no shame in another woman mingling with the females of the family.

"What was it like?" Pal leaned forward. Lola suppressed a start at the curiosity lighting Pal's features, so unusual was the emergence of anything resembling human emotion on that sharp little face.

"Odd. They'd feed me, of course. They're the most hospitable people on earth. Even the poorest people would at least offer tea. But when it was a full meal, they'd often put me with the men for dinner. It's like I was an honorary man. I suppose I should have been flattered, but it made me so uncomfortable, I'd go eat dessert with the women. They were more fun, anyhow."

"How's that?"

Lola laughed at the memory, and then again at the welcome re-alization that not all of her memories of Afghanistan were bad. "Be-cause the women spent a lot of their time making fun of the men."

"What was the food like?"

"Scary."

Actual mischief crept into Pal's eyes. "Like yours?"

"Just for that, I'm taking the last of the coffee." Lola emptied the dregs into her cup and prepared a fresh pot. The food in Afghanistan had to have been unsafe for a western gut, the vegetables washed in water swimming with bacteria, the meat obtained from a market where it hung, buzzing with flies, all day in the sun. "But it was so good I couldn't help myself. I ate it all!" she said. "The fruits and veg-etables were nothing like the ones here, all good looks and no taste. The flavor was so intense. And for the most part, I never got sick. Just lucky, I guess."

"Just immune from eating your own cooking," Pal muttered.

"Let it go. Unless you want kitchen duty," Lola shot back, warm-ing to the beginnings of repartee, reminiscent of the same sort of smartassery she shared with Jan.

Pal obliged by returning to their earlier subject. "Did you make any friends? Among the locals, I mean."

"Not really. Mostly I just interviewed people and moved on," Lola began. "But there was one—" She stopped, teetering, fighting for balance at the lip of a bottomless chasm.

"Who?"

Lola closed her eyes against the images at the forefront of her brain, but that only threw them into sharper focus. The chasm yawned. Lola swayed. She grabbed at the table. "Never mind. Not important."

A chair scraped. Footsteps. Hands on hers, clasping them tight, pulling at her, turning her in the chair. She opened her eyes. Pal crouched before her. "You want me to spill my guts to the whole fucking world about the worst thing that's ever happened to me? I say you'd better start talking."

Lola forced the words. "I can't. I haven't. Ever."

Pal's grasp tightened. The tiny bones in Lola's hands crunched. "You can. I'm living proof. What was that little lecture you gave me about not cowering before the shit that scares us? Well, right back at you. Close your eyes if it makes it easier. But start talking. Get it out."

Lola squeezed her eyes shut. "His name was Ahmed. He was a fixer," she began. She felt herself leaning even farther over the edge, Pal pulling just as hard against her fall. She steadied herself. And, against all odds, kept talking.

———

Lola awoke in her bed, with little idea how she'd gotten there and none of how much time had passed. She had a memory of Pal leading her to the room, her arm around Lola's shoulders, and urging her into bed beside Margaret. "You did great," Pal whispered so as not to wake the girl. "You're going to need to sleep now. You'll feel better when you wake up. We'll finish my interview and do the DOD report then." Lola couldn't even muster the energy to tell Pal she could have shouted without disturbing Margaret.

Lola's throat was dry. She opened her eyes. The light hurt. She squinted against it, almost expecting to find herself back on a Kabul street, bloodied bits of human flesh beneath her feet, the grievously wounded flailing about, screaming for help or, worse yet, lying in the grey silence that precedes expiration. Pal had said she'd feel better after sleeping. She wasn't sure. She went first to the bathroom and then the kitchen, waiting in the doorway as the room swam into focus, the humble Formica table, the long counter, Pal standing at it, doing something with food. Pal glanced her way.

"Welcome back to the world. It's nearly lunchtime, and we've got a long afternoon ahead of us. I'm fixing some food for us, and Margaret, too. Poor kid. She's been so good out there all morning. She's teaching Jemalina some tricks, apparently. God help us."

A can opener sat on the counter. Lola sniffed. Tomatoes. Oh, Jesus, she thought. Not ravioli. Something sizzled in a pan. A familiar, buttery smell. Lola let herself hope. "Is that—?"

"Grilled cheese. Tomato soup, too. Canned, but it's all I've got. I know it's hot food on a hot day, but comfort seemed the way to go. Here." She set a plate and a bowl in front of Lola, and called Margaret indoors. Lola finished her sandwich before her daughter had even settled in her chair, breaking yet another rule, this one involving waiting to eat until everyone was seated. Pal raised her eyebrows, buttered another piece of bread, and slapped it into the pan, topping it with thick slices of cheddar and another piece of buttered bread. "Do you mind waiting for yours, big girl? Your mom had a long night and she's in the middle of a long day. What say we take care of her before you and I eat?"

Margaret swelled at the "big girl" and nodded assent. "I'm teaching Jemalina how to fetch," she announced. Bub's ears stood up at the word "fetch."

"Sometimes she beats Bub to the ball." The ears flattened. Bub's lip curled.

Lola held her bowl to her mouth and slurped directly from it. The more quintessentially American the food she inhaled, the farther Afghanistan receded.

"Rude, Mommy."

Lola tilted the bowl high. Pal retrieved it and refilled it before she could even ask. "How can a chicken fetch a ball? It's too big for her beak," Lola asked in the interminable seconds before the bowl returned.

"She rolls it. Do you want to see?"

Pal stepped in with Lola's soup and a second sandwich. "Your mom and I have a lot of work to do this afternoon. Why don't you teach Jemalina a new trick, and then tonight, we can have ourselves a regular chicken circus? I'll call Delbert and invite him up to watch. Maybe he can bring some popcorn."

"Or ice cream." Margaret cut her eyes toward Lola, who'd begun to think of Wyoming as the Land of No Rules.

Pal returned to the table with a sandwich and two plates. She cut the sandwich in half and put a piece on each plate. She went back to the stove and upended the pot over two mugs, filling each one about halfway. "One for you," she told Margaret, "and one for me."

She sat down. Raised her own sandwich. Took a bite. Swallowed. Put it down. Reached for her mug. Another swallow. Licked a bit of soup from upper lip. Back to the sandwich. Lola held her breath. It was the most food she'd seen Pal eat since she'd met her. Margaret watched open-mouthed.

Halfway through her sandwich, Pal raised her eyes. She looked from Lola to Margaret and back again. "What?"

Lola caught Margaret's eye and shook her head. "Nothing," she said, rearranging her face so as not to reveal the relief welling within. It was just a start. Pal had a long way to go. But she'd planted her feet firmly on the path. "Nothing at all. Eat hearty," she said to Pal. "We're going back to your story next."

THIRTY-ONE

PAL BLAMED GRADUATION NIGHT. "The party. It was epic." It was at Skiff's place, in town, with the understanding that everybody would stay over. His parents barbecued early, then collected car keys and tactfully absented themselves when the kegs arrived.

"Wait," said Lola. "Kegs, plural?"

"It was graduation."

"How many graduated?"

"Seventy-five. Eighty, maybe."

That sounded about right. Thirty was about the same size as Magpie, which had graduated sixty-five the year Lola got stuck covering graduation. "How many kegs?"

"Three or four. I can't really remember. More than two."

Lola tried to remember her own high school party math. She counted on her fingers. "A six-pack per person, then. At least."

"Liquor, too."

"No wonder you enlisted," said Lola. "You'd have to be just that drunk to think it was a good idea."

"Oh, we were all pretty trashed. Except Mike. He doesn't drink. Didn't."

Lola knew that some of the reservation kids looked at the alcohol-fueled devastation around them and went straight-edge from the start; no drinking, no drugs, often with a good dose of religion. "Was it a church thing with him?"

"No. He wasn't one of those Jesus Indians. But he watched alcohol kill his mom. It almost killed Delbert, too, but he got straight when his daughter died and he had to raise Mike."

Something tugged at Lola's memory. "I thought Mike graduated from the rez school. What was he doing at the Thirty party?"

Pal's face went fond. "He was my, uh, shot blocker."

Lola reminded herself that she was only about fifteen years older—okay, maybe closer to twenty—than Pal, to whom the difference likely loomed larger. But she couldn't let that one pass. "I'm familiar with the term cock blocker."

Pal had the good grace to blush. "I just wanted to be able to have a good time and not worry about anything."

Lola had only experienced Pal as taciturn at best, and downright rude. She tried to imagine the lighthearted high school girl, tossing back that mane of hair, holding out her cup for another beer, razzing the guys, Mike hovering, smiling but protective. She wondered how much fun the night had been for Mike. He'd been a good friend, she thought.

"Sometime after midnight, we got into one of those now-what conversations," Pal said. "You know, 'School's over. Now what are you gonna do?'"

"And?"

"Skiff said he was signing up. Town boy like him, not going to college, what else was there for him? At least the ranch kids have the whole legacy thing going on. Soon as he said that, T-squared got all macho and jumped in. 'Us, too.' And Cody. He'd go along with whatever anybody else was doing."

Lola could see the idea taking hold in beer-soaked brains, images arising of uniforms, guns, regular paychecks, somebody else making all the tough decisions for them. Nobody ever pictured the downside, she thought. But she'd been just as bad, angling for Afghanistan, knowing it was *the* story, without stopping to think about what getting the story entailed. Yet again, she kicked her own memories aside. "How'd you and Mike get sucked into this clusterfuck?"

"Oh, come on." Pal's eyes met hers. "Indian guy's gonna sit there and let the white boys march off to war while he stays home with the women?"

"Right." Lola knew Mike probably would have enlisted anyway. But if he'd signed up later, he might have come back alive—or if not alive, at least dead at the hands of his enemy, rather than his so-called friends. She imagined that Pal had already come to that realization a few thousand times or so since Mike's death. No wonder the woman drank herself to sleep each night. "What's your excuse?"

"I couldn't let Mike go alone." The same sort of simple, naked truth that, months later, had sent Mike flying to Pal's defense against the odds. "Besides, we figured everybody would have forgotten about it the next morning."

"But they hadn't."

"Nope."

They drove over to the recruiting office in Casper together, squashed into Skiff's dad's double-cab pickup, Pal on Mike's lap, all of them red-eyed and in a fair amount of pain, cussing up a storm each time Skiff hit a pothole. "We had to stop twice so's folks could puke," Pal said. "Cody. And Tommy. Lightweights." Her lips thinned in disdain. "We hit a gas station on the edge of town so they could clean themselves up. It probably didn't matter. That recruiter, he must've thought it was Christmas. He couldn't fill out the paperwork fast enough."

Lola could imagine. A half-dozen ranch- and sports-toughened young people, none—not even T-squared, not at that point—with serious brushes with the law, all with good-enough grades, all of them able to pass a pee test despite their clear predilection for overindulging in alcohol. They found themselves in basic training before they knew it, overseas a blink later, plopped down in the midst of a desert country, albeit surrounded while on base by the comforts of suburban America, most of them unavailable in Thirty. "My big adventure to a foreign country and I might as well have been in Casper," Pal said. "Burger King, movie theater, everything."

"What was it like?"

"Hot. Boring. You can only watch so many movies, play so many video games. And the sand got into everything. I'd brush whole handfuls out of my hair every night and the next day it would be back again."

Lola remembered the way she'd double-bagged her laptop and camera and satellite phone in zip-top bags, then wrapped them in an extra shawl and stashed them in the trunk of whatever vehicle they were traveling in that day, only to recover them filmed with dust when she retrieved them at night. She shook sand out of her clothing, her shoes and, on the rare occasions when she had a working shower at her disposal, she rinsed grit from her hair, her ears, the crevices of her knees and elbows. One day she'd walked into a tailor's shop, handed him a few afghanis for the use of his scissors, and chopped her hair down to within an inch of her scalp. She started to say as much to Pal, then remembered why Pal had cut her own hair. She steered the conversation back to the steadying details of the mundane. "What about when you went on patrol? What was that like?"

"Hotter. All that gear. You think you can't stand it for fifteen minutes and the next thing you know, you've been out there two, three hours. More. I never drank so much water in my life as I drank there. And I didn't even drink as much as the guys."

Lola knew that drill, too. "So you wouldn't have to pee."

They shared a knowing grimace. "The real penis envy," said Pal. "Not having to drop your drawers."

Pal's story largely followed the outlines of the texts Mike had sent his friend. The larky early days, the initial combat forays before the brutal realization that when you shot at people, they shot back—and sometimes shot first. The fact that shooting was the least of it. The way they started looking at everyone and everything they encountered. The kid running toward them with a soccer ball—what was in that ball? The dead donkey by the side of the road. Was it bloated with the gases of decomposition? Or did it conceal a bomb? The thrumming tension that translated into increasingly rough hijinks in camp. The normal sarcasm ramping up, turning ugly. Along with the inevitable rejoinder to any protests: "Can't take a joke?" The backslap that slid low, turning into a hand on the butt. An unasked-for adjustment to her flak jacket. Fingers sliding across her breasts. "Oops. What? You think I did that on purpose? Get over yourself. Bitch."

"Are they born with that script?" said Lola.

Pal forced a laugh, a small shattering sound. Her lips trembled. They'd come to the day the group visited the village, Lola realized. Once Pal filed her complaint with the DOD, she was going to have to tell that part of the story over and over again. Lola held up her hand. "You've already told me this next part. How about if I just summarize what I remember you saying, and you tell me if I've got it right. And if I get anything wrong, for God's sake, let me know about that, too. Here goes." She spoke steadily, making notes on her own words as Pal nodded silent agreement, concentrating on her pen moving across the page so as not to see Pal's face.

"That's right," Pal said finally. "You've got it all now." Her voice was steady.

"Thanks. I know it's hard to go over the … incident."

Pal's voice grew stronger still. "Rape. Call it what it is. I'm done hiding from it."

Lola held up her mug of cold coffee in a sort of toast. "How do you feel about using your name?"

"What the hell? In for a penny, in for a pound. In fact, I've got a better idea."

"What's that?"

"All those notes you just took? Can you type them up into a statement for the DOD, too?"

"Sure. And I'll file a copy of the complaint with the story. But just for extra insurance, do you mind if we get the statement notarized? People love shit when it's notarized."

Pal had sounded so certain moments before. Now her voice wobbled anew. "Notarized? In a town the size of Thirty? How long do you think it'll take to get back to Skiff exactly what's in that statement?"

Lola leaned back in her chair. "This is the easy part. You don't have to get it notarized in Thirty."

"Then where?"

Lola waited for Pal to figure it out.

"The reservation!"

"Bingo. And once it's notarized, I'll fax a copy to InDepth."

"Assuming you can find a working fax on the rez. There's one more thing."

Lola looked up. She was pretty sure they'd hit everything on her mental checklist.

"We've got to tell Delbert."

That night, Jemalina demonstrated her prowess at fetch, rolling a ball past a glowering Bub to return it to Margaret. The chicken also fell onto her side and stretched out her neck and feathered feet when ordered to play dead, to loud applause from Delbert, Pal, and Lola. "Maybe she's really dead?" Lola whispered. "Shoot," she said a moment later when Jemalina arose, shook out her feathers, and accepted a bit of bread from Margaret.

Delbert put his hands on the arms of the porch chair and heaved himself upright. "Miss Margaret, you have provided us with a fine evening's entertainment. Thank you. And thanks to your chicken, too. Dolores Wadda will be pleased to know she's earning her keep." He bowed toward Margaret. "Wherever did you learn to do this?"

"YouTube."

"Say what?"

"It's videos. Mommy lets me watch them on her phone."

Lola had a dim memory of Margaret's favorite video, one in which a seven-year-old demonstrated how she'd trained her 4-H chicken. "I can do that," Margaret had said at the time.

"You can't," Lola had retorted. "She's seven. You're five. And you don't have a chicken."

Showed you, Margaret's glance said now.

Pal rose. "Margaret, it's time to sleep. Your mom told me I could put you to bed tonight." The idea was to give Lola time to talk privately to Delbert. Lola walked with him to his car. "Hey." She nudged a front tire with her foot. It sat low and squashed, throwing the car off to one side. "You're working on a flat here."

"Aw, hell." Delbert spat tobacco. He whipped around at Lola's next words, sending the stream wild, splashing across the car door.

"Do you still have Pal's guns?"

"I do. Why?"

"I thought maybe you could bring them up here. Now that she's getting better and all." Lola listened to herself lie and wondered if she had ever fooled anyone in her life. Delbert, however, was still focused on his car.

"Won't be able to get them up to you for a couple of days. This thing will barely get me home. Any chance you can call the garage in town, tell them I'll need a new tire? I'd call them myself but," he rubbed a toe in the dirt, "phone got cut off last month."

In her hurry to cover the embarrassment of his admission, Lola only made things worse. "Don't you have a spare?" Lola knew better before he even answered. He'd probably been driving on his spare for months. This time, she thought before she spoke. "Maybe I'll run down tomorrow and get those guns. Pick up that tire for you, too. Save somebody a trip." She changed the subject before he could question her further as to why she wanted the guns.

"I know you're worried about that tire," she said. "But can you wait here until Pal gets Margaret to sleep? She has something she needs to tell you. And I need to be there when she does."

———————

Pal arranged two of the kitchen chairs so that they faced one another, placing herself in one, Delbert in the other, knees nearly touching. She took his brown, twisted hands in her small white ones. Lola sat across the table, "record" button pushed on her phone, pen in hand.

"I'm going to tell you something hard," Pal said. "Lola here's writing a story about it. She's going to take notes while we're talking. But when I'm done, if you decide you don't want her to write about this part, you can tell her. And she won't. She'll erase everything and we'll put her paper notes in the woodstove. She promised."

"That's right," said Lola. It wasn't how things were usually done. But it was the right way.

The wrinkles in Delbert's face remapped themselves, starting in a smile that mocked Pal's serious tone, moving to puzzlement and then to apprehension. "Hell, girl. Whatever it is, just say it. I got a tire going fast down to the rim. You don't want that wreck of mine stuck in your front yard."

So Pal said it. She talked for a long time. Delbert bent over her hands, clinging to them as if to keep from falling altogether. He took one harsh breath after another. "You're saying—"

He raised his head. "You're saying—"

He dropped Pal's hands, rose, and unkinked his back to the extent that he could, achieving a semblance of military attention. "My grandson, he didn't fall asleep on watch."

"No." The word like a black line of certainty beneath this new information.

"Didn't put everybody else in danger."

"No."

"Died in defense of a fellow soldier."

"Yes."

"That being you."

"Yes."

"Killed by his own countrymen."

"Yes."

"Not a coward."

"Never, Delbert. Not for a minute. Those other guys. They're the cowards."

Delbert launched the separate movements required to turn and face Lola. "You go ahead and write that story. You write it all."

THIRTY-TWO

LOLA'S PHONE RANG AS Delbert's lopsided taillights disappeared over the hill. She didn't have to look at the number to know who it was.

"Hey, Charlie."

She wished she'd forced something resembling warmth into her voice. But the long interview with Pal and then the wrenching conversation with Delbert had left her simultaneously drained and wired, the story buzzing in her head, her fingers itching to type. "Look. It's been a tough day. It might be better if we don't talk tonight."

Charlie cut her off. "I don't care that you had a tough day. Or why. And I don't want to talk. At least, not on the phone anymore. It's too easy for you to avoid me. I'm wrapping up training. The deputy's ready to go solo. I'm handing the weekend shifts over to him and heading down there."

"What? I don't think that's a good idea—"

"I don't, either. But I don't feel as though you've given me much choice."

"Charlie—" She spoke to dead air. "Goddammit."

She turned to go back into the house and nearly ran into Pal. "Who's Charlie?"

"Margaret's father."

Pal blocked the doorway. Behind her, the scent of berries hung heavy in the kitchen's lingering heat. "And?"

"And I don't want to talk about it." Lola paced the kitchen, an old habit, physical activity a prelude to writing. She wasn't ready yet. She'd give herself about another hour of fidgeting before sitting down to work. "Come on. Let's deal with those strawberries." She pushed past Pal and retrieved an old newspaper from the stack by the front door and spread it across the kitchen table, then scrounged in the cupboards for a couple of colanders. She hefted one of the flats from the counter and sat it in front of Pal's chair, and the other in front of hers.

She calculated. If Charlie left first thing in the morning, it would take him at least nine hours to get to Thirty, despite his propensity for miles-gobbling speed. Some years earlier, Montana had abandoned its "reasonable and prudent" speed limit that effectively amounted to no speed limit at all. But Charlie saw no reason to change his ways, especially given his expectation of professional courtesy at traffic stops. Lola decided she could afford to worry about Charlie later. By the time he arrived, the story would be done.

She retrieved a paring knife from a drawer and sat down and plucked a strawberry from the flat, slicing off its top. She tossed the cap onto the newspaper and the berry into the colander and selected another. "This morning," Lola said. "You were ready with that shovel. Didn't you see it was me?"

"No." Pal popped a strawberry in her mouth. "These haven't quite turned, you know. We don't have to use all of them for jam. We can save some just for eating."

"As far as I'm concerned, we don't have to use any for jam. How could you not know it was me?"

"You parked next to the house. I couldn't see your truck from the front door. And I didn't hear you pull up. I'd just stepped out of the shower and gotten my clothes on, when I heard somebody walking across the porch."

Lola took a moment to appreciate the fact that Pal was showering upon rising. "Who'd you think it was?" Even though she knew.

"You know damn well who."

"Do you really think he'd come after you?"

Pal let the question sit there, gave Lola a good long time to think about Mike, sprawled in fatal surprise on the hard earth, blood spurting from the gash in his neck, scarlet as the stains on Lola's fingertips.

"Okay. He would. But he probably won't. He thinks I've got no story. And he's got no way of knowing that you've contacted the DOD. Which you hadn't even done this morning." And yet, Lola thought, Pal had been frightened enough to seize a garden implement. Lola gave serious thought to getting in her truck and heading downhill to Delbert's on the spot, retrieving the guns despite the lateness of the hour. The memory of the silver truck looming in her rearview mirror, and her desperate jouncing flight across the rocky valley floor, welled afresh. She tamped it down. "Here's what I'm going to do," she said. "I'm going to write my story tonight. I'll write it out longhand. We can go to town in the morning. I'll type it into one of the library computers, and send it from there."

Pal cast a dubious glance at the berries. "Then we shouldn't be capping these now. Don't you want to start writing your story?"

Lola shook her head. "I like to wait a little while after I've interviewed people before I start writing. It helps everything come together in my mind. This is the perfect brainless activity."

"But they'll go bad before we can start cooking them."

Which would give her a great excuse to throw them out, Lola thought, even as she acknowledged yet another hopeless instance of wishful thinking, about as productive as her fantasies about a dead or disappeared chicken. "I'll be done with the story by noon. Those berries will hold that long. Besides, you smash them up for jam, right? It's not like they need to be perfect."

Pal's fingers moved over the berries in a blur, caps raining onto the newspaper. "I suppose. How long before your story goes public?"

Lola tried to match her own speed to Pal's, and ended up slicing the berries nearly in half in her haste, throwing away almost as much berry as she saved. "No idea. I've never dealt with these folks before. It'll take them awhile to get the story online. There'll be editing, and probably some lawyering."

"These berries go quicker if you just use your fingers. Like this." Pal slid her nail under a cap and flipped it onto the newspaper, a green speck against Lola's great berried blobs.

Lola tried it. A line of juice ran beneath her nail. Pal was right. It was faster. "By the time the story goes up, Charlie will be here. We don't have anything to worry about from Skiff," she said, as much to reassure herself as Pal.

"Charlie's coming here?"

Lola capped another strawberry. It sailed into the colander, landing with the thud of fruit against fruit. Her colander was barely a quarter full. Berries mounded high in Pal's. Lola looked at the flat. She'd barely made a dent. "Yeah. He's heading out in the morning." She slid her nail into another berry.

"Maybe things are going to be okay on my end," Pal said. "But it sounds as though you've got a whole lot of worry coming your way."

Lola typed her story into the library's computer with hands swollen and sore from capping the berries the night before, her fingertips darkened by strawberry juice that defied efforts to scrub it off. Margaret sat across the room, in a beanbag chair in the children's section, surrounded by every book she could find with a chicken on the cover. Lola glanced through the window. Pal waited outside, with a coffee she'd poured into a double thickness of super-size soda cups. The librarian had let them know in no uncertain terms that the coffee was to remain outside. So Pal stayed with it, and every few minutes Lola rose from her chair and opened the library's front door and leaned out and took a gulp, notching grim satisfaction at the librarian's aggrieved sigh as the scorching heat shoved up against the air conditioning.

Each sip jolted her synapses anew, fueling a fresh burst of typing. Within minutes, her fingers would slow, her eyelids droop, her shoulders slump. Once, she felt hot breath in her ear. "Mommy. Go get more coffee." Once, the librarian. "Ma'am." When, Lola wondered, had she made the transition from miss to ma'am? "We don't allow sleeping in here. Besides, people are only supposed to use the computers for twenty minutes at a time."

"Do you see anybody else in here?" Lola asked. "But look. I'm leaving." She performed another near-stumble toward the door, took another gulp of tepid coffee.

"How much longer?" said Pal. "You know it's freaking hot out here, right?" She had her own supersize cup in her other hand, filled with ice. She rolled it across her forehead.

"Give me some of that." Lola flipped the lid of Pal's cup open without waiting for permission and snagged a couple of reduced ice cubes, dropping one down the front of her shirt and pressing the second to the back of her neck. "Oh, sweet Jesus. That's awful. And good. Just what I needed." The story was taking longer than she expected. She was glad she'd left a very reluctant Bub back at the house.

"Just get your ass back in there and keep typing."

Lola pushed back through the door. "Here I am again," she announced. "Start that twenty-minute timer of yours." But the librarian opted to ignore her for the hour it took before she hit the send key on the story, and printed out Pal's statement. During that hour, Pal went back to the convenience store and returned with a coffee refill. Lola figured she'd probably spend the rest of the day peeing. Maybe, she thought, she should just sleep on the bathroom floor when she got home. Of course, the way she was feeling she could probably sleep in the middle of the street outside the library. She fumbled for her phone, glad she'd thought to save the InDepth.org editor's number on speed dial. She wasn't sure that, at this point, she could have managed to dial the numbers in correct sequence.

"I'm printing it out right now," he said in response to her call.

"I'll fax you a notarized statement in a little bit, too."

"We've got the lawyers standing by. Should be pretty straightforward, given all the documents you're filing with it. Nice job on the photos, too, by the way. Stay close to your phone. I'll probably be checking in all day with questions."

"Of course." No need for him to know she planned to turn the ringer to high and lay beside the phone so she wouldn't sleep through his calls. She emailed herself a copy of the story, deleted the file from the library's computer, and directed a frosty smile toward the librarian. "We're out of your hair now. Thank you. Margaret? Time to put the books away."

People who reshelved books improperly or not at all were among Lola's pet peeves. "I'm sorry," she mouthed silently to the library gods as she stacked Margaret's books and left them on one of the small tables in the children's section. "You've been so good," she said to Margaret on the way out. "We just have one more stop to make." Although, Lola thought, it was likely to be a lengthy stop, given the fact that they'd hit the reservation offices right about the time people were taking their lunch breaks. She wondered if she could possibly drink even more coffee, then reminded herself that, at least for this brief moment, Margaret should get her undivided attention. "You deserve something special for how good you've been the past few days while Mommy was working."

"Mommy's always working," Margaret observed, larding her request with guilt before she pressed her advantage. "Pop? Ice cream?"

"Only if you can eat it or drink it in the car," Lola said, too exhausted to object. "Otherwise, I'm going to embarrass you and Pal by falling asleep in the ice cream shop. Speaking of whom—where is she?"

She and Margaret stood in the shade of the library's awning where, moments before, Pal had perched upon the library's wide outer windowsill, twin cups of coffee and ice in hand. The cups remained, sweating circles onto the brick façade. But Pal was gone.

Lola looked up and down the street. No Pal. A large silver pickup, side defiantly dented, rolled toward them, the driver's hand raised in mocking greeting as the truck passed.

THIRTY-THREE

"Is he gone?"

The whisper hovered on the wind's exhalation.

Lola spun around. No one. "Where are you?"

"The alley."

Lola checked the street. The truck was gone. She and Margaret hastened around the library's corner and found Pal pressed into a side doorway, face blank, eyes dead. Her lips barely moved as she spoke. "He already made one pass. He knows."

Lola checked the street yet again. Still empty, but for her own vehicle parked at the curb. Not for the first time, Lola rued its look-at-me red paint job. She tried to infuse her voice with a certainty she in no way felt. "Doubtful. He probably saw my truck, and drove back around to check things out. He's gone now. You can come out."

Pal flattened herself against the door. "Can't."

Lola looked to Margaret. The girl moved to Pal's side and took her hand. Lola took the other. "Yes, you can," Margaret said. She tugged at Pal's hand. Pal didn't move. "You come now. We're going to—" she shot a glance at Lola—"get some ice cream and then we're going to the rez and then we're going home. Mommy's going to take a nap. You can, too. I'll be good. I'll stay right in the room with you so you don't have to worry."

Pal's feet moved, slow and jerky, as though separate from her body. Lola and Margaret guided her to the truck.

At the ice cream parlor, Pal held the cone before her lips, eating it with those same automatic movements, but finishing it nonetheless.

At the reservation, she walked without assistance behind Lola and Margaret into the Eastern Shoshone tribal headquarters and explained in coherent sentences to the one person who miraculously had opted out of her lunch break that they were doing some business for Delbert St. Clair, and could they please use the fax? Which, in further evidence of the existence of miracles, was working.

And at home, Pal shook off Margaret's repeated suggestion that she lie down and instead arranged a pillow and blanket for Lola on the bathroom floor and positioned Lola's phone by her head and herself outside the door. A belated thought wriggled through the murk in Lola's brain. She'd meant to stop by Delbert's and pick up the guns. But she'd driven right past his house, slumped over the steering wheel, barely-open eyes concentrating on the last couple of miles of road. "Damn," she murmured. Then, to Pal, "Shovel?"

"What's that?"

It was too late. She was asleep.

———

When Lola awoke for good—she'd peed exactly as much as she expected, and she also had vague memories of a couple of befogged conversations with the editor—the air was redolent of strawberries.

She put her hands on the side of the tub and pulled herself to her knees, then grabbed for a towel rack and pulled harder, until she was standing. She made the mistake of looking in the mirror. She bent over the sink, turning on the cold water and splashing it on her face until it was numb. She turned off the water and toweled her face, making sure to avoid a second encounter with her reflection.

She followed her nose to the kitchen. There, Margaret stood on a chair at the counter, wielding a potato masher against a bowlful of strawberries with such force that her face, hands, and clothing— along with a good portion of the surrounding real estate—were splattered with red juice. Pal stood beside her, methodically smashing berries with somewhat less force but more effectiveness, the contents of her own bowl a pulpy mass.

"That looks disgusting." Lola's voice came out in a croak.

"*You* look disgusting. Don't you have a comb? And some clean clothes? You know, the last time I checked, there was a shower in that bathroom."

Lola thought Pal was enjoying their role reversal just a little too much. Bub arose from a spot in the far corner, and circled the room to get to Lola, sticking close to the walls on the way. Lola saw movement under the table and realized the cause. Jemalina had settled herself there, on a nest of shredded, scarlet-blotched newspaper.

"Good Christ. What's that chicken doing in here?"

"Quarter, Mommy. She was lonely. Besides, she likes strawberries and Bub doesn't."

"She can't eat strawberries outside? Oh, never mind." A few hours of shut-eye, Lola thought, and the entire order of the universe had been upended. "Is there coffee?"

"No more coffee for you. How about some juice? And I thought we might go for a run later." Pal elbowed Margaret. Giggling ensued.

Lola hadn't thought Pal capable of laughter, let alone something as frivolous as a giggle. She brushed past the treasonous pair and made the coffee herself, holding a mug under the stream as it began to flow from the coffeemaker, not substituting the pot until the mug was full.

"Ahhhhh." Her eyelids lifted. Joints became limber. Her ears, attuned moments earlier only to the gurgle of the coffeemaker, picked up a tinkling sound, simultaneously glassy and metallic. "What's that noise?"

Pal lifted a wooden spoon from her bowl, splattering the counter with red, and pointed with it toward the stove. Two outsize cast-iron pots sat there, one covered, its lid jiggling as puffs of steam escaped. "We're sterilizing the jam jars. If you must poison yourself with more coffee, finish it fast. We're about ready to start cooking down the berries. You can do that. All you have to do is stir. Even you won't be able to ruin it."

More giggling.

A basketful of intact strawberries sat on the counter. They'd saved the best for eating. Lola picked one up and started to run her thumbnail under the cap. Then she remembered how long it had taken her to scrub the worst of the stains from her fingers. She found the paring knife in a drawer and sliced off the cap and popped the berry in her mouth, savoring the burst of flavor against her palate. She put down the knife and lifted her coffee mug.

"What do I have to do?" she said around the strawberry.

"Here." Pal handed Lola the bowl of mashed berries and the spoon. "Put these in that pot. Add Margaret's. Dump in that sack of sugar. Stir until it dissolves. Squeeze those lemons over the pot. Make sure the seeds don't get in. Heat it until it simmers. Stir it up good so it doesn't burn. Keep stirring. That's it. Think you can handle that?"

Lola tilted the bowl over a pot that could have held all of Jemalina and a couple of her friends besides, something Lola thought would have been a better use for the pot. The strawberries slid out of the bowl with a sucking sound. Some missed the pot and slopped onto the floor. Lola looked askance at the sugar. "Do we need that much?"

"It's half what my mom used. Hey. Keep stirring or you'll ruin it. I'm going to take Margaret and clean both of us up."

Lola dragged the spoon through the mashed berries, pinwheeling the white lines of sugar deeper with every swipe. Bubbles rose to the surface and broke noisily, a backbeat to the clinking jars. The mass of berries was surprisingly heavy. Her arm ached. She heard water running in the bathroom. Then a cracking sound—once, twice, three times, the old danger signal. Bub lifted his head. The chicken clucked. Lola glanced through the window. Nothing. She knew those cracks as gunfire. If she'd been in Afghanistan, she'd have assumed ill intent, bandits at best, insurgents a more likely and far more dangerous scenario. Here, it was probably somebody plinking at prairie dogs. Afghanistan had been years ago, she reminded herself. Time she got over it. Still, she listened hard. Nothing, other than the shower, still running. She picked up the paring knife and, still stirring, decapitated another berry one-handed, sucking the sweetness from it as she checked the window again. A line of dust hung above the ridgeline, signaling an oncoming car. Her heart jumped. She glanced at the clock. Two in the afternoon. Early for Charlie, but not too. She forgot to stir. She forgot that she'd resented his proposal. Forgot that they were in the midst of a fight. Forgot everything other than the fact that he was finally here, that for the first time in days, everything wasn't going to be on her. She left the spoon in the bubbling strawberries and crossed the kitchen in giant steps. She flung open the door, arms raised to wrap around him, face lifted for his kiss.

"Well. This is quite the welcome."

A foot wedged into the doorway. Lola looked first at the unfamiliar cowboy boot, then the face. Skiff Loughry grinned down at her, even happier to see her than she'd been to see Charlie.

THIRTY-FOUR

FEAR ASCENDED THE MUSCLES in her calves, her thighs, her back. Bub's hackles stood up like saw blades.

For each step Lola took back, Skiff took one forward, a halting dance of retreat and pursuit. He closed the door behind him. "Where is she?"

Lola listened. The preserves simmered thickly, bubbles plopping and bursting. The glass jars shivered against one another in their boiling bath. But no water running, not any more. Nor voices.

"Out," Lola said. "Probably on one of her runs. You should go look for her."

"Nice try." Why was he still smiling? "I just drove up that road. I didn't see her anywhere."

Lola's chest heaved with the effort of breathing. Margaret, she thought. Margaret. She tried to remember what Skiff had just said. "Sometimes she runs the ridge. You should go up there."

"I'm not going anywhere. Guess what?"

Lola wet her lips and took a half-step sideways. If she could get past him. Get outside. Maybe they were out there. Maybe Pal had seen Skiff drive up. Maybe she'd helped Margaret crawl out the window. They could get in Lola's truck. Lola had out-driven Skiff once. Pal could, too.

"What?" she said. "Why do you want to see her, anyway?" Maybe, Lola thought, she was overreacting. Maybe this was a friendly visit.

"I've got a friend in town goes out with a girl on the rez." Skiff looked as though he'd smelled something bad. "What can I say? No accounting for taste."

Something flickered behind him. Motion in the hallway. So Pal and Margaret—oh, God, Margaret—were still in the house. Lola raised her voice to a half-decibel below shouting.

"Skiff, why should I give a shit about your friend? Why, Skiff?" Putting a little English on his name. Afraid to chance another glance at the hallway, but hoping they'd heard.

"Because, *Lola*." A mocking imitation. "My friend's girlfriend works in the tribal offices. Says she faxed something for a couple a whitegirls. Says it was pretty interesting."

Another motion, this time at her feet. Jemalina streaked past, beady eyes intent upon Skiff's feet, only to find her beak bouncing off his cowboy boot. She let out a surprised cluck and regrouped. "What the hell was that?" Skiff said. "What's that thing doing in the house?"

"I ask myself that every day," Lola said. Maybe she could stall him with humor. Even get him to leave. "I throw her outside. She sneaks back in." She forced a smile, all teeth and no eyes. Skiff laughed. She felt Bub relax a millimeter against her leg. Jemalina hunched, flapped her wings, and launched another attack. Skiff stepped to one side, reached down, grabbed Jemalina and snapped her neck with a single twist. He flung Jemalina's body across the room.

"No!" Lola shouted. She'd hated the chicken and its last act had been to defend her. She took a step toward Skiff, intending to— what, exactly? She didn't have to decide. Bub was across the room in two long bounds, the second launching him airborne, the whomp of his body against Skiff's sending them both to the floor, attached by dint of Bub's teeth sunk to bone in Skiff's thigh. Bub snarled and Skiff hollered, and then Skiff's hands were around Bub's neck. Lola leapt into the fray, dropping to the floor beside Skiff and pummeling his face with her fists. He let go of Bub, which was good. But he turned to Lola, which was very, very bad, she decided as he locked his hand around her wrist and hauled her upward. He was exactly as strong as he appeared, jerking her around in front of him with no more effort than if she'd been an empty flour sack. Bub picked himself up off the floor, arching his back and hacking. He lifted his head and bared his teeth again, hindquarters bunching in preparation to spring. Skiff dropped Lola's wrist and drew back his leg. His booted kick landed squarely on Bub's chest. Bub yelped once and fell limp.

Lola whirled and leapt for the door, grabbing the paring knife from the counter as she went. Skiff moved fast to cut her off. He stepped squarely in the wet slickness of spilled berries and careened toward her, arms cartwheeling, grabbing at her for balance, catching at the front of her T-shirt, tearing it to the waist. She flung up her arms to push him away, forgetting that she still held the knife. The thin blade caught him under the chin, sliding through the soft part of his throat. He bellowed with anger and drew an arm back and landed a fist so hard against the side of her face that she crumpled, dropping the knife and catching at the counter for balance. She bent over it, things blurring black.

Skiff's harsh breathing filled the kitchen. Lola moved her head slowly from side to side to clear it, and pushed herself upright and turned to face him, her back against the stove. She felt the heat of the pots, bubbling away behind her. Skiff pressed a hand beneath his chin. He lowered it. Blood ran from the cut.

"Look what you did," he said. "Look what you did."

"Like you did to Mike," she heard herself say.

"No," he said. "Not like that at all."

"You're right," she said. It hurt to talk. "This was an accident."

He put his hand to his chin again. Blood oozed through his fingers and dripped onto his shirt.

She looked away. Her gaze fell upon the knife. He saw her looking at it, and kicked it. It spun across the floor toward the door. She lunged away from him, but he was faster, catching her by her arm and jerking her around so hard that she lost her footing. He let go of her and she slammed against the floor.

"Stop," he said. "Don't you know when you're done?"

She pushed herself up on all fours. He put his boot to the small of her back and shoved her back down. She lay there, face in the spilled berries, arms reaching for the door.

"Stop," he said again.

She pulled her arms back and locked her hands behind her head, her elbows covering her ears so she couldn't hear him. He was saying things and she shook her head. No. Whatever it was, no.

His booted toe nudged her. "Turn over."

She shook her head, and he drew his foot back as if to kick her.

"No," she whimpered.

He laughed. "Then turn over."

She pushed herself up on her hands, and rolled into a semblance of a sitting position, hugging her knees to her chest. Her nose ran. She tasted blood in the back of her mouth.

He stood above her, straddling her. "You hurt me," he said.

Her head throbbed.

"Do you have any idea how much trouble you're in?"

She leaned over and spit blood. Then she raised her face to him. "I don't care," she said.

"Well, you should," he said. He held out his hand. "Here. Get up."

She let him pull her up, then dropped his hand and backed away from him, leaning against the stove for support. The pots burned her back.

He looked her up and down. She wished she'd worn a bra. "You stay right there," he said. "I'm going to check the house. Then I'm coming back for you. Don't even think about moving. You know what I'm capable of." He turned away, toward the hall. There was no mistaking his walk for anything but a swagger, Lola thought, cocksure in his certainty that she was too cowed to disobey.

Lola felt blindly behind her, reaching for something, anything. The pots. She turned. Her fingers closed around the scalding handles of the kettle holding the jars. Muscles tore in her back as she hoisted the heavy pot in a single motion. Holding it high, she swung toward Skiff, who turned at the sound of her escaping scream. She opened her hands wide and the combined weight of the pot and the force of her spin sent it flying from her hands and into his face. The iron rim caught his brow. It tilted, splashing boiling water across his face and down his chest and over his hands as he raised them to protect himself. Lola screamed again as Skiff Loughry crumpled to the floor in a mess of hissing water and breaking glass and the faint fizz of dissolving flesh.

"Hey. Lola. Hey."

Lola summoned a superhuman effort and turned her head toward the door. It opened a crack. Pal stood outside. Lola raised her hands, heavy as weights, in a warning.

"Don't let Margaret in here." Lola would not have thought herself capable of a full sentence, words as much of an effort as action, but there it was.

"Then come out here. Can you?"

Lola took a step. "I guess so." She felt something beneath her foot. She raised it and saw the knife. She picked it up and slid it into her back pocket. She reached the door.

"Fix your shirt," Pal whispered.

Lola pulled the edges of her shirt together and slipped out onto the porch. Margaret shrieked.

"It's your face," Pal said. "It looks like blood."

"It is," Lola whispered.

Pal ran a finger across the mess on Lola's face and held it before her. Blood mingled with a brighter, stickier mess. "Look, Margaret. It's just strawberries." She licked it. "Guess we're blood sisters now," she whispered to Lola. She held her finger out to Margaret. "Taste."

Margaret shook her head, but swallowed her cries. She let Pal place her shaking body in Lola's outstretched arms. Maybe, Lola thought, as she held her daughter against her, feeling every place where Margaret's body touched hers, kissing her again and again, there had been another moment in her life that matched this reunion with her daughter, both of them alive and safe. She couldn't think of one.

Behind her, Pal's words tumbled disjointed. "I'm so sorry. So sorry. I left you in there alone. But Margaret—"

Lola stopped her. "You did right."

"I wanted to get the truck and go for help. But I was afraid if he heard me leaving, he'd—" Pal left unsaid whatever Skiff might have done. "Margaret. She was so good." Pal's voice broke. In the last twenty-four hours, she'd told Lola the worst thing that had happened to her, all in a droning monotone. Lola turned to face her.

Pal's teeth were sunk in her lip, blood welling but the tears successfully held back.

"I be'd quiet," Margaret said. "Bad man gone?"

"He's not gone," Lola said. "But he's not going to hurt us."

Margaret twitched experimentally. "Get down?"

If she put it in the form of a question rather than her usual demand, she wasn't ready, Lola thought. Besides, she herself wasn't ready to let go. "Not yet."

Pal moved to where Margaret couldn't see her face and mouthed a question. "Is he—?"

Lola shook her head. Pal looked toward the door, but stayed put. They were going to have to go back in there, Lola thought. Or, at least one of them was. They couldn't leave Margaret alone on the porch. A halloo interrupted her thoughts. Margaret, looking over Lola's shoulder toward the road, saw the source first. "Delbert!" she squealed. Her wriggling turned assertive. Lola opened her arms. Margaret flew down the porch steps and toward the man hitching up the road on his bad leg, a shotgun in his hand. He held the gun far to one side as Margaret reached him.

"Saw that big outfit of his go by," Delbert gasped as he approached, his face pale with pain. He pointed with his chin toward Skiff's silver truck, hard by the side of the house. "Couldn't call. Tire's flat. Got up here as fast as I could on foot. Shot three times, hoping you'd get the message."

"I heard," Lola said. But she'd ignored her own instincts when she'd heard the three shots sometimes used as a distress call. "I'm sorry," she said, apologizing to herself as much as Delbert. Apologizing to all of them.

Delbert looked at Lola holding the remains of her clothing together, and unbuttoned his blue work shirt. "Here." Lola turned her back and fastened it around her. Margaret took Delbert's hand, leading him toward the porch. "Mommy? Where's Bub? Where's Jemalina?"

Lola pointed toward the kitchen with an exaggerated turn so that Margaret wouldn't see her face. "In there. In fact, if you can stay here with Delbert, I'll go in and check on them right now."

Pal moved to her side. "I'll go with you."

Lola thought Pal had already had one confrontation with Skiff too many. "You don't have to," she said.

Pal set her jaw and Lola saw the steel in her. "Yes," she said. "I do."

THIRTY-FIVE

"BRACE YOURSELF," LOLA WHISPERED as they slipped through the door. No warning would have sufficed. She pressed her fist against lips to stifle her own reaction to what was left of the man on the floor.

Skiff lay on his back, atop the shards of jars. Blood pooled beneath him. Lola looked away and looked back, at the bits of glass embedded in his skin where the broken jars had found purchase, at the nubs of eyelids, at the raw meat that had been his face, at the splinters of bone protruding from the gash on his brow. Strawberries and burnt sugar, cut by the coppery tang of blood, scented the kitchen. Pal tiptoed around Skiff and turned the burners off, never taking her eyes away from the man on the floor. His gaze rolled from her to Lola and back again. Blisters bubbled yellow across his lips.

Lola crept to his side and forced herself to take one of his hands, thinking to pull him away from the broken glass. The slippery, softened skin slid from his hand like a glove. Skiff's mouth stretched in a guttural scream. Lola jumped back. She wiped her hand on her jeans. Bits of skin clung to the denim. The moaning took on a dual quality.

"There." Pal pointed. A few feet away, Bub lifted his head. It fell back again.

"Bub!" Lola knelt beside the dog. "Oh, Bub." She slid her hands beneath him and rose with infinite slowness. Despite her care, he trembled in her arms, whimpering. She moved to stand beside Pal, giving Skiff a wide berth. "I guess we've got to call 9-1-1." But she didn't move. She tried to imagine the call: "A man attacked me and I nearly killed him."

But no one had seen the attack. Skiff—if he survived, and he probably would, given that his injuries were above his chest, where his heart appeared to be damnably chugging along—would surely tell a very different story. *Story.* A wriggle of hope in her chest. Her story, with its account of the rape and Skiff's subsequent threats, would be online soon, if it weren't already. That would help. But as Lola knew from too many years of covering the legal system, the person with the worst injuries got the most sympathy. Pal's experience—assuming anyone believed her, and rape victims were the least believed victims on the planet—would pale beside Skiff's grievous wounds. As for Lola, all she had to show was a bloody nose, along with some bruises and a torn shirt. The deepest wounds, the ones to her psyche, remained invisible.

Words bubbled up in her brain, breaking the surface like the strawberries slowly quieting in the pot. *Murder.* No. Skiff was still alive, albeit only just. If he survived, *aggravated assault.* Nowhere near as bad as murder, but still a felony, enough to put her in prison until Margaret was a teenager. *Self-defense.* But no suspicious, hard-eyed juror would ever fall for that one, not when there were no witnesses and a guy's eyelids had melted away.

"Fuck oh fucking fuck. What the fuck do we do now?" Later, she could never remember whether the words had been hers or Pal's. The answer, though. That came from Pal. Who reached behind Lola, slid the forgotten paring knife from the back pocket of her jeans, and said, "You take the dog and go on back outside. I'll handle this."

———————

Lola took her phone from her pocket and looked at it a long time. In the end, Delbert slid it from her limp hand and called 9-1-1, requesting both sheriff and tribal police. The ranch was, after all, within the reservation boundaries, something that would complicate things, given that the FBI also was summoned whenever there was a felony on the rez. "An ambulance, too," Delbert said. "We got a man bad hurt here." He paused. Lola could see him considering the implications of his words. "And a couple of women in pretty bad shape. They fought him off. There's a child, too, scared out of her wits."

Lola slumped on the porch steps and awaited the impending swarm of activity. There'd be cop cars from all the agencies, lights twirling red and blue in the monochrome landscape. The ambulance. Even a fire truck, dispatched with each ambulance call, never mind that smoke was nowhere on the horizon. "A regular circus," Lola murmured, one hand sunk deep in Bub's fur, kneading his shoulders. Margaret sat beside her, one hand clutching Lola's sleeve, the other stroking Bub's head.

The dog would be fine, Delbert had assured her. "Got the wind knocked out of him. Maybe a broken rib or two. He'll take it easy for a few days. Sleep a lot. That'll let him heal."

Tears wet Margaret's face. "Jemalina won't heal."

"No, honey. But she was very brave. She tried to save me, just like Bub." Lola allowed herself the lie. Jemalina had been doing just what she always did, funneling her natural pure meanness into one last dash to destroy someone's feet. The unthinkable came out of Lola's mouth. "When we get home, we can get another chicken. Maybe some baby chicks. Would you like that?"

Margaret lit up. Delbert snorted.

Pal had been in the house a long time. "I'll handle this," she'd said. Knife in hand. Lola could think of only a single interpretation. Well. Skiff had it coming. What had he said to Pal at the parade? "Karma's a bitch."

Damn straight, Lola said to herself. How bad would it be if, when the various law enforcement agents finally trooped into the kitchen, Skiff had expired? Justice, albeit unofficial, would have been served. Lola's gut tugged at her, a reminder that she knew better. In their twisted way, Skiff and the others had thought they were serving justice on Pal, and on Mike, too, that night in Afghanistan. They'd concocted a palatable story that everyone was happy to believe. *This is different*, she told herself. The mantra of rationalizers. Her gut knotted tighter.

She continued her silent argument with herself. There was her story. She'd have to update it now, with the attack, and likely with Skiff's unfortunate death. Lola had never knowingly written a false word in her life, had never understood the impulses that drove plagiarizers and outright fictionalizers. Now it dangled before her, beckoning. It wouldn't be active fiction to write that Skiff had died of his wounds, said the beguiling whisper within. More like one of those sins of omissions the nuns of her childhood were always harping on. She could write, truthfully, that Skiff was alive when she left the kitchen. And that when authorities arrived, he was dead. So unfortunate. End of story.

Come closer, the scenario whispered, crooking a seductive finger. Because there was Pal. The truth would see her tried for murder. After everything she'd been through. Hadn't she suffered enough? Lola started as the words ran through her mind. The very words used by Dave Sparks, by the high school principal, by Skiff himself. *Let's just let this lie. Everybody's suffered enough.*

The wriggle turned into full-blown nausea. She gagged and pushed herself to her feet. She had to stop Pal, if it wasn't already too late.

"Mommy?"

"Lola?"

Two sets of worried eyes turned upon her. Bub whined and tried to push himself up.

"No, Bub. Delbert, Margaret, it's okay. I just need to talk to Pal. You wait here."

Before they could catch her, she was through the kitchen door, closing it behind her in a way that warned Delbert not to follow.

————

Pal stood over Skiff, the knife dangling in her hand. He was very still, eyes staring ceilingward, unmoving.

Lola held her breath. Forced it out, along with the same question Pal had put to her earlier. "Is he—?"

Pal nudged Skiff with her foot. A creaking sound emerged from those spongy lips. "Nah."

Lola found herself on the floor, butt planted firmly on the linoleum, hands braced on either side of her. "I thought you would—" Unable to finish a sentence despite herself.

"Yeah. I thought so, too." Pal poked at Skiff again with her toe. The creaking continued. "For sure, I wanted to." She lifted the knife to her own throat. "Just like he did to Mike."

"Careful!" Lola came partway up from the floor. Pal dropped her hand and Lola sank back.

"It would have been so easy. All this broken glass. Hell. I don't even need the knife. Nobody would have thought twice."

"True." Probably. Although, among all the law enforcement officers due to arrive momentarily, inevitably there would be one like Charlie. Unconvinced. Dogged. Worrying the inconsistences like a dog on a bone. Hating the *unfair* of the results, but unable to stop himself from pursuing the truth.

"You're going to go through hell." Lola couldn't help but point out the obvious. "I've seen rape trials. They're bad enough when the guy's a stranger. But if the two people know each other? You have no idea. I once saw a lawyer lay a cardboard cutout of a woman down on the floor and climb on top of her, trying to show the jury things couldn't have happened the way she said."

"Good God."

"I was so shocked I couldn't tear my eyes away from him to see how the jury took it. He was a little guy, round as he was tall. He had a hard time getting up."

Pal's almost-smile flickered. "It's not going to go much better for you. You're involved in your own story now. Isn't that against the rules? Seems to me I remember Jan talking about stuff like this."

Lola felt ridiculous, sitting there on the floor, but couldn't seem to get up. "It's problematic, that's for sure." She stretched out her leg and gave Skiff a nudge, and tried to feel ashamed of the jolt of satisfaction when he emitted a cry. "Why?"

"Why what?"

"Why didn't you?" Lola drew her finger across her throat and looked at Skiff.

Pal shrugged. "It would have been one more lie. After so many. Mike didn't take the coward's way out. How could I?" She chewed at the raw spot on her lower lip. "Not that I trust the justice system to get things right. Especially not the military justice system, not when it comes to this stuff. I don't know. Maybe I'm crazy. Hey, Skiff." This

266

time, she delivered a real kick. He obliged with a real scream. Lola scrambled to her feet.

"Roll those big bare eyeballs of yours over this way. Got something I want you to see."

Skiff began to shake all over, the raw exposed flesh of his face quivering.

"Pal, he's going into shock. We should get a blanket."

Pal's voice was as unyielding as her grip on Lola. "No. You stay here. I want you to see this, too." She dropped Lola's arm and raised the knife.

"Jesus, Pal." Lola grabbed at it.

Pal was too fast. The knife flashed, coming down across her own arm, carving across an exuberant bloody X across the final single scar there. "That one's for you, Skiff. I'm done with all of you now." She threw the knife down beside his body, and left the kitchen, Lola close behind her.

Pal stopped in the doorway and lifted her hand to her forehead, heedless of the blood coursing along her arm. Lola followed her gaze. A line of dust rose above the road. "That'll be the police," she said.

The vehicle topped the rise, alone, not the cavalcade she'd expected. Lola narrowed her eyes. Margaret figured it out before she did, on her feet in a flash, skimming down the road toward the approaching car, sounding the first note of joy Lola had heard in a very long time.

"Daddy!"

THIRTY-SIX

MARGARET WAS IN CHARLIE's arms as soon as he opened the door, the horn beeping as she wriggled onto his lap. They sat in the car a long time. Lola could hear them talking, Margaret's high, excited tones, Charlie's low rumble, but couldn't make out the words. She waited on the porch with Delbert and Pal, each shooting sidelong glances her way.

Charlie finally detached himself from the seat belt, if not from Margaret's embrace. He approached slowly. Margaret still exuded joy, but Charlie's face telegraphed low expectations. Lola tried to see the group on the porch as he saw them—an elderly, shirtless Indian man. A near-bald young white woman, her forearm bare and bleeding. And Lola herself. She touched her hand to her face. Gooey bits of strawberry still lingered around her hairline. Delbert's shirt hung nearly to her knees, but failed to cover the streaks of strawberry and fast-browning blood on her jeans.

"Hey, Charlie." Lola dropped introductions into the silence. Charlie touched his fingertips to Delbert's, then switched to a whiteman-style grip for Pal. He turned back to Lola. "Anybody going to offer me some coffee?" In a different tone, it could have been a routine question. The way Charlie said it, it was a dare. A gust of wind kicked up some grit and carried the faint rise and fall of sirens toward them.

"Not a good idea," said Lola. She moved so that she was between him and the front door. He handed Margaret off to Pal and brushed past her. Pal thrust Margaret into Delbert's arms and followed them both inside. Charlie stopped and stood unmoving as the sound of sirens grew and grew, filling the air around them, drowning out even the anguished moans from the man on the floor.

―――――――

In the end, Lola never had to explain anything directly to Charlie. He introduced himself as a sheriff from Montana, mumbling the part about his relationship to Lola, and that was all it took for the ranks of tribal cops and deputies and EMTs and a late-arriving FBI man to bring him into their circle as they questioned Lola and Pal. Delbert was allowed to stand off to one side with Margaret and Bub, as well as Dave Sparks, who had followed entirely too closely the parade of cruisers. Why oh why, Lola wondered, had Dave picked this particular moment to get aggressive about journalism? She belatedly decided she'd liked him better as a slacker. Dave pointed his Leica at her. She forced herself to stare into the lens. She would never, she vowed, be that person ducking away from the camera, hand up to shield her face.

"Lola," he called. "What's going on here?"

Charlie, in full sheriff mode, stepped between them. "Who are you? You know this is a crime scene, right?"

Dave introduced himself. Lola saw Charlie register the name, knew full well he had the kind of steel-trap mind that would have held on to Margaret's days-old mention of "Mommy's friend, Dave," as well as Lola's own dismissive postscript that Dave was "just another reporter."

"No interviews, not now. They're still in the middle of their investigation. And no pictures of the child," Charlie warned. "She wasn't involved." Margaret flapped a wan hand at Dave. Charlie turned back to Lola. Earlier, he'd looked as angry as she'd ever seen him. Now she realized that was just a warm-up.

"Charlie—" she started. Something behind her snagged his attention. They were bringing Skiff out of the house. Lola and Charlie moved toward Margaret to shield her from the sight. Charlie got there first. His look warned Lola away. Dave elbowed past her, shooting rapid-fire photos as the EMTs maneuvered the gurney down the steps. The ambulance brapped its siren, warming up for its screaming mission to Casper where, no doubt, Skiff would be loaded onto a med-evac flight bound for Seattle in a déjà-vu of the trip made by Patrick Sounding Sides after his beating by T-Squared. A tribal cop climbed into the ambulance with the EMTs, on the off chance that Skiff might summon something resembling speech on the way. A bit of luck, that, Lola thought. No matter what Skiff said, if he said anything at all, the tribal cop soon would know Pal's version of events, starting with the allegation that Skiff had killed one of the tribe's own months earlier in Afghanistan.

"All the background you need is right here," Lola had told the cops. "Look. I wrote a story about it." She worked at her phone, typing in the address for InDepth.org. Her story popped up on the screen, photos of Pal and Skiff prominent amid the initial lines of type.

"Let me have that." A cop reached for the phone.

"Why don't I just email it to you? Then you can forward it to all of these folks. It's got documents, everything."

Charlie, who'd listened without speaking, spoke up now. "You wrote a story? On your furlough?"

"Not for the *Express*. For a website." Lola felt another demerit land in the column against her.

"Come on, Margaret." Charlie took his daughter's hand. "Let's wait in the car. I've heard enough here."

Enough, Lola thought, to know she'd deceived him about her reasons for staying in Wyoming. To know she'd also lied about working instead of being on vacation. Both of those things were, possibly, forgivable. But he'd seen the unmistakable evidence sprawled on the kitchen floor that she'd put his child at risk, not just forgetting-to-hold-hands-across-the-street peril, but true, mortal danger.

Which meant that, as uncomfortable as the questioning from the cops, it was nothing compared to what she was going to face later from Charlie.

———

Later came too soon. The evidence technicians packed up their gear and collected their evidence bags. Officers and deputies folded notebooks and put them away. They pressed business cards into her hand. "We'll be in touch." A promise, not a courtesy. "Don't go anywhere for a couple of days. Not without checking in with us."

Charlie waited beside his car until the last left. "I'm taking Margaret to town," he said. "Bub, too. We'll stay in a motel. The sooner we get her away from here, the better." He whistled to Bub. The dog hesitated and looked at Lola. She nodded permission and he limped behind Charlie, glancing over his shoulder every few steps, waiting for her to follow.

What about me? Lola couldn't figure out a way to ask without sounding plaintive. She liked dealing from a position of strength. Forget asking, she thought. Thirty only had two motels. She could find him easily enough. "I'll be down later," she called. Not giving him a choice about it. Besides, she needed time to update the editors at InDepth.org about the story. "We'll talk then."

Charlie started the car and rolled down the window. He started to say something, but bit it short. They'd always tried not to fight in front of Margaret. "Suit yourself," he said.

Lola allowed herself a moment of self-pity, bitter and satisfying in its predictability. She decided it was a good thing his proposal was likely off the table. As uncomfortable as it had made her, that sort of discomfort paled beside the task of explaining to him how a story, even for a second, had trumped Margaret's safety.

"Speaking of the story," she reminded herself. She couldn't put it off any longer. She dialed the number for InDepth.org. The editor answered on the first ring. "Lola!" She held the phone away from her ear as he enthused about the response to the story, the comments and the web traffic it had engendered. "It's blowing up," he said. "Great job."

She waited for his enthusiasm to wind down. Finally, silence. She took a breath and lobbed the grenade. "There's been a development."

———————

By the time she clicked off her phone, the Winds sat in black judgment against a violet sky. The air wrapped her in gooseflesh. Pal waited on the porch steps, a quilt folded around her shoulders, another in her lap. Lola dropped beside her and took the second quilt, welcoming its embrace. The porch light threw a pale circle onto the dirt and sage. Something stirred at its edge, low and sinuous. A snake curved its way toward the warmth beneath the house. Pal leaned down and picked up a handful of pebbles and tossed them. The snake coiled tight and shook its rattles. "Get out of here," Pal said. "Where's that chicken when we need her?"

"Want me to get the shovel?" Lola made an offer she wasn't sure she could fulfill. Her weariness ran bone-deep. She remembered when she'd tried to explain Pal's PTSD to Margaret. "It hurts her soul." Her own soul felt as though it had been battered into something she barely recognized. She'd expected Pal to kill Skiff, and had done nothing to stop her. And if Pal had killed him, Lola had been prepared to leave that detail out of the story. The latter had been unthinkable—except that, of course, she'd thought it anyway.

At least the story was out of her hands, safe from her worst impulses. The editor at InDepth had responded exactly as he should have when she'd told him of the day's events. First, he'd cursed. Then he'd cursed some more. "We'll put somebody else on it. You can't be your own subject. But you already know that."

"Of course I do," she'd said. "Of course." Needing to repeat it until she steered herself back on course. The effort drained her. The shovel, propped against a wall not five feet behind her, might as well have been miles away. The snake lowered its head and slid a foot closer to the house. Lola bent and felt about on the ground until she found a stone about the size of a walnut. She'd been a pitcher on her college softball team. The stone had real velocity behind it when it struck the snake's body. This time, it didn't bother with the coil-and-hiss routine, but slithered off into the sagebrush with a flick of its too-long tail.

"Cool." It was the first time Lola had heard anything resembling appreciation in Pal's voice.

"Not really." Years earlier, Lola had turned that same skill on a man who was trying to kill her. The object she'd thrown had hit his horse. Both man and horse had died in the resulting fall. At least she hadn't seen their bodies. She thought of Skiff, writhing on the floor. "Maybe I should stop throwing things at people."

Pal drew her arm back and slapped Lola.

Lola drew back, hand to cheek. It hurt. A lot. "What was that for?"

"You did what you had to do. Skiff was like that snake. Turn your back on him for a minute and he'd have killed us both. And maybe Margaret, too."

Lola's heart lurched.

Pal was on her feet, hands on hips. "You had no problem telling me to go ahead and file my complaint, even though you and I both know exactly what sort of hell I'll be going through as a result. You thought I was tough enough to take it. I think you're tough enough to take this. Cowboy up, sissy."

"Sissy?" Something bubbled up in Lola's chest, pushing past the stone there. Her shoulders shook with the force of it. To her absolute and utter shock, it escaped as laughter, incredulous at first, gaining strength, turning into whoops that bent her double. "Sissy?" she gasped past it before it overtook her again.

The next time she came up for air, she saw Pal on the ground, contorted in laughter of her own. She fell beside her, letting mirth chase the bad spirits from her body and, yes, her soul, leaving her limp and cleansed and, finally, quiet. Beside her, Pal sat up.

"All better?"

Lola tilted her head back. The upside-down peaks of the Winds were visible, just, a jagged inky line against a charcoal sky. "Hell, no. Not by a long shot. But getting there."

"Good. Then it's time for you to pick yourself up and go to Charlie."

A moment earlier, the laughter had still lingered within Lola, pushing against her chest, tugging at her lips, threatening to burst free again. Now it vanished. Lola tried to coax it back, if not the laughter itself, at least the lightness.

Too late. It was gone.

THIRTY-SEVEN

CHARLIE HAD BYPASSED THE low-end chain motel on the Thirty's eastern edge for the old-fashioned motor court on the west end of town, hard by the river. Its rooms, each with a postage-stamp concrete patio and two plastic chairs, faced the water. Flowers bobbed in boxes below the windows, their colors muted in the light that shone above each room's entrance.

Charlie opened the door before Lola could knock. "Heard somebody coming," he said. "Figured it was you."

Lola started to enter the room, but he shook his head and put his finger to his lips. "She's asleep." He pushed one of the chairs toward her. Lola sat. The plastic was cold through her clothing. She was glad she'd donned a sweatshirt before heading into town. She tucked her hands into its pouch. Charlie lowered himself into the chair beside her and tipped it back against the wall. The river slid past, whispering over rocks, eddying among the grasses in the shallows. It glinted like liquid metal in the moonlight. A damn shame, Lola thought, that Charlie had chosen such a pretty spot to end things. She'd have preferred the chilly anonymity of the chain motel.

Charlie waited. That old trick. Thinking she'd crack and speak first. He could just think again. Lola closed her eyes and let her breathing slow. She had a few tricks of her own, one of them an ability to catnap when stressed. She feigned sleep and then it arrived, fast and fitful, a shallow dip below the surface, just deep enough to return her to the kitchen and the moment when her hands opened, launching the pot. Crunching, splashing sounds. A scream. Glass breaking. Thud of body to floor.

"Lola." A hand on her arm. "Wake up."

Lola surfaced with a gasp. Skiff vanished. Charlie's face hovered over hers, concern softening his features. "God," Lola breathed. "Thank you." She wanted to pull him closer, to soak in the strength that, much as she refused to admit it, had sustained her these last years. He withdrew to his own chair, his face once again set in lines of implacable anger.

"You want to tell me what happened out here? Start at the beginning. Don't even think about leaving anything out."

———————

Lola left some things out anyway; mainly, the dalliance with Dave. She could only handle so much self-destruction. She wasn't suicidal.

"Honestly, we thought we were safe," she said at the end, her voice hoarse with the effort of prolonged whispering. "The story was going online. You were on your way. We had no way of knowing his friend was hanging out with that girl from the rez."

"But he'd chased you. Nearly ran you off the road. And you didn't even call the cops when you realized it was him." Each word dropped distinct and heavy onto a scale already lopsided with her failings.

Because when she'd told Pal about how Skiff had chased her, Pal finally decided to talk. To have called the sheriff at that moment might have given Pal time to change her mind. Lola knew better than to say those things aloud. It didn't matter.

"You and your stories. They'll always come first."

"It was a hell of a story." The word slipped unbidden from her lips, words that could only make him angrier. But it was the truth. "A *hell* of a story," she repeated. "Even without what it turned out to be. Those deaths, those arrests, those kids who left Wyoming whole and came back dead or broken inside. It's happening all over the country and nobody has to think too much about it because our fabulous all-volunteer military is filled with people from rural areas or inner cities, and nobody gives a rat's ass about what happens to people in those places."

Charlie started to say something but Lola bulled right over it. "And then Pal. Do you know how many thousands, how many tens of thousands, of women and some men, too, are assaulted in the military? And in this case, we're not just talking assault, but murder. Those assholes were going to get away with everything. But she stood up to them. And I helped her do it. That's what I do, Charlie. Sometimes it's dangerous—not nearly as dangerous as what Pal did, but still. It's dangerous the way your work is sometimes dangerous, too, but you don't see me going all whiney and crybaby about how you should stop. How many times have you gotten up from the dinner table when a call came in? What about Margaret's birthday last year? You left her party because of—what? A goddamn truck wreck?"

Charlie's protest turned defensive. "A truck that spilled steers all over the road. And I didn't have a choice. I'm the only law in the county outside the rez. But you have a choice. There's other reporters out there."

Lola had already pounced. Now she dug in her claws. "But it was my story. I don't give away my stories, Charlie. Just like you don't give away your cases. This is who I am. Just like the Becker Babes are who they are."

"Who?"

"Never mind. If you hadn't figured all of that out after six years, then you had no business asking me to marry you."

Lola rose from her chair. She stood over him, no longer bothering to whisper. "And you have no business implying I'm a bad mother, either. I'm a good reporter and I'm a good mother. The two aren't mutually exclusive, just like being a good sheriff who's on call around the clock doesn't mean you're a bad father."

Charlie tried to interject something. Lola held up her hand to stop him. "No. This whole proposal thing has been your show from the start. Maybe I'll marry you someday." Lola thought about the marshmallow dress. The sticky makeup. "Maybe not. But for sure, it's not going to be because you bullied me into it. And if this means ending things between us, so be it."

The words hung there, as much of a surprise to Lola as they no doubt were for Charlie. Beyond them, an immense blackness, populated by specters of separate homes, shared-custody arrangements, awkward social situations involving extended family and Charlie with a new girlfriend hanging on his arm. Lola wanted to shove past Charlie into the room, take Margaret and flee with her into the night. Life without Charlie, she could handle. Maybe. Life without Margaret, even part of the time? Incomprehensible. But they'd arrived at this point, and there was no turning back.

Charlie pushed himself slowly from the chair, only inches away from her when he stood, close enough for her to feel the warmth of his body. She leaned in. He held her so close that the buttons on his shirt mashed into her cheek.

"Maybe you're bluffing, Lola. I know how you like to do that. It's how you get half your stories. Well, I'm calling your bluff. The proposal goes. Forget I mentioned it. But I hope you stay."

THIRTY-EIGHT

THE WOMEN STACKED SMALL squares of red crepe paper in piles of six, pleating each pile with brown fingers so gnarled as to seem incapable of such dainty work. Each woman selected a long green wire from the pile in the middle of the table and wrapped one end tight around the middle of the pleated sheets. They wielded scissors with deft sharp snips, triangling the ends of the sheaves, bits of red paper floating down around their ankles like bloodied snowflakes. The paper rustled and whispered a conversation of its own beneath the elders' desultory voices.

"Cold's holding off. Good thing. Want to get these in the ground before a hard freeze."

"But not too long before Veterans Day. Don't want them to be all faded for the ceremony. Hey, Dolores. Why you make your flowers so big, hey?" Laughter all around, eyes glazed with age crinkling at the corners, hands lifted to cover toothless grins.

"She wants Mike's grave to shine bright."

Dolores, a big woman, puffed larger, suddenly fierce in aspect, not unlike the chicken she'd pawned off on her unsuspecting victims some months earlier. "Don't he deserve it, though?"

Smiles vanished. The women's hands stilled. Even the paper held its breath.

"That other boy. The one killed ours. He's in jail now, right?"

"Long time. They got him on the murder. Still working through the rape thing."

"Huh. Maybe in jail, he finds out what that's like. That girl gets justice one way or the other. Bet he cry for his mama. Big boys like him, they always cry. So brave until it's them." Lips stretched in expressions too frightening to be termed smiles.

The eldest among them, a woman so small her head barely edged the tabletop despite the cushion thoughtfully placed beneath her bony rear, took it upon herself to bring the flower-makers back to their proper mood. "So, Dolores, you've moved yourself right in with Delbert. You got your man."

Scissors flashed in Dolores' hands. She spoke righteous as the new preacher at the reservation's fundamentalist church, who no doubt would be scandalized by the women's conversation. "Him and that girl, they're setting up to ranch again, just like Delbert and her father used to do. Going to get themselves some cow-calf pairs, see if they can make a go of it. Last thing he needs to worry about is cooking, keeping house."

"Oh. You're *looking after* him."

Dolores fluffed a carnation so assertively she shredded the petals. She tossed it onto the floor.

"He keep you up all night? That why you're so clumsy today with your flowers?"

Shoulders shook. Laughter pealed. Order was restored.

The cold held off, one balmy day after another, aspen trembling golden on the flanks of the Winds, sky an ethereal blue, even the wind briefly becalmed. Harsh edges seemed softer. Wyoming briefly became the place on postcards, calendars, tourism brochures. Newcomers publicly complimented themselves for their great good sense in moving there. Old-timers held their tongues and spent as much time outdoors as possible, storing up the bluebird days against the inevitable.

The Shoshone elders scooped armfuls of the paper flowers into black plastic leaf bags and handed them off to young people with strong thighs and backs, who spent a weekend pulling the old, faded flowers from the humped graves in the Sacajawea Cemetery and inserting the new stems into the ground, one close by the other, until a scarlet blanket adorned each grave. At the last minute, Dolores decided she didn't trust anyone else to give the job the attention it deserved. Despite her arthritis and Delbert's various aches and pains, they spent a long afternoon kneeling beside Mike's grave, placing flower after flower, stopping frequently to sit and stroke the surface of the dirt, crumbling the larger clods and patting them smooth.

Two weeks later, they were back. Winter came with them, the sky grey and heavy and unyielding as steel, a great weight pressing down on the small crowd assembled at the cemetery. A rude wind spit snow into the wrinkled faces of the elders, tore at the eagle feathers on the veterans' war bonnets, tossed the buckskin fringes dangling from the lances, and snatched the honor song from the drum and carried it away. The veterans, Delbert among them, slitted their eyes against it and held heads high. Pal waited off to one side with Shirl Dillon. She had insisted that this shattered man, who now bore the shame that once burdened Delbert, join them. "Your son, Cody," she said, "at least he was sorry. He punished himself. Not like those others."

Charlie and Lola and Margaret stood beside them. Margaret tugged with mittened hands at the scarf wrapped around the lower part of her face. Lola's own hands were bare. She clasped them together against the cold, the fingers of her right hand worrying the tiny diamond ring on the third finger of her left. The ring was a compromise—Lola's acknowledgement of someday, along with Charlie's that something flashier would have represented too strong a push. Charlie took her hands in his own, enfolding them in warmth. They turned toward Mike's grave. A veteran, one of the younger ones, pulled a bugle from beneath his arm, where he had tucked it for warmth. He raised it to his lips. Lola's eyes met Pal's. The two women nodded, then faced front as the sound of taps rose and bumped against the sky and hovered there above them as Mike St. Clair was finally accorded the honor he deserved.

THE END

ACKNOWLEDGEMENTS

So many people to thank: The empress of editors, Terri Bischoff, and the rest of the Midnight Ink crew—development coordinator Kathy Schneider, publicist Katie Mickschl, freelance editor Gabrielle Simons, proofreader Melissa Mierva, book designer Bob Gaul, and cover designer Ellen Lawson; also, to agent Barbara Braun.

Deep gratitude to Glenda Trosper of the Eastern Shoshone Tribal Council, who patiently answered my questions; J.J. Hensley for an early read; Tom Avril, whose story about his Aunt Pearl's Fourth of July celebration I appropriated for my own purposes; and my niece, Gina Florio Sous, for lending the name of her diabolical cat, Jemalina, to my fictional and equally diabolical chicken.

The Badasses, the lovely Badasses—Jamie Raintree, Kate Moretti, Aimie Runyan, Andrea Catalano, Orly Konig Lopez, and Theresa Allen—helped keep both my writing and my sanity on an even keel.

Profound appreciation for my partner, Scott Crichton, and his unwavering support for this crazy writing life. All love to my children, Kate Breslin, whose fearlessness gave me my Margaret, and Sean Breslin.

© Silkati Photography/Missoula, MT

ABOUT THE AUTHOR

Veteran journalist Gwen Florio has covered stories ranging from the shootings at Columbine High School and the trial of Oklahoma City bomber Timothy McVeigh, to the glitz of the Miss America pageant and the more practical Miss Navajo contest whose participants slaughter a sheep. She's reported from Afghanistan, Iraq, and Somalia, as well as Lost Springs, Wyoming (population three). Her journalism has been nominated three times for the Pulitzer Prize and her short fiction for the Pushcart Prize. *Disgraced* is her debut Midnight Ink novel. Learn more at http://gwenflorio.net/.